ONE MORE TIME

ROBERT J. TILLEY

Cover Design by the author.

Order this book online at www.trafford.com
or email orders@trafford.com

Most Trafford titles are also available at major online book retailers.

Printed in Victoria, BC, Canada.

ISBN: 978-1-4251-2452-6 (sc)
ISBN: 978-1-4251-2453-3 (eBook)

*Our mission is to efficiently provide the world's finest, most comprehensive
book publishing service, enabling every author to experience success.
To find out how to publish your book, your way, and have it available
worldwide, visit us online at www.trafford.com*

Trafford rev. 05/20/2010

 www.trafford.com

North America & international
toll-free: 1 888 232 4444 (USA & Canada)
phone: 250 383 6864 ♦ fax: 812 355 4082

This book is dedicated to my wife Jan, for her patience during its prolonged gestation.

By the same author:
A NOVEL, 'THE BIG LOSERS'

PROLOGUE

Weatherby was halfway home when he remembered the sample swatches he was supposed to be taking to Detroit the next day.

He swore. He was late, and already it had been a day compounded of small irritations; machinery faults, a delayed delivery that had intermittently kept him on the vidphone for much of the afternoon.

He hesitated, but only briefly. His train was due to leave just after eight, and if he waited until the morning before picking them up there was always going to be the risk of running late and not making it to the station on time.

He swore again, and went back to the works. He collected the swatches from his office, and was on his way out again when he heard the hissing sound.

It seemed to be coming from the main storeroom; what sounded like a sudden exhalation that lasted for several seconds, then stopped. He hesitated again, then dug out his keys and opened the storeroom door.

He detected the smell when he was halfway down the central aisle that divided the banks of shelving. There was an unfamiliar mustiness there, faint, but still discernible against the normal slightly acrid odour generated by the rolls of fabric that filled the shelves. He moved on, curiously sniffing the air and peering around him, and then it happened.

He'd almost reached the far end of the room and was set to investigate an adjoining aisle when he suddenly found himself somewhere else. He wasn't in the storeroom any more. He was in a dark place of some kind, immersed in what at first seemed like total blackness. For a second or so he thought he'd gone blind, but then his eyes adjusted sufficiently for him to realise that he hadn't.

He could just about see, his surroundings faintly illuminated by the light that was filtering dimly thorough what looked to be a regularly-spaced series of windows, located some distance above his head and identifying the perimeter of the area in which he stood. Somewhere in the gloom there was the sound of steadily dripping water, accompanied by a faint echo each time it made contact with the floor. The smell that he's detected in the storeroom was all around him now, musty and slightly oily.

He stepped back in instinctive retreat, and was dazzled by the sudden flare of light that greeted him. He shielded his eyes, blinking frantically, then gradually focused on the blessedly familiar scene; the rows of shelving units and their multi-coloured contents, a mobile ladder unit that he'd passed during his exploration.

Weatherby said, thickly, "Jesus." He wondered if he'd suffered some kind of brief fit. But he was still on his feet and everything appeared to be functioning normally. He hesitated, thoughtfully, then picked up a ruler that lay on an adjacent shelf, and cautiously poked it out in front of him. The ruler disappeared, and so did part of his hand. He snatched his hand back again, and saw his knuckles reappear, still whitely gripping the ruler.

"Jesus," he said again. He sat down on a stool, breathing heavily and staring blankly into space. After a minute or so, he eased himself back onto his feet and moved gingerly back down the seemingly unoccupied aisle, holding the ruler stiffly at arm's length in front of him.

Approximately a quarter of it gradually disappeared again. He halted, and moved the visible remains from side to side. Two feet to the left, the missing part reappeared, and the same thing happened a little over a foot to his right.

He said, aloud, "Four feet six, give or take a couple of inches." He was irritated to notice that his voice sounded hoarse and shaky. He continued to move the ruler about, gradually locating the limits of the phenomenon and forming a picture of it in his mind's-eye.

As far as he could make out, it extended a little over eighteen inches above his head, commencing there with a more or less sharply defined point. Convex lines descended from this, reaching the limits of their curve somewhere around knee-height, then gradually closing inwards again at floor level.

He pinched his chin, thinking about it. It was rather like the top two-thirds of an unserrated leaf, he thought, with the bottom third embedded in the storeroom floor. He wondered if it really did extend below the floor, and just how accurate his mental image of it was.

He roused himself and left the storeroom, cautiously negotiating his way back to the door down another aisle that seemed mercifully unaffected. In his office, he took a flashlight from a desk drawer, hesitated thoughtfully, then unlocked a cupboard and took out an almost-empty decanter. He drank the contents, carried both items back to the storeroom, indulged in a few seconds deep breathing, then set his jaw determinedly and walked towards what he's found.

Again, there was the musty near-darkness, this time relieved by the beam from the flashlight. He carefully placed the decanter on the cement floor, positioning it as centrally as he was able to gauge in front of the opening, then straightened up and stared around him.

He'd already deduced that wherever he was it was night-time, and that he was in a large, high-ceilinged building of some kind. A few yards to his left, there was a stained and mildewed wall, punctuated at the top by the windows that had identified the perimeter during his initial visit. He moved closer to it, and cautiously began to circumnavigate the area.

A pair of large corrugated metal doors that he passed failed to yield when he pushed them, and he detected no artefacts of any kind in the body of the room as he continued around it. Not far from his point of entry, identified by the reassuring glint of the decanter, he found an office, its door ajar. Inside, there was a badly scarred wooden desk and a brace of wooden filing cabinets, all of them covered in dust and grime. He checked the cabinets and the desk, but apart from a multitude of spiders' webs, all he found was rusty metal paper-clips and a few petrified rubber bands.

He circled the walls with the flashlight beam. Eventually, it settled on a calendar, suspended alongside the filing cabinets. He moved closer, squinting against the play of the light. The calendar had a picture on it, a horse and buggy on a country road. There was lettering beneath it, badly faded now, separating the picture from the yellowed date pad. He looked closer, stiffened, blinked, then re-read the barely legible statement 'COUNTRYSIDE CALENDAR for 1937'.

He felt a chill go over him. The room was cold, but until then he'd been too intrigued by what was happening to have really noticed the contrast in temperature between where he was and the storeroom. But suddenly he felt as though the warmth of the present had been stripped away and he was being touched by the deathly coldness of the past, the stale breath of decaying time.

Was he really in the past?, Weatherby wondered. And still in Leyland? For all he knew he might have been on the other side of the continent, nowhere near Pennsylvania even. But that didn't feel right somehow. Although he had a purely marginal interest in such intangibles as time and space he knew they were inextricably linked, so he didn't see why he should necessarily be somewhere else in the strictly geographical sense. He hadn't been raised in Leyland and didn't know much about the history of the Bush Hill industrial estate where their synthetic fabric manufacturing works were located, but it didn't seem illogical to assume that the building was an earlier occupant of the same piece of ground, only ninety years or so before, depending on how old the calendar was in this time.

During his walk around the perimeter he'd found another door, locked with rusty bolts, situated in a far corner. He went back to it, wrestled the bolts open, and went outside, instantly shivering as a cold gust of wind caught at his clothing. He tugged the lapels of his jacket together, and walked around the corner of the building. There was a narrow concrete path there, fringed by a single-strand wire fence, with grass rustling on its far side.

He followed the path to where it opened out onto a shallow forecourt, and beyond that an unlit road that terminated at the wire fence. He pulled his jacket tighter to him, and walked along the front of the building, playing the flashlight across its surface. Something caught his eye, a discoloured metal plate, located to the left of the double doors that he's failed to open. He focused the beam, and read 'MOSTON ENGINEERING', a name that meant nothing to him.

En route to the road, he found a fallen 'FOR SALE' sign, but there was nothing else of interest when he reached the far side, just open ground that appeared to gradually fall away into the darkness. Looking back, he vaguely detected other structures that led away from the one that he'd emerged from, bulking enigmatically in the gloom. Occasional lights appeared and drifted along the horizon, accompanied by faint traffic noises, some of them heavy-sounding. A wash of more subdued light showed beyond that, reflected on the underside of low clouds, further indication that he was close to both a main highway and the outskirts of a town.

The direction and distance of the town and the location of the lighting pretty much confirmed his initial idea, that he was still in the vicinity of Leyland, and that the building was somewhere close to the site of their works, possibly even on it. He chewed his bottom lip, thinking hard, then re-traced his footsteps back into the building. He paused by the decanter, braced himself, slitted his eyes, and stepped over it, re-emerging into the brightness of the storeroom.

Back in his office, he took a bulky portable radio from a shelf there, and rummaged until he found an extension-lead. He returned to the storeroom, plugged the extension into a wall socket situated a few yards from the still-invisible enigma, then cautiously stepped back through it, taking the radio and lead with him.

He carried them into the nearby office, placed the radio on the desk, attached the lead, and switched on. He only half expected it to work, but it did, initially emitting the faint sound of music, almost drowned out by a fierce crackle of static. He searched carefully through the bands, occasionally catching a distant hint of more music or barely intelligible voices. One voice suddenly magnified slightly, faded, then magnified again as he juggled the control.

It was a newscast, about hostilities of some kind. He listened carefully to the listing of unfamiliar place-names that were abruptly punctuated by one that he recognised. He hurriedly ducked his head closer to the speaker, breath suspended, confusedly trying to memorise details and vaguely conscious of the sudden clamminess of his hands.

The war report finished and was replaced by domestic news. He continually moistened his lips as he listened, breathing hard now. After a minute or so, he switched the radio off, wiped his hands on his handkerchief, and returned to the storeroom. He locked it, then continued to the office and 'phoned his partner.

He told him what had happened, and for the next couple of minutes suffered Stoltz's initial sarcasm that eventually gave way to irritable defeat. Stoltz joined him half-an-hour later, his irritation rapidly deflated by what Weatherby showed him.

Back in the storeroom, they faced one another, sombrely.

Weatherby said, "This war business. You know about that stuff. Where does that put this place, as near as you can figure?" He approximately re-stated the newscast details that he'd managed to retain.

"The Germans captured Schlusselburg and cut off Leningrad's communications," Stoltz said. "It didn't do them any good, though. They never took it, of course."

"When was that?"

Stoltz frowned, thoughtfully. "Some time in September. I'll have to check."

Weatherby groaned with impatience. "What year, for Christ's sake?"

"1941," Stoltz said. He pursed his lips, raised his eyebrows, and grinned, a little tremulously. "Very interesting. You realise what that means?"

"It puts it two or three months before Pearl Harbour," Weatherby said. Unlike Stoltz he was no student of history, but he knew that much. He did a quick mental calculation. "That was eighty-seven years go." He swallowed, finding his throat quite painfully dry. "Right. So what are we going to do about it?"

"If it stays like it is, that's going to be for scientists and government people to figure out," Stoltz said. "It's a cinch we can't keep it to ourselves." He paced restlessly for a few moments, then paused, snapping his fingers. "Sammy Stockton. He was something to do with military intelligence. He ought to know somebody." He grimaced. "Of course, you realise what a couple of chumps we're going to look like if it goes away again before anybody else gets here. It'd sure be worth it, though, because I hate to think what'll happen to our set-up if it doesn't."

Following a brief silence, Weatherby said, "They couldn't just shut us down without any kind of explanation, though. There'd be too much talk. What could we tell the staff? There's no way of knowing how long it's going to last, either. What if it's here for quite a while, maybe even permanently?"

Stoltz stared at him, baffled. "You're making it sound like that'd be good news. How could it be, for Christ's - ?" He stopped, suddenly pensive, a glint of comprehension in his eyes.

During the preceding decade another industrial estate had been developed alongside the new turnpike on the other side of town, in the process relegating Bush Hill to something of an inconveniently-sited and now barely half-occupied backwater. Maintenance costs on their present place had risen appreciably over the last couple of years as well, and for the past few weeks they'd been eyeing some unexpectedly vacated premises that were for sale on the new estate, frustratingly deterred by both the asking price and their calculations relating to the inevitable loss of production time that would result from relocating. Aggressive competition was adding another factor to their predicament, despite their realisation that such a move could eventually lower their overall costs and possibly salvage their progressively ailing business.

"When you really think about it, even a couple of days could be enough," Weatherby said. "Maybe even less than that. As long as they get confirmation that it exists, there's no way that they'd just let us carry on afterwards like nothing had happened. Even if it closed again right after that, they'd still want to secure the place, put people in here in case it came back, try to check out the cause, that kind of thing. Whatever, we'd still have to relocate, and that'd mean compensation, right?"

Stoltz moistened his lips. "Right. Of course, that's right. I wonder how far we could push this?"

"My guess is that they'd want to keep us happy," Weatherby said. "Within reasonable bounds, of course, but I imagine there'd be room for a little negotiation. I mean, when you consider what we've got here…" He shrugged, riding the swell of a steadily rising tide of relief and optimism now.

Stoltz nodded eagerly, barely able to contain his own excitement. "I guess so. Anyway, the sooner we get this show on the road the better. I'll see if I can get Sammy's number. Let's hope he isn't ex-directory."

He fished out his mobile and punched it with a shaking forefinger.

1.

—

FOR THE ATTENTION OF
DEPUTY CONTROLLER ONLY

14.22 hours/3.3.2028

Sorry I was so cryptic this morning, Rob, but even though we were on the direct line I didn't dare say anything more than I did, and when you've heard what's on the other cartridges you'll understand why. Right now the priority has to be making sure that it goes no further than is absolutely necessary, and that includes our own people; you've obviously got to be in on it as soon as possible, though, and since I have to get to Washington in a hurry and we're going to miss one another by five or six hours I can't see any realistic alternative to doing it this way. Make sure you clean everything as soon as you've heard it; I'm taking the originals with me, and the fewer copies there are the better.

As of this moment only three people know the actual details of what Lohmann's chosen to drop on us, by the way. If he's still alive that'd be four, although for reasons that I'll get to later I very much doubt it, but whether he is or not – and despite his admitting at one point to being a congenital liar – I still can't see any reason not to believe that at least it's a fundamentally accurate account of what he's been up to. His lying skills must've been pretty considerable, though, and obviously extremely useful as far as his time in the field was concerned. There was that early wobble with the draft police, I know, but he clearly honed that side of things to a very much sharper edge afterwards; fooling

1

psych and Urich would've been way beyond most of us, but he did it, which I'm sure you'll agree says quite something about his eventual abilities in that department.

Anyway, that aside, given the way that things developed it's hardly surprising that he didn't speak out before he did, and in any case he freely admits that his reasons for doing it at all were as much to do with his personal affairs as it was with the rest of it, an opportunity to air his maudlin conscience over what happened to his wife. At least it's a mercy that it ended up in his sister-in-law's lap, despite the obviously strained relationship. Understandably, she wasn't at all appreciative that he left her to decide what to do with it , but we have to be extremely thankful that if he was going to unload it at all at least it was with someone bright enough to recognise its potential to do massive harm that there'd be no way of undoing. I shudder to think of the consequences if she'd taken it to one of the networks or, God forbid, one of the sensation sheets, but Phyllicia Waters is clearly nobody's fool, and of course Kennway's always been a responsible editor.

I'm not going to say anything about my own conclusions, not right now; it'll be best if you listen to what Lohmann's had to say first, and I'll tell you my own thoughts on it afterwards, although I suggest you give yourself a little time to digest everything before you get to them; you really do need to approach this with as open a mind as possible, and it's obviously essential that I don't influence your initial thinking in any way. Before you get started on the cartridges, read the copy of Waters' statement first, then burn it – don't shred it, burn it. I really can't stress the necessity of keeping this under wraps too much, so the less documentation there is the better.

Right. So she went to the Globe on Tuesday and played Kennway the cartridges Lohmann had sent her, and yesterday morning Kennway came on the line and said that he needed to see us; he told me that he knew what we'd been doing here, and that he was in possesion of information relating to it that we didn't have and that ought to be discussed urgently, but in view of its obvious importance it shouldn't be over the 'phone. He suggested that he came down here with the informant and the evidence, and since it was already clear that they knew where we were I agreed and told him to wait at his office until our people collected them.

The fact that he had our number and knew about any of it was enough of a jolt, but needless to say it was the bit about knowing things that we didn't that really grabbed me. Anyway, they flew down yesterday afternoon and we spent most of the night listening to the cartridges, and I made these copies at the same time. Like I say, I daren't even start to think about what would've happened if we hadn't been dealing with fundamentally reasonable people, but she's known Kennway a long time and decided he wouldn't go off half-cocked, despite his journalist's instincts, which is why she chose him to confide in. It was still a very chancey move, of course, but I can understand her wanting that kind of leverage at back of her while she was putting us in the picture; she obviously felt that because of what Lohmann had told her about the security angle she could've been putting herself at risk if she'd approached us without any kind of safety-net, and I have to admit I can see her point.

Kennway told me that he'd made his own copies when she'd played them to him, but he gave his word that nobody else was in on it, and come the finish he said he'd wipe them as soon as they got back. They'd already discussed the implications of releasing them, and concluded that if they were - or if they leaked, of course - whatever we chose to believe the repercussions would be catastrophic, so at least we didn't have to waste time debating the issue. Neither of them was prepared to commit either way at the time, incidentally, which is understandable given their limited understanding of cosmology and quantum theory; I have my own ideas now that I haven't had a chance to put to them yet, and to be fair we are dealing with something that's bound to lead to a lot of confused thinking, anyway.

It certainly puts me in mind of our own mixed feelings at the start of it all; excitement at the prospect of being in on a key event as far as broadening our understanding of the workings of time and space was concerned, especially as it meant putting the record straight on a particularly vital segment of our own history, and regret that it was happening after we'd squandered our chances the way we have. I can't imagine that at the time anyone involved seriously considered the possibility of us finding ourselves in a situation where we –

Actually, I think I'd better just leave it there. I've said more than I intended to, and without getting into specifics I'll only be clouding things even more than I'm sure I already have, so just drop everything else you were planning on doing, put Mal in charge, then lock yourself away and listen to what Lohmann's elected to tell us. You don't really need to hear the preliminaries at this stage; altogether there's something like eight, nine hours, and the early stuff isn't essential, most of it about how the hole was found and the setting up of the programme, his recruitment and training and how we knew it was all going to finish with the fire, and bearing in mind what happened then I hardly need point out the irony of that. I've set the first one to where he tells her about going out on his initial trip; strictly speaking a lot of that's inessential as well, but it's intriguing to hear his early reactions, the way he saw the situation before he started to let his imagination take over.

Anyway, they're all yours, and I'll be extremely interested to hear your own conclusions when I get back. Wipe this now, before you get started on the rest of it, and don't forget what I said about burning Waters' statement as soon as you've read it, either.

2.

"No later than eight," Bridges said. He listened to the confirmation at the other end of the line. "Right, I'll see you." He put the 'phone back in its cradle, and stood up. He said to the pale-complexioned man standing by the window, "No later than eight, O.K.?"

Lohmann looked back at him. "I'm sorry? I was — " He gestured outside. He looked a little lost, Bridges reflected. Well, it was understandable. It had taken him a while to adjust, too, accept the reality of what was happening.

He said, patiently, "Don't forget you'll be 'phoning them before eight every morning, when you get back here. Any time you anticipate being later than that, let them know as soon as you can. But whatever you do, report in. It could cause a lot of complications if you don't."

Lohmann nodded. "Sure, of course." His eyes drifted back to the window. Bridges joined him, staring out at the craning forest of buildings, now patterned with grids of light and their hard angularity diffused by the gently falling curtain of snow. In the distance, the roof of one of the silhouetted skyscrapers periodically glowed with the overspill from an enormous flashing sign that read 'HAPPY NEW YEAR'.

Not altogether appropriate, maybe, Bridges thought. He glanced at Lohmann, conscious of his tension beside him. "Well, this is it. New York, 1942-style. How does it feel?"

Lohmann laughed, a slightly breathless sound. "Pretty darned cold. I guess their summers were a bit more comfortable than ours, though." He gestured outside again. "There certainly have been a few changes. In quantity, that's for sure. It hasn't fully sprouted yet, I guess you could say."

Bridges nodded. "That's as good a way of putting it as any." He checked his watch. "Anyway, I have to be out of here. Mastin's on his

5

way, so you'll be having some more company soon. That's been a lucky break, having somebody you know pretty well helping you settle in for your first week. You two go back quite a way, I was told."

Lohmann smiled. *"Fifteen, sixteen years. We met in college. It was just shared interests at first, but we got quite close after a while. He's in New York and I'm in Philly, but we've kept in touch on the personal side as well as professionally."*

Bridges studied him as he talked. He was paler than usual, he decided, and despite his claim to coldness there was a slight sheen of sweat visible on his cheek and forehead. It was the kind of evidence of nerves that was to be expected at this stage, and in most respects he seemed to meet the requirements ideally. Like all the people selected for survey duty he was unattached, and his profile had been well inside the acceptable parameters; politically and religiously sound, responsible, basically serious, tending towards introversion, libido at the lower end of the scale, no evidence of problems with drink or drugs.

He seemed as safe a bet as any of them, Bridges decided. He mentally shrugged, and said, *"Anything else you want before I go? I have to be across in Queens by seven."*

Lohmann bit his lip. *"No, I don't think so, thanks. Artie'll be here soon, and then we'll be getting a meal, I expect. I'm not really hungry, but I haven't eaten much today, of course."* He smiled again, self-consciously. *"Mustn't let all this excitement put me off my food."*

Bridges said, *"I didn't have much appetite for the first couple of days. It takes a while to get the feel of things."* He picked up his hat and re-settled it on his head. *"O.K., that's it, I guess. Any problems, you've got the number."* He shook hands, went to the door, and paused. *"I almost forgot. Happy old New Year."*

Lohmann laughed his slightly breathless laugh again. *"Thanks, same to you. I'm sure it'll be an interesting one, anyway."*

3.

——

If Artie hadn't been there to steer me for a lot of the time during those first few days I know I wouldn't have gotten through them as well as I did. He had his own schedule to take care of, of course, but we still met up in the afternoons and compared our findings from the previous evenings, and he helped to ease me into things in a more general way as well, so that really did take a lot of the pressure off that I know I'd have felt if he hadn't been around.

He'd been recruited onto the programme a little earlier than me, and although it was his first time out and he'd only been there a couple of weeks he already gave the impression of being totally relaxed, which meant that he was able to blend into things in a way that I've never been able to, even in our own time. He always was a much more comfortable social animal than me, though, able to mix with strangers in a completely unselfconscious way, something I've always envied him, but that kind of unforced gregariousness just isn't part of my nature, regretfully. Anyway, I'm still grateful for that time; we were always pretty tight in a lot of ways, but the shared excitement and the element of danger that was a permanent part of the situation brought us particularly close together while it lasted. Actually, talking about Artie and remembering our friendship is a singularly painful business for me now and always will be, but I'm not going to explain why that is at this point; it would only confuse things, and in any case the only sensible way to tell you all this is to do it chronologically, so please bear with me on that.

It's fair to say that a lot of my preconceptions about how things would be were reasonably accurate, but real knowledge of that kind only comes from direct experience, of course, and at least some of my ideas had to be revised in a hurry. Even though I had

Artie to lean on for at least part of the time I found it pretty scary to start with, too. It wasn't really to do with the acclimatisation barrier, either; there was so much to occupy my attention, so many totally engrossing points of interest that I didn't even consciously think about that aspect of it initially. It was more a question of feeling that I was an intruder in a foreign country where I had no right to be, and although I spoke the language and broadly understood the customs and social codes I was still very conscious of the fact that there were pitfalls that I didn't know about and had no way of guarding myself against. That's stayed with me to some extent even now, but my initial worry lost its edge fairly quickly because everybody was so wrapped up in their own affairs and everything moved at such a frenetic lick that at least I didn't find it difficult to stay anonymous, become just another speck in the crowd, an enormous relief, I'll tell you.

The main topic of conversation was the war, of course. I heard it practically everywhere I went; in shops, diners, the subway, the hotel. Most of it was based on shock and worry, because it was still only a matter of weeks since they'd been pitchforked into it, but already there was talk of the Utopia some of them believed would come when it was all over and a world-wide recognition of the futility of butchering one another was coupled with what they saw as the endless possibilities of technology.

I guess that's the principle difference between now and then, in the strictly human sense that is. Despite all the hardships, the long haul out of the Depression and the trauma of suddenly finding themselves directly involved in what was turning out to be the biggest war in the whole history of the human race, there was still optimism. It was based on a relatively short-term view of the future, but given the circumstances that was hardly surprising; the problems they were facing then were more than enough to occupy most of their thinking. But they were genuinely hopeful, never seriously doubting that they could take on this latest challenge and eventually win.

To be honest, I couldn't help resenting that kind of blind optimism a little, even though I accepted it was needed in their situation. The size of the hole we've been digging ourselves into's all too evident now, of course, but they were still totally unaware of their part in it, far too busy demonstrating their determination and ingenuity; improving *this*, replacing *that* with something brighter and more efficient, concentrating totally on the needs of the moment and far too dazzled by their vision of the way things would be after they'd won to consider such an eventual possibility.

I'd expected the popular culture of the time to reflect all of this, but I hadn't really been prepared for the impact it actually did make on me. It was everywhere; bright, bouncy music, movie theatres on practically every block, most of them screening escapist froth of one kind or another. A lot of the music was nondescript, of course; novelty numbers, sentimental songs of variable quality, patriotic stuff at marching tempos, that kind of thing. But there was jazz, too, and even though most of it'd been diluted by commercial pressures the feeling was still there, echoing the treasure I was finding on 52nd Street and that was waiting for me up in Harlem, all the legendary people and places that I'd never dreamed would become realities for me.

Despite that, there were always things that dulled the shine a little, of course. It was impossible to get away from continuous reminders of the war, and they soon put my own real interest in the period in perspective, frequently uncomfortably so. Another thing I found hard to take initially was the amount of aerial pollution, particularly in the places where I was going to be doing my research. It was bad enough on the streets, but the air in the clubs and restaurants and dance halls was worse in its way; smoke and sweat and perfume and sometimes cooking smells as well, a mixture that turned my stomach just thinking about it. There was no escaping it, though, so I just kept on reminding myself that it I was going to make full use of the opportunity that I'd have willingly given a sizeable slice of my life for it was essential that my camera-toting jazz buff persona looked to be totally at home in those settings, happy to accept that side of it as a normal ingredient of the scene.

The camera was actually my sound-recorder, by the way, although it was a real camera, too, based in a model that was current then, with the recording unit built into parts of the casing. Anyway, apart from it and the protective weapon I'd been issued with – I'll be getting to that in a little while – that was my total equipment, because it was reasoned that the less I carried that could prove impossible to explain away if I should be unlucky enough to find myself in a situation where I had to answer awkward questions, the safer I'd be. Needless to say, that was a prospect that bothered me a lot during the early days, but like with the smoke and smells business I reminded myself of the unique chance I'd been given, and for the time being at least I gradually relaxed, because as far as I could tell wherever I went nobody ever gave me more than an occasional passing glance.

I'd been re-christened Michael Cranmer – most people kept their own names, but obvious German ancestry was seen as best avoided just then – and my personal documentation had me still coming from Philly, but instead of a musicologist and jazz historian on the Marsham faculty I was an enthusiast of independent means; unmarried, 4F because of all-too genuine back problems, and my story was that I was doing research for a book that I was in the process of writing. I had no family any more, but there were various ostensibly reliable people at various respectable addresses who could be contacted to verify all of this if the need arose, an arrangement that didn't quite reach that stage, but I'll be getting to that, too, in a while. It was a near-miss that I still have nightmares about, even though it's turned out to be a key incident in directing me to where I am now, on the verge of a truly monumental change that I still find hard to believe, although I know it's true; I actually am in a situation where needs that have been missing from my life have been provided, something that I'm going to be eternally grateful for.

I'm not going to bore you with any real details about happened that first time out; they're irrelevant to why I'm telling you all of this, anyway. During the first few days I visited most of the places on and around 52nd Street that I've read about so many times; taking pictures, recording, watching and listening to people who in some ways I felt I already knew as a result of all the years of familiarity with their music, but even that hadn't fully prepared me for the sheer raw immediacy of a lot of what I heard.

There's an irreplaceable intimacy about live performance, of course, but especially so with jazz. Its fundamental ingredients are the same as any other music, but it's the way they're used; the special rhythmic feel, the element of improvisation, its tonal qualities, all the things that make it such a uniquely moving musical form. Something that non-enthusiasts don't really understand is that it's a particularly illuminating means of personal address, the solo part, that is; a mode of expression that talks to the listener in a way that's far more revealing than words often are, because the player is really out on the line, telling their individual story, and whether what they have to offer is basically no more than a bag of tricks or pure poetry, the truth of what they're saying's always there for people who have the ears to hear it. In fact, it isn't over-stating the case to call it the most human of all musical forms, because it really is capable of depicting the whole range of our sensibilities, and that makes it a kind of musical catharsis that touches a very special nerve in someone like myself, so that even when the poetry's only marginally present I still feel privileged to be on that particular emotional wavelength, able to receive that message and be moved by it.

Lecture over, Phyl. I really didn't mean to get into that, but even at this late date I'd like to think that despite your own aversion to jazz you understand at least a little just how much this all meant to me. Anyway, it was a magical time as far as I was concerned, in some ways the happiest I'd ever known, and you'd have hated every aspect of it. The settings were crowded and noisy and generally unhygienic, things that I normally hate myself, but even then it had a kind of innocence, and I loved practically every minute of it, like a kid let loose in a candy store, an experience he'd never dreamed was possible before it actually happened.

52nd Street really was a musical cauldron then, with just about every imaginable ingredient thrown into it. It wasn't all true jazz, although I accept that that has to be a personal opinion to some extent, because what is and what isn't has always been a notoriously tricky area of definition. Whether it was or not, though, it still wasn't all necessarily good music, because in one respect jazz is no different to any other form of creative activity; there's the cream, and then there's the rest, with the rest making up the bigger part of it. But there must have been more of the cream concentrated in that block of converted brownstones than anywhere else in the whole history of jazz; great names working just a few yards from one another, all of them making contributions that I was there to preserve, performances that'd be revered long after they were dead and gone, and none of them giving a thought to the possibility of that kind of memorial.

Posterity never entered their minds; I'm sure of that; what they were doing at that moment, the job at hand, was all that mattered to them. It was probably one of the greatest and least valued outbursts of spontaneous creativity in the whole history of humankind; incredibly skilled artists plying their trade in places that have pretty accurately been descried as upholstered sewers, often playing to people who could only hear the excitement and none of the artistry. There was always a genuinely appreciative core, but a fair percentage of the audience simply wasn't tuned in to what was really happening, service personnel a lot of them, more interested in the women and the drinking and the general feeling of being with a crowd. It was an aspect of the situation that irritated me at the time, to start with, anyway, but whenever I began to feel like that I'd concentrate extra hard on the music, using it in the same way that they at least partly were, I guess, to drown out some of the deeper feelings I found nagged away inside me a lot of the time.

There's always been one particular facet of the way things were then that's soured my image of the period to some extent, of course, and I've never tried to evade or minimise it, because it's simply the way it worked at that point in history. I've thought about the racial situation a great deal over the years, especially during the time that Donna and I were together, naturally. I'm sure it'll always exist, although in quite a few ways it isn't anything like as bad was it was then, that I can guarantee. There were a few people that crossed the colour line like we did, of course, made mixed marriages or had other intimate relationships, and a few black musicians played with what were predominately white bands, but racial prejudice was still often a savage and brutal sort of business. There wasn't a lot of it among the musicians, not overtly at any rate, but most of the downtown clubs, including the 52nd Street ones, practised a white-only policy. Blacks could perform in them, of course – generally for less money than whites would have been paid – but they weren't welcome as customers, not at that time.

It was blatant, too, in no way shame-faced. Whites still travelled uptown to Harlem to take in what was happening there, although not as many during the 1930's. It wasn't part of my regular beat, not at first, anyway, and although it wasn't anything like the no-go area it became later, whites weren't normally greeted with open arms, so it was best to have somebody black with you, at least until you became a familiar face.

Artie provided me with my entree to that scene; the fact that he was Afram meant that he'd avoided that kind of problem, and Harlem was where he spent most of his time. He took me with him on the last two evenings of that week so that people could get a look at me, introduced me to a few acquaintances he'd made, and that paved the way for the solo trips I made up there after he'd gone back to base and during later survey outings. At that time I was pretty amused to see the way that he'd adapted to those particular circumstances; I think the rest of the Rutgers' staff would have been tickled, too, if he'd turned up there in the zooty outfit he'd gotten himself, but there was always a touch of the street in his makeup, and that had made it relatively easy for him to slot into the Harlem jazz community. He hadn't needed to put on much of a performance, just slightly exaggerate what came naturally, and it was obvious that he was already accepted as one of the regular crowd that frequented those places.

Because of the sheer concentration of the musical activity on 52nd Street I did most of my research and recording there that first time out, but despite the quality of most of what I heard I couldn't really detect much evidence of the evolutionary changes I was particularly hoping to find, not then. For the most part that kind of thing was still restricted to a couple of Harlem clubs, Minton's and Monroe's, and those were the places where I often got my biggest kicks. Even there, though, the changes to the music that I heard were still very much at the embryo stage, so what resulted was often like the contents of rag-bag, fragments of old and new all mixed together, more of a tantalising hybrid than a truly unified form, but still intriguing.

I'm not going to go into a lot of detail about why these changes were taking place, but you need to know the basic reasons if you're going to understand that part of what's been happening to me. It principally got started because some of the younger black musicians got tired of being restricted by the normally pretty simple chord patterns they used to improvise on and a style of playing that had become more or less standardised by then, especially when they had to put up with second-raters sitting in on the after-hours sessions where they went to let off steam, and these guys reacted by gradually piecing together an altogether more demanding musical vocabulary that eventually led to what was in effect a real quantum leap in all departments and effectively split the jazz community right down the middle. It made it more difficult to steal ideas, too, at least for a while, and that was another factor. Whitey has always profited from copying stuff that originated with black musicians and bands, and there was understandable resentment about that, so it was a way of reasserting themselves, reminding people who the real originators were, and at the same time discouraging people who couldn't handle these changes from trying to mix it with them.

It was a key period in the evolutionary sense, but any chance of comprehensive documentation was sabotaged when the Musicians' Federation called a ban on all commercial recording activities by its members that was due to start in August that year and last for the next eighteen months or so. The issue was the amount of air-time being given over to records rather than live music; they wanted a token payment whenever that happened, which wasn't exactly unreasonable, but it all backfired badly, because although they eventually got what they were asking for the strike was a major factor in kick-starting the end of the big swing band era and simultaneously wiping out any chance of collecting and preserving decently recorded aural evidence of what was happening at the really creative end of the music right then.

Actually, I had a very good reason to be grateful in a strictly selfish way, because if it hadn't been for the gaping hole that that left it's very possible that our little sub-section of the programme would never have existed. This changing musical climate's turned out to be relevant in a very personal way, too, although I had no way at all of even suspecting that until a good deal later. Anyway, for the time being I just did what I was supposed to do, observed and recorded and kept a fairly low profile, but made sure that my face got known at the same time. There was so much to soak up and the time went so fast that it was a real shock when I started to experience the warning signs I'd been told to expect, signalling that it was time for me to head on back to base.

I'd barely thought about that side of things until then, which might sound unlikely, but I was already totally addicted to what I was doing. I was in no way unusual in that respect, either, because everybody who'd been selected for survey duty was an historical junkie of one kind or another. Social, military, the sciences, the arts, it didn't matter what the specialism was, in that situation all of us were hooked to an extent that no non-addict could possibly hope to understand.

On my twelfth day there I woke up around noon feeling nauseous and breathless, and my heartbeat was pretty irregular, too. It was disturbing, of course, but I didn't panic; in fact, my first reaction was a mixture of disappointment, jealously of the guy I was alternating shifts with, and concern about how it might affect my own position as far as future assignments were concerned.

The instructions we'd been given about that kind of situation had been very precise, though, so I notified my ground staff contact and then caught the first available train to Leyland, and all the time the symptoms very gradually worsened, which was when I started to get things into a more realistic perspective.

Learning about the three-week limit and the reason for it had been a shaker, but of course we'd been assured that as long as we struck to the rules we'd be O.K., at no serious risk. The delayed-action protective shots that had been introduced after the unanticipated changes to the blood components of the two preliminary surveyors who'd died had meant that there'd been no more problems of that kind, we'd been told, and in any case, they said, they'd both managed to make it back before the changes killed them, so we had no reason for undue concern.

Despite all of that I hadn't even made it half-way through my allotted time there, which to say the least of it was alarming. It's hard to believe now, but until that moment, when it was affecting me directly, I simply hadn't allowed myself to think too deeply about that aspect of it all. Being accepted onto the programme had pretty much obsessed me at the time, so I'd somehow managed to convince myself that what they'd told us about the shots was bound to be right, and as long as I headed back to base as soon as the warning signs appeared the injection would kick in and see me safely there, where they'd be waiting to normalize things.

Right then, though, I really began to sweat, wondering just how foolproof the stuff they were pumping into us was. We'd been told it was an adaptation of something that NASA had cooked up when they'd still had a budget generous enough for them to be able to plan a manned expedition to Mars, which meant that it must have been modified for our use in one hell of a hurry, so there simply wouldn't have been time for proper checks and counter-checks and field-testing.

From the point of view of the overall situation that degree of haste was understandable, of course. Don't forget, because of what had been learned from the research on the Bush Hill estate and the derelict building where the hole was, the people in charge had been able to deduce that they had less than a year and-a-half to complete everything. That was little enough, especially in view of what was happening at that particular point in our history, but they still saw it as priceless, and I guess that on balance they took a reasonable gamble in assuming that we'd get an uninterrupted run, that it actually would stay open for the whole of that time.

But it still meant that at most they had less than eighteen months to do it all, and of course they hadn't become fully operational for almost three of those because of the time it had taken to set up the programme. When you think about how much they achieved in that time, it really was an incredible exercise in get-up-and-go; converting the old agricultural college into temporary training and living quarters, buying and adapting the premises on the other side of the hole that had been Moston Engineering works – the name T.& M. Research was dictated by the contemporary newspaper reports, by the way – recruiting and training personnel and so on, but it still left them with only fifteen months or so to trawl what they could before the fire the fire that seems to have been responsible for closing it happened. Like I told you, they have no idea why or how it happened; the possibility that it originated – *will* originate, I guess – in Stolz and Weatherby's old premises seems the likeliest explanation as far as it goes, but whatever the cause they've had plenty of time to get ready for it.

There were a lot of scare stories about spies and espionage floating around during the war years, so it's hardly surprising the press played up the mystery angle the way they did. It must have been a real puzzler, too; no locals employed at T.& M. Research, no bodies found when they raked over what was left, no indication of what kind of activities had actually gone on there, and especially the fact that nobody claiming a connection with the place showed up, then or ever. What actually happened to the hole is the really intriguing part, of course. It's only logical to assume that that was when it closed, whether as a direct result of the fire or something else there's obviously no way of telling, but there was no hint in any of the newspapers that it'd been found, and there's apparently no trace of a mention in any government files of the period, either.

Whatever, as far as our people were concerned they had no realistic option except to interpret it as telling them that that was the end of the programme, at least for the time being. Unless the hole re-opened sometime, or another one like it turned up – which'd have to be in circumstances where it'd be possible to keep it under wraps, like the existing one – it looked to them as though what we'd been given for the past eighteen months really was the whole thing, a once-in-a-lifetime opportunity to study our own history at first hand that they simply hand't been able to resist, despite the unknown quantities and possible dangers involved.

Knowing what was going to happen eventually was no kind of consolation right then, of course, and in any case there wasn't anything I could do except hope that I made it back before I became another fatality. I carried on sweating and fretting for as long as it took to get to Leyland, and by the time I got in I really did feel pretty terrible; extremely nauseous and breathing like an asthmatic in the middle of a bad attack, a throbbing headache, and my pulse was sluggish and all over the place. Back at base they put me to bed right away and gave me a shot and I went out like a light, very fast, and when I came round a couple of hours later I felt fine; no queasiness or headache, a steady pulse, breathing normal, no trace at all of what I'd been going through.

There were no problems at the physical I had the next morning, either; it didn't take long and I was given a clean bill of health. I told the medic about how I'd felt, and he said it sometimes took a little while to balance the booster dosage as far as individual needs were concerned. He'd make sure I had the necessary increase next time I went out, he said, but I didn't have anything to worry about; there'd been nothing in the results of my checkup to suggest that I wouldn't adapt quickly to the level of dosage that'd allow me to extend my trips to the maximum three-week stay.

That was a tremendous relief, of course. The question of physical risk had become my first concern, although the possibility of being taken off field-work and restricted to base duties for the duration hadn't been much less of a worry. I'd cleared that hurdle, though, and afterwards I made it through the psych check as well; in fact, before experiencing what I'd gone through that was the part of the de-briefing that in some ways I'd dreaded more than the physical, but I obviously managed O.K..

Anyway, I was in the clear, so I checked in at the section and gave Jack Walden, our section head, a preliminary verbal report – just to clarify, he's an ex-journalist who'd been running the department of jazz studies at Cornell, a good organiser – and we discussed the trip, how I felt it had gone generally. In some ways it was a relief to be back, to have made it without coming to any actual harm and to know that I'd been cleared for future trips, but even while we were talking I was feeling restless, wanting to get back to the smoke and the noise and the music, the whole intoxicatingly chaotic scene I'd been forced to leave behind for the next three weeks.

At least I had enough to occupy me for the first of them, which did help a little. I put together a detailed report and transferred and filed the stuff I'd recorded, then after I'd cleared it I drifted around Maine for a few days, but found it impossible to settle, really relax. Letting us out for a touch of our own normality so that our feet stayed on the ground to some extent made sense, I suppose, but in practise it didn't work all that well, not as far as I was concerned, anyway. Eventually I simply gave up trying and spent the rest of the break hanging around base, manufacturing work for myself and itching to get started again, and I was more relieved than I can tell you when it was time for me to go out on my second trip.

I had no kind of premonition at all about what the whole business was going to mean to me in the personal sense eventually, not then. That didn't hit me until quite a bit later, and it was only after a couple of things happened that on the face of them were both freakish coincidences that I got any kind of inkling. One improbable incident wasn't enough to make me automatically curious, but two was something else, and after the second one I began to wonder if they could possibly be linked in some way, if there could actually be some kind of pattern to what I was involved with, even if I could be an essential part of it.

That persisted until very recently, and although I'm pretty sure now that my initial reactions were right after all, I have to admit that it's still left a question mark, albeit a very small one. My ideas about existence have always been uncertain, anyway, and they're certainly no more clear now; if anything, in some ways they're more confused that they've ever been. It could be that as a believer you find that kind of possibility a lot easier to go along with than I do, Phyl; whatever, despite what I've come around to accepting I'm just going to give you the facts and leave it you to draw your own conclusions, but even if you decide that temporarily seeing myself as a possible candidate for that kind of consideration has been the height of egotistical blasphemy, I think you may at least understand why I've had the nerve to tentatively ask myself the question.

Anyway, my second and third trips went smoothly enough. There were no real recurrences of the scare that I'd had at the finish of my first time out, by the way, because I made sure I was out of there in good time; I did experience mild symptoms on a couple of later occasions, but they didn't worry me too much because I was already on my way back to base before they surfaced.

Whether pre-destiny's at back of it all or not, it was while I was there the fourth time that the first really significant thing happened.

4.

—

The room was almost filled when the plump-faced man with the crew-cut and broadly-checked jacket entered. He nursed his drink, gazing searchingly through the haze of smoke, slightly disconcerted by the absence of white faces other than his own.

Whites did come here, he knew; an associate who'd preceded him from Fargo a couple of months earlier had assured him that that was the case. There'd been no blatantly open indication that he was unwelcome when he'd come in, either, but he was already conscious of the fact that his presence was attracting a few thoughtful or straight-faced glances.

Take it easy, he told himself. There was no real feeling of threat in the air, nothing to inspire alarm. Even so, he was already feeling isolated, as though an invisible barrier was separating him from his surroundings and the other people there. Then he saw the man near the far end of the room, seated with his back against the wall, his head turned in the direction of the small, low stage occupied by the musicians, watching the activity there.

He looks white, the crew-cut man thought. In the subdued lighting it was hard to tell for sure, but the clean-shaven profile looked Caucasian. He worked his way across the room, and halted beside him. "Pardon me." The man looked up at him, clearly startled. "Is anybody else sitting here?"

The man stared at him without replying. The crew-cut man guessed him to be in his early thirties, possibly a decade older than himself; small-featured and thin, the drawn planes of his face contrasting with his own rather bland pale plumpness. A camera was hung around his neck, its lens exposed above the hanging case-flap. He said again, rather shortly, "Are you on your own? Is this seat taken?"

The thin-faced man stirred to slightly embarrassed movement. "No. No, it isn't. I'm sorry. I wasn't really with you just then."

"That's O.K.," the crew-cut man said. He sat down, relieved by the belated politeness. These places attracted all kinds, he knew, and he could have been considered a little out of line just then. He took out cigarettes and put one in his mouth, hesitated, then proffered them. "Smoke?"

The thin-faced man shook his head. "No, thanks."

The man with the crew-cut put the pack on the table and lit the cigarette with an initialled lighter, then turned his attention to the stage. It was sparsely occupied. Besides the obligatory piano, bass and drums the only other player was a slightly-built young Negro holding a trumpet, presently tacit and seated to one side listening intently to the piano's oblique, fragmentary explorations that were being backed by a steady bass line and firm, frequently punctuated drumming.

The pianist hunched bulkily over the keyboard; a heavy, bowed figure that watched the traverse of his fingers with apparently bemused intensity. Some of the patterns he made had a crab-like quality to them; oddly discordant shapes that to the crew-cut man's ears were rhythmically uneven, their eccentricity fuelled by the drummer's own occasionally perverse placement of accents.

It's kind of weird alright, he thought. He essayed a small, wry smile. Kenny had been right about that. Well, at least he could say that he'd checked it out, speak with some authority. And anyway, he had plenty more time, another five evenings when he could catch up with the less esoteric happenings to be found in other parts of Harlem and over in 52nd Street.

The pianist finished his solo to a scattering of applause, looking up almost vacantly to the young trumpet-player as he worked through the closing bars. The trumpet-player lifted his instrument to his mouth and began to play, the trumpet angled towards the floor just beyond the stage. His tone was restrained and cloudy, and his phrases sparsely noted; quiet, mostly legato music that was almost drowned by the steady drone of talk that filled the room. He worked his way carefully through two choruses of the standard that they were playing, tacking on a brief coda as the music drifted to a subdued conclusion.

What applause there was was fairly perfunctory, thinly augmented by one or two encouraging shouts. There was a lull as the pianist and *bassist conferred and the drummer lit a cigarette, staring out across the room. The drone of conversation rose steadily in volume.*

Well, the crew-cut man thought, disappointed. So this is Minton's. So what. He glanced at the thin-faced man, still sitting with his back to the wall, his head lowered now. "Kind of slow tonight."

The thin-faced man stirred. "It's still early. It'll pick up in a while." *His voice, like his face was politely withdrawn, muted by caution.*

The crew-cut man gestured towards the stage. "I thought they queued up to blow in this place. A friend of mine told me there were more guys up there than customers, almost, when he was here. Monday's supposed to be the big night, right?"

The thin-faced man elicited a small smile. "They'll be along. There were a couple of triers up there just now, but they cut out when the going got a bit too hard."

"Too weird, you mean?"

The thin-faced man smiled again. The smile sat awkwardly on his features somehow, as though it didn't really belong there. "You could say that." *He studied the crew-cut man guardedly, and nodded towards the stage.* "Did you like what they were doing just now?"

The crew-cut man shrugged. "It was O.K., I guess. The trumpet sure wasn't much. He wants to work on putting an edge on his tone. No bite, you know what I mean?"

"It could be that that's how he hears it," *the thin-faced man said. His look was still guarded, but touched with appraisal now.* "Maybe he likes a softer sound."

The crew-cut man felt a slight stirring of annoyance. He shrugged again. "That's up to him. He'd get buried in a section, though. Any idea who he is?"

The thin-faced man said, after a pause, "No. He hasn't shown before when I've been here. The regular guy's out sick, I heard."

So you don't know everything, the crew-cut man thought. He glanced towards the stage where the bassist was now re-tuning his instrument while the pianist quietly fed him single notes. "How about the rest of them? Is that the one called Monk?"

The thin-faced man nodded. "Yes. The bass player's—" *He broke off and turned his head towards the back of the room as someone shouted a greeting, echoed by others.* "I guess things should heat up in a little now." He smiled his uncomfortable, non-committal smile again.

The crew-cut man followed his gaze and saw a broad squat man carrying a tenor saxophone case edging his way past the tables, exchanging greetings as he approached the stage. Now, that's more like it, he thought. He exposed his teeth in an anticipatory grin as Ben Webster stepped up onto the stage, greeted the people there, and began to unpack his instrument. He said, "I heard Duke was in town. The kid with the trumpet might be smart if he took off now. Men and boys, you know what I mean?"

The thin-faced man nodded, blank-faced. "You could be right."

There's no could be, pal, the crew-cut man thought. He held his elation in check as he watched Webster confer with Monk and the bassist and drummer, screwing the goose-neck of his saxophone into position then tuning to the piano. The trumpet-player was still there, making what he guessed were unnecessary adjustments to his instrument. There was a touch of electricity in the air now, the kind of anticipatory pressure that precedes a storm. Webster seated himself on a vacant chair and re-set his sling, taking his time. He stared out into the room, his head nodding slightly, then suddenly still as he closed his lips over the mouthpiece.

For three bars the saxophone was unaccompanied; a gush of soft-edged metallic resonance that swept out across the room, instantly establishing a medium-tempoed foundation in which the notes were embedded with tersely positive precision. At the beginning of the fourth bar, the drummer softly commenced a press-roll, pushing it to a crescendo as the bar ended and the rhythm jumped into full flow.

There were shouts from the audience as the music surged from the stage, the tenor's sonority backed by the steady drive of the bass, the punctuations of the piano, now laid firmly on the beat, and an urgent wash of cymbal response; an instinctively integrated torrent of sound that shimmered and pulsed with its own unique elated vitality, contrasting sharply with the subdued hesitancy of the previous performance. There were still traces of dissonance detectable in the pianist's chording, but now they added an element of spice to the overall texture of the music, contradictorily but effectively complementing the relatively straightforward harmonic conception of the saxophone. Behind them, the rhythm simultaneously supported and propelled, completing the formula. There was no hesitation detectable, no uncertainty of any kind. Already it was of a piece, giving clear notice that nothing less than triumphant resolution was anticipated, to come in its own imperiously dictated time.

Grinning, his right foot pumping urgently in unison with its pulse, the crew-cut man glanced towards where the young trumpet-player was watching Webster, his trumpet held lightly against his chest with both hands. His pose was relaxed, but there was a slight stiffness about his face, a patina of tension that he couldn't disguise. Deep water, my friend, the crew-cut man thought. Too deep for you by a long, long way. He felt a flicker of sympathy as the tenor's full-throated declamation continued to cascade out into the room, drowning the remnants of conversation at the crowded tables.

Webster's solo was relatively extended, an ostensibly off-hand display of muscle-flexing that concluded with a raspingly repetitive figure and a single explosive, breath-saturated note that was almost like a spit of contempt. Monk took it up as Webster turned away and made conversation with the bassist while applause and approving shouts came from the body of the room.

Jesus, the crew-cut man thought. He joined the clapping, enthusiastically. That's _really_ talking. He glanced at the thin-faced man, still backed against the wall, his head tilted now as he stared towards the stage and the activity there. There was no visible response to the music that the crew-cut man could detect; no movement of any kind, no indication of pleasure or approval. He was frowning slightly, his face thoughtful, as though the music had failed to penetrate his preoccupation with a matter of greater concern.

How blasé can you get?, the crew-cut man thought. Slightly irritated again, he lit another cigarette and returned his attention to the stage where the trumpet-player was watching Monk with the same simulated calm that he had afforded Webster. You don't fool me, buddy, the crew-cut man thought, sourly. Your guts are tied up in reef-knots right now. He drew on his cigarette, the continuing rise and fall of his foot additionally fuelled by a touch of acerbity.

Monk's solo was shorter than Webster's; explorative playing that now took on some of its former metrical eccentricity; riff-based, closely intervalled phrases and occasional extravagant runs that were separated by extended periods of inactivity, its apparently piecemeal structure held together by the positive interplay of bass and drums. It terminated with a two-handed attack that contained what could have been a touch of burlesque, an implied recognition that in the present context a degree of deference to tried and tested ingredients should be acknowledged, a good-humoured nod to earlier innovators and the foundations they had laid.

The trumpet-player raised his instrument and began to blow as applause and one or two mildly ironic cheers came from the audience. He began simply, with a series of flattish-sounding, widely spaced notes, some of them sustained across a bar or more; soft, almost vibratoless sound that was nevertheless rounded and firm. The density of the rhythmic backing lightened, gradually adjusting its texture to provide a sympathetic cushion for the light tone and fragmented phrasing. It was a pattern that continued for the first two choruses, a period of careful stabilisation that concerned itself more with rhythmic placement than harmonic exploration.

Gradually, the line became more complex and idiosyncratic, echoing something of the pianist's solo style; still based on the legato approach with which it had started, but now interspersed with more widely intervalled phrases and contrasting flurries of notes that were not always cleanly executed; another contradictory compound that somehow managed to preserve a sense of form and continuity. As the solo progressed, the crew-cut man became conscious of the increasing complexity of the rhythmic backing and the way that Webster's pose had become suddenly watchful, his heavy-lidded eyes fixed on the trumpet-player and his hands motionless in the saxophone keys.

The trumpet-player finished, concluding with a final downward chromatic run that ended in the instrument's lowest register. Better, the crew-cut man acknowledged. Not really good, but better. He joined in the applause as Webster leaned across to the trumpet-player and said something, holding his arm. The trumpet-player nodded and smiled, rather shyly, his fingers still flicking at the valves of his instrument. There was something a little cat-like about him, the crew-cut man decided, a quality that on reflection had been mirrored in his playing; a kind of thoughtful if not always certain toying with the harmonic and rhythmic structure of the music, as though it had been a captive mouse or bird; some new and not altogether predicable plaything, to be *nudged and prodded with cautious respect before familiarity permitted the eventual emboldened dissection.*

He glanced across the table, surprised and vaguely discomfited to see that the thin-faced man was smiling now. The contraction of the facial muscles was still a somehow uncomfortable exercise, touched with something that could almost have been regret, but there was genuine pleasure as well, even a touch of constrained exultation.

Well, O.K., the crew-cut man thought. He mentally shrugged, sensing that in some way this response implied that he personally had been excluded from the full reality of what had just happened; that beneath the surface of events had lain subtleties beyond the range of his own appreciative capabilities. If that's what you dig, he thought, flatly. But he wasn't that good, believe me. Still irritated, he returned his attention to the music, now pared down to the fragmented line of the bass, punctuated by nudging interjections from the piano and drums.

The bassist concluded his solo and Webster re-entered with twelve bars of richly textured, solidly structured music that was firmly anchored in the rhythmic foundation behind him. The trumpet-player responded with a chorus of his own; soft-toned and relatively restrained, but in no way deferential; a lightly skipping exercise that was in direct contrast to Webster's more firmed-footed approach. This alternation continued for several choruses before Webster set up a riff and the trumpet-player joined him. The music finished to a lot of applause.

The crew-cut man said, after a pause, "He could make it, but he'll have to fill out his sound and work on those runs." He reached for another cigarette. "Not bad for somebody that young, I guess. He's got plenty of time to get it together, build up his lip." He glanced at the thin-faced man again, this time startled by the sudden bleakness that he saw on the drawn features. "I mean, a few years on the road—" He broke off and turned his head as voices rose behind them. More people had entered, several of them carrying instrument cases. He recognised two of them; Roy Eldridge and Lips Page among the less familiar faces.

He grinned broadly, relieved to find himself back on familiar ground. "Well, now. It looks like he might be going to get a real run for his money. He'll find it tough trying to stay with these guys." He turned back to the stage, in time to see the young trumpet-player snap his instrument-case shut, exchange a few words with Webster, then step down and melt into the crowd. A minute later he caught a last glimpse of him as he went through the door at the far end of the room.

He shrugged again, reaching into his jacket for his lighter. "I guess he got smart. O.K. for a preliminary, but not so hot when it comes to the main bout."

The thin-faced man said, "Maybe so." He looked and sounded suddenly tired. He glanced at his watch, and rose. "I guess that does it for me." He nodded, without smiling, and turned away, threading his way through the crowded room towards the exit.

You're not really so hep, buddy, the crew-cut man thought. All that what's-different-has-got-to-be-good stuff. If you really knew what it was about you wouldn't take off when the real action was due to start. And it wasn't going to be a wasted evening after all, now that Ben and Roy and Lips and some other real pros were on the scene. He settled in his chair, lighting his cigarette and smiling in anticipation as the new arrivals began to congregate on the small stage.

5.

—

It'd be impossible for me to describe exactly how I felt right then. Although I'd struck gold, the foreknowledge I'd taken back with me had thrown a shadow across the whole business, not simply what had happened that evening, but in a more general sense as well. In fact, that general shadow had been gradually adding itself to my existing reservations for quite a while before that, but the truth is that I'd chosen to ignore it as best I could because I didn't want it to sour things any more than was absolutely necessary.

I still didn't consider the wider implications all that much, not immediately, because my mind was completely taken up with Buddy Henry and what I knew about him. Before that evening I'd only ever heard him soloing briefly on a handful of radio transcriptions that had been subjected to fairly rough treatment before they'd ended up in more caring hands, but even after that they'd never been really successfully restored.

Despite that, his playing had lodged itself firmly in the back of my mind, and because I'd heard those same individual qualities back there at Minton's I'd eventually recognised him, musically first, then physically. In fact, those transcription solos had been a revelation when they came to light a few years back, not just to me, to jazz historians generally. Even the mush that had gradually accumulated over them and never been completely removed hadn't been able to disguise the totally personal sound that he'd made; soft but broad, cloudy but paradoxically clear as well, truly unique. It had a kind of serenity, too, the sound of someone who'd found his direction, and I think that was the most moving aspect of the whole thing, adding tragedy to the mix, because I knew that only a few months from then he was due to die, and in pretty horrific circumstances.

He was twenty-two years old, and he came from Wichita; he'd learned trumpet at high-school and spent the previous four or five years serving the usual apprenticeship, playing in mid-western territory bands then moving up the professional ladder when he joined the Benny Valentine band while it was on tour. It wasn't long after that that he'd made the radio transcriptions for a small radio station in Omaha, playing with a contingent from the Valentine band, and a few weeks later he'd died in a hotel fire, leaving those few fragments as his only recorded legacy.

Known photographs of him were almost as rare, all of them showing him in group settings, most of them blurred publicity half-tones of the Valentine band. It'd been impossible to pick out any real facial detail on any of them, but even so, as soon as I'd recognised his playing I could see that it was him; the puffed-out cheeks that only partially filled out the small face under the contrastingly large forehead and deep cranium. What I'd caught at Minton's had confirmed a belief that I'd held ever since hearing the transcriptions; that he was years ahead of his time, someone whose playing contained clear pre-echoes of the future, and an individuality that I was convinced would have coloured the voices of the emerging generation of he'd lived long enough for his message to have been absorbed and understood.

He was virtually unacknowledged in his own time, the usual fate of far too many creative pioneers who dare to wander that far ahead of the crowd, hoping that people will catch up with them eventually. But even that kind of belated recognition was going to come far too late to benefit him in any way. The reaction of the guy who'd shared my table at Minton's and the general indifference of the audience until Webster's presence had helped to focus some attention on him must have been typical of the kind of treatment that he'd grown accustomed to during his relatively short playing life. Creativity that's that far ahead of the game can be a lonely business, and the dividing line between rejection and acceptance a tough one to make it across. But he had a quality that I sensed *would* have made it in the musical climate of the not-so-distant future, and that meant that his own playing as well as his influence could have been a key factor then, maybe even bringing him the rewards that he deserved.

A sad aspect of jazz history is that it's peppered with might-have-beens, people who could and should have made it, but never did. Some of them failed because of their own inherent weaknesses or misguided beliefs, and others actually did make it, but only for a short time and often for the same reasons.

But Henry wasn't one of those. He was snuffed out in circumstances that might have been of his own making – smoking in bed, something like that – but even if it was his own fault that didn't make his dying when he did any less tragic. Hard drugs weren't much more than a fringe problem just then; they took their real toll a few years later, but he wasn't going to live to see that, or have the chance to become one of its victims. He was going to die because of an accident, and that meant that as far as the jazz audience was concerned both he and they were going to be robbed anyway; him of his life and talent, and them of the contribution that he would have made, almost certainly a vital one.

In actual playing time, the extended performance I'd captured that evening had enormously increased the evidence of that contribution, and despite the far from perfect circumstances it had been recorded on equipment that was going to do him something like full justice at last. Even though I'd remembered at the time of making the recording what the future held for him, my initial reaction when I'd realised who he was had been mostly excitement, the joy of making a prize capture, especially because it had come right out of the blue, and it was only when he quit and left the club that the tragic side of it really hit me, making it impossible for me to stay and listen to what was going to happen after that.

I felt helpless and frustrated for the rest of that evening, damning the fates for being so coldly uncaring and depressed in a more specific way than I had been since first going through the hole. But next day I told myself that there was no point in that kind of thinking, because the time allotted to him was set and there was nothing at all that I could do to change that. What I had to do was accept the situation for what it had been, a once-only opportunity to really put the record straight on his behalf. There was no chance of his being rewarded in what was left of his life, but at least his paragraph could be revised, his contribution shown in its true light. So on that point at least I was able to console myself a little; still saddened by it, but able to appreciate that what had happened had been of real value, a kind of posthumous tribute to someone who might have elevated himself to the ranks of the giants if circumstances hadn't worked against him to prevent that happening.

But even though I'd resigned myself to seeing it in a more positive way, the general depression stayed with me, and over the next few days I found I was being reluctantly forced to recognise that for some time my attitude had been changing, that I was seeing the situation as a whole very differently to the way I'd viewed it when I'd first gone there.

Everybody dies, that's the one totally inescapable fact of existence, and as far as a lot of the other musicians I'd listened to and recorded, I knew pretty much exactly when that would be for them. Some were going to go on living for a reasonable span, some weren't. But initially at least that was something I hadn't really considered in any deep emotional sense, and I guess I'd seen my attitude as simply being realistic, accepting the inevitable in a mature way and simultaneously ensuring that I didn't wander too close to the objectivity parameters that the programme planners considered acceptable.

It wasn't really like that any more, though, and it hadn't been for some time. Against my better judgement I'd gradually begun to view these people as real individuals, subject to all the pressures and ailments and calamities that afflict all of us; a far more unsettling business that I'd bargained for, and something that I instinctively resisted because of the way that it might affect my own immediate future. I knew from conversations that I'd had at base that the limits calculated by the psych section were generally considered realistic, not unreasonably demanding; after all, compassion's a normal part of human nature, and none of us could be expected to shut it off completely. But it all came down to a question of degree, just how far that kind of thing could go before the people in charge decided that it had reached an unacceptable level, and because of that I'd tried to keep it at arm's length, refused to acknowledge that it was actually happening to me.

But the Buddy Henry thing had forced me to admit a few things to myself. I remembered how I felt during my first couple of trips, my irritation at some of the service people in the clubs, their obvious indifference to the real qualities of the music that was being played there, and that was a recollection that emphasised just how much I'd changed since those early days. Without consciously thinking about it, I'd begun to view that kind of thing in a much more understanding way, seeing it for what it often was: a fundamentally tragic situation, where life-affirming music was serving as a narcotic, dulling the uncertainties and fear that haunted them, however unconsciously that might have been, temporarily at least shutting out the dreadful possibilities of an uncertain future. They didn't really dig the music, but that was their business. They still benefited from it, because for a little while the images of death and mutilation were blotted out by a pulse that echoed the pumping inside their own still-intact bodies, and although the finer points of what was being played might have eluded them they knew that dead men don't tap their feet and snap their fingers.

But it went even further than that. I'd begun to see myself as a kind of uniquely situated voyeur, someone whose foreknowledge placed them in an almost god-like position, and not just in a general way, either; the Buddy Henry business had underlined just how specific it could be. And what was to prevent me from getting into a conversation with any of the people that swarmed all around me, eventually finding out their names and a few personal details? The chances were that somewhere among our own files it'd be possible to find out what happened to that person; the broad pattern of their life, its development and eventual ending.

I guess there are some people who'd revel in that kind of situation, actually enjoy it as a kind of temporary omnipotence. Not too many, though. I think most people would react as I did; feel a mixture of sadness and sympathy, a kind of deepened recognition of the brevity of life. I'd begun to really look at faces then, too; not in the furtive, glancing way that I had at first, but actually studying them, feeling a degree of kinship that I don't recall feeling before, not ever; wondering about them, worrying about them even, wanting to express this new awareness in some way.

I told you earlier about how the military people had wanted to use the hole to try and wrap the war up in short order, and despite all the terrible implications why that had been decided against, and the truth was that even though I'd begun to feel the way I did the non-participation policy still seemed to me the only rational way to go. Looked at logically, history *has* to be a fait accompli that in all probability's immutible anyway. But even if it isn't, there could never have been any guarantee that the kind of interference they envisaged would ultimately have been beneficial. With the global situation as delicately balanced as it is the planners obviously followed the only sensible course open to them when they decided that trying to tamper with the already recorded pattern of events, however well-intentioned, might somehow work against us in ways we simply couldn't imagine, actually exacerbate the process of decay.

So despite my changed feelings I didn't see that I had any choice, either; I simply had to bottle them up as best I could while I just carried on doing what I was there for. It was never quite the same after that evening at Minton's, though. The music didn't stir me any less than it had before, but I had these other things on my mind as well. I began to get irrational impulses, too; a couple of times I felt an almost irresistible urge to grab the microphone wherever I was and tell the people there that in the end they were going to win the war, that kind of thing. But who'd have believed me? Why should they? It was a crazy time, even crazier than now in some ways, riddled with just about every kind of over-heated lunacy. They'd simply have decided that I'd had too many drinks and bundled me out of the place, never knowing that what I was offering them was the truth, a valid promise of ultimate victory.

Fortunately, I'd calmed down a little by the time I got back to the base. The feeling was still there, but I'd managed to rationalise it enough to accept that it was something I was simply going to have to live with, an inevitable part of the situation. I was still worried about how the psych people would view it, but in the event there was no problem at all; I was told that my reaction had been perfectly normal, that it was a phase that everybody out in the field went through sooner or later, and it was very unlikely that it'd bother me to the same extent in the future. The way things turned out they couldn't have been more wrong about that, but for a while at least I did feel more settled, and my next time out put a real shine on it, too, because it turned up the real highlight of my time in New York, even more of an event than my Buddy Henry find, at least that was how it felt when it happened.

Apart from Henry I haven't bothered to tell you who any of the people I'd been listening to actually were, for the obvious reason that they'd have meant absolutely nothing to you, but one other name I feel I have to bring in at this point is Charlie Parker. That's partly because he was one of the genuinely pivotal people ever to appear on the jazz scene and a key figure as far as the changes that were taking place then were concerned, but principally because the way he played on three consecutive nights during the last week of that trip was something very, very special.

We'd been covering him as best we could ever since the start of the programme, which wasn't always easy, given all the ducking and diving that was a normal feature of his life-style, but right then he'd settled into something of a routine after he finished what was his regular gig at the time, playing with a band that had a residency at the Savoy ballroom. Monroe's had become one of his favourite places to jam; I'd caught him there several times on previous trips and he'd always produced remarkable music, but on the nights I'm talking about there was particularly clear evidence of the new vocabulary that he was gradually developing, and he was obviously inspired by his latest discoveries, consistently reaching a level of creative virtuosity that was truly dazzling, in some ways as good as anything he ever played, at least as far as what was recorded's concerned.

Although for me it was like hitting the mother lode I realise that it's a matter of complete indifference to you, and the only reason I'm telling you about it at all's because it made what happened at the start of what turned out to be my last New York assignment particularly hard to take. It was a terrifying experience in itself, but what made it even worse at the time was that it seemed to be telling me that that was the end of my dream, the whole thing abruptly wrecked by what I saw as a ludicrous coincidence that I'd had no way at all of anticipating or guarding myself against.

I'd only been there a couple of days at the start of my next trip when it happened. I'd just finished what by comparison with the Parker experience hadn't been a particularly productive trawl of the usual places and was back at the hotel I was using then, sitting on the bed unlacing my shoes, when somebody knocked on the door.

6.

—

There was a brief pause, then a voice beyond the door said, "Who is it?"

Mancuso said, "Mr. Cranmer? Could we see you for a minute, please?"

There was another pause, then the muffled sound of footsteps, and the click of a key in the door. It opened, hesitantly.

Mancuso said, again, "Mr. Cranmer?" The man in the doorway nodded. He looks scared already, Mancuso thought. He held up his identification wallet. "I'm Lieutenant Mancuso, and this is Detective-Sergeant Pennebaker. We're police, attached to the Draft Authority. We'd like to check something with you. It shouldn't take long."

The man in the doorway said, "Is there a problem?" His voice was a little clogged.

"Not if you're who it says you are in the hotel register. Can we step inside for a minute?"

The man hesitated, then moved back, reluctantly opening the door wider. They went into the room.

Mancuso looked it over, briefly. It contained the usual hotel bedroom furniture, none of it new. Apart from a newspaper and a camera on the dresser and a shirt draped across the bedside chair, there was little evidence of occupancy. He turned and faced the man as he closed the door and moved away from it. Pennebaker drifted around the room, occasionally tapping surfaces with his forefinger, his eyes bored.

Mancuso said, "Are you on your own here?"

The man nodded. He was fairly tall, an inch or so above Mancuso's five feet nine and-a-half; a gaunt figure in a nondescript brown suit, dark brown shirt and beige tie. His face was pale and shadowed, the eyes hooded by a high, slightly receding forehead. It was an intelligent face, Mancuso decided, *not quite what he'd expected. He mentally compared it with the photograph in his inside jacket pocket. Well, it could be, but he wouldn't bet on it at this stage.*

The man said, "You want identification, is that it?"

Mancuso nodded. "That's it."

The man moved toward the bed. "I keep it under the mattress when I'm not going out again. I only just put—" He stopped as Pennebaker drifted in front of him. He stepped back, and tried to laugh, a failure that produced only a breathless sound. "It's on this side, about half-way up. You people sure are careful."

"It's the only way to be," Mancuso said. He took the papers that Pennebaker extracted from the wallet he was holding, and studied them. After a minute, he handed them back to Pennebaker, who studied them in turn, leisurely. He shrugged, and placed them with the wallet on the dresser top.

The man said, "Well?"

Mancuso ducked his head. "I don't know. They look O.K."

"Then what's the problem?"

Mancuso stared at him. "The problem is they could be phoney. You know anybody called Salter?"

The man shook his head, frowning. "Salter? No, I don't believe I do."

Mancuso continued to stare at him. "A PFC called Billy Salter jumped the stockade back in March. We got a picture of him."

"Are you saying I look like him?"

Mancuso nodded. "You look a lot like him. You could be a little older, I guess."

"What was he inside for?"

Mancuso smiled, thinly. "He was selling medial supplies that belonged to the army, that's what. Why are you in town, anyway?"

The man took a deep breath. "I'm doing research. For a book I'm working on."

"What kind of research?"

The man tried to smile, a weak contraction of the facial muscles that failed to reach completion. "It's going to be a kind of sociological treatise, really, a study of current trends in popular music. New developments, certain ethnic influences, things like that."

"That so?" The voice, too, Mancuso thought. It didn't really fit. Salter was from Tennessee, a down-country boy, and this guy's accent was altogether more neutral. "Sounds kind of unusual." He maintained his stare.

The man tried to smile again, another failure. "Yes. It is a pretty limited field right now. Of course, these things—"

"Know anybody else in town?"

There was a brief silence. The man cleared his throat. "No, not really. Just people I've talked to in bars, restaurants, clubs, that kind of thing." He sounded really frightened now. There was a sick sheen on his pale face, and his eyes looked hunted, close to desperation. Even if he isn't this Salter, there's something wrong, Mancuso decided. He just didn't tie together. They'd better take him in, run a check. He looked just about ready to fall apart, anyway.

The man said, hoarsely, "Look, the fact is, I'm expecting somebody. Can't this wait until tomorrow? You really have got it all wrong, you know." It sounded furtive, totally unconvincing.

"I thought you didn't know anybody in New York. Who are you expecting?"

"Well." The man hesitated again. "A friend. You know."

Mancuso nodded. "Sure. I think you'd better come along with us, anyway. If we clear you, you could be back here in a couple hours." He tilted his head towards the door. "Let's go."

The man said, fretfully, "Would it be all right if I left her a note? I mean, she's not just—" His voice tailed away.

Was that all it was, Mancuso wondered, making it with some guy's wife? He studied the patently guilty face, thoughtfully. No, it had to be more than that. He shrugged. "O.K., make it short."

The man licked his lips, then began to slide a hand inside his jacket. Beside him, Pennebaker said, "Hold it." He reached out and took hold of the man's arm, then pushed his other hand inside the jacket. He fumbled around, then withdrew it, holding a fountain-pen. "O.K., go ahead."

The man took the pen. His face was grey now, and his hands were shaking. Mancuso folded his arms and rested the backs of his legs against the base-board of the bed, watching him as he unscrewed the fountain-pen cap and slipped it into his side pocket.

In the seconds that remained before he blacked out, Mancuso's curiosity only became alarm when he saw Pennebaker's collapse. The sequence of events was completed almost instantly, and yet it was as though a minute fragment of time had somehow expanded so that its individual components transmitted themselves at a speed that enabled him to watch them in detail, at first uncomprehendingly, and then with shocked helplessness.

The pen, he thought, idly. Why would he do that, put the cap in his pocket, instead of pushing it onto the butt end? Still unalarmed, only mildly curious, he watched as the man took his left hand away from his pocket and placed his thumb at the base of the pen, turning it suddenly towards Pennebaker.

Pennebaker's head jarred back, a flinching movement that abruptly collapsed along with the rest of his body. His fall was untidy; a loose-limbed, flopping descent that took him floorwards like some inexplicably boneless corpse. He was still moving downwards when the pen was turned in Mancuso's direction, shocking in its sudden threat. Simultaneously, he felt a sharp prick of pain below his right eye. There was a blurred, sliding image of wall and ceiling, the embrace of the bed covers meeting his back, and then nothing, all of it smeared into oblivion by the descending wash of darkness that engulfed him.

7.

—

When the tall one had hit the floor it sounded like the clap of doom to me, the signal for people to start banging on the door, demanding to know what was going on. In retrospect I guess it wasn't really all that loud, but when it was all over I just stood there, desperately trying to hear past the drumming in my ears and shaking like a leaf in a gale, listening for any kind of reaction, especially from the room underneath. I could hear a radio playing somewhere, dance music, but apart from that and the sound of traffic down the street there wasn't anything as far as I could tell.

After my hands had steadied down a bit, I de-armed the pen and put it on the dresser. When I pulled the needle out of the one on the bed I found it had hit close enough to one of his eyes to remind me of something that had always bothered me, the fear that if I ever had to resort to protecting myself like that I'd blind somebody in the process, and it's a thought that still makes me squirm.

I put the needles back in the pen, then washed my hands; I'd been told that that was essential, in case I cut or scratched myself after handling them. Then I got the dark one off the bed and tied and gagged both of them with strips of bedsheet. It was probably a pointless waste of time, actually; I knew they'd be both out for at least a couple hours, and I didn't imagine that I had that long before a call went out that I'd slipped them, but right then it seemed like a sensible thing to do. When I'd finished that, I changed into my spare suit, packed my stuff as fast as I could, and went out into the corridor, locking the door behind me.

It seemed obvious that the hotel people were in on what was happening, maybe even to the extent of it being them that had tipped off the authorities. It was pretty common practice for hotels and flop joints to be issued with photos of wanted people, and I automatically assumed that that was how they'd mistakenly gotten on to me. So I couldn't go by the desk, especially carrying a suitcase, not without stirring up more trouble. But I had to get out as fast as I could, because when the two cops failed to reappear somebody would be bound to check out what had happened to them.

There was a service door at the end of the corridor; it was locked, but we'd had a couple of hours on that during emergency procedure training. It wasn't that easy, principally because my hands were still twitching, but I managed to open it eventually, all the time scared witless that somebody would come out of one of the rooms or the elevator. But they didn't, and I made it down to the bottom without meeting anybody on the way.

I could see an open door halfway along the bottom passage, and I could hear voices coming from where it led to, some kind of argument. I took a chance and kept on moving, and they must have been too busy with what they were disagreeing about to notice me as I went past. The door at the end of the passage was unlocked, and I went outside into a yard that had bins and crates lined up against the walls. I got up onto one of the crates and checked what was on the other side of the wall that continued from the side of the hotel; it was an alleyway, without anybody in it as far as I could tell, so over I went. I got out into the street and walked a little way, then I flagged a cab, and when we got to the station I bought a late edition and sat behind it in the coffee-shop until the train for Leyland came in. It was pretty full, so I parked myself in the club car and hid behind the paper until it pulled out.

Can you imagine me doing those kinds of things, Phyl? I find it hard to believe myself, because all my life I've ducked situations where there was any real physical danger involved. I guess the fact that I'd wittingly allowed myself to get into something that obviously contained a large element of risk underlines how much what I was doing meant to me, and I can tell you that the belief that none of us knows what we're actually capable of when it comes to the question of self-preservation until we're really tested is one hundred percent right. I'd have done considerably more if the circumstances had demanded it, I know that now, and I'm just thankful I didn't have to.

Although I didn't kid myself that I was completely out of the woods, I felt almost elated at that point. In some ways I felt completely exhausted, too, mentally and physically, but I remember that my principle reaction was self-congratulation, the feeling that although I'd been right out there on the line, I'd handled it, no real sweat. The fact that I'd ignored standard emergency procedure – the initial stage, at least – by not referring the police to the people who were set up to vouch for me had been deliberate, because it simply hadn't felt right in that particular situation. If they really had been convinced that I was this Salter, somebody who was actually on the run in their own time, then I sensed that that could have put my back-up in all kinds of trouble, too, if I'd brought any of them into it. I had no way of knowing how my decision was going to sit with the people in charge, of course, but for the time being at least I still felt that I'd been right to handle it like I did.

I made it back to Leyland O.K., but by the time medical had finished with me I was still feeling drained, obviously a reaction to it all, so I decided to skip psych until later, after I'd cleaned up and rested. I went to Walden's office first, though; he'd just started his day, all neat and clean-shaven, while I was a real mess; my suit had dirt marks on it from where I'd climbed over the hotel wall, I had a face-full of stubble, and I was badly in need of a shower by then as well.

I told him what happened, just a straight list of facts. During the train ride I'd had time to consider the implications of it all, and although I still felt that I'd done the right thing that had cooled me down considerably, because they weren't good. The police on the other side of the hole had a picture of somebody who looked enough like me for them to think that maybe they'd found the guy they were looking for, but after what had happened anyone with that face was going to be immediately up-graded to someone that they'd want to get their hands on again particularly badly. What made it far worse was that the pen idea wasn't exactly new; in fact, intelligence agents on both sides were using something like it at the time. So that put this Salter and me right up there on the most-wanted list, not simply as an army defector now, but probably as a suspected foreign agent as well.

Walden listened to it all, then he told me he'd have to take it higher before any kind of decision was made. He agreed that under those particular circumstances I'd probably been right to keep the backup people out of it, but there was no way of telling what sort of a reaction it would get from the brass. He said that in fact mine was the third piece of bad news to hit the programme during the past couple of weeks, and although it was obviously serious and likely to affect our own operation, it was still overshadowed by the other things that had happened.

Two more surveyors had just gone missing, he told me. He didn't know all the details, but one of them was overdue a fortnight by then and the other one a week; the fortnight one was from the theatre and the other one from economics. The theatre surveyor was a woman, the only one in that sub-section. He asked me if the names Carrie Bethal and Martin Glass meant anything as far as I was concerned.

Although I was still immersed in my own problems, that shook me quite a bit. I hadn't known Glass, but I remembered Carrie Bethal because she'd been in the same primary training group as me; dark, attractive in determined kind of way, a small woman, very intense. She'd come out somewhere close to the top of the bunch and immediately gone into the intermediary high-flyers group, while a few of us had to do a re-run of some of the material. The thought of somebody as vital as that being hit by what we'd been warned about, probably reduced to a vegetable before suffocating or having her heart quit on her, was horrible, a truly nightmarish image that I found very frightening, especially after my own experience the first time out.

I told Walden that I'd known her slightly, and we talked about it for a while. It had been accepted that they were both no-hope situations by then, he said; they both had to be dead, either killed in some way, or trapped there by circumstances beyond their control and unable to make it back in time. There was even the possibility that they'd become so engrossed in what they were doing, some project of the moment, that they'd simply ignored the first warning signs and delayed their departure until it was too late, collapsed and died on the way back to the base. It underlined what a uniquely vulnerable situation survey staff were in, he said, and just how important it was to stick to our instructions, and that was something that was being reiterated very strongly before anyone went out again.

It was a depressing conversation, and I was almost glad to get back to discussing my own problem. Walden repeated that he shared my view that given the circumstances I'd handled it in a sensible way, but he was very thoughtful, and I could understand why. New York was a big town, but because of what had happened I'd suddenly become a very bad security risk, and there were going to be a lot of people looking for me as a result. For me to go back there in the foreseeable future would be impossibly chancey, I could see that, even if I kept well under cover during the daytime and restricted my activities to the world of jazz clubs and dance halls and after-hours places. It could even have been that the draft police had latched onto me while I was leaving the last place I'd visited that evening and tailed me to the hotel; after all, I'd only assumed that it was the hotel people that had tipped them off and that they'd been waiting there for me.

But New York was the hub, where all the important things were happening to the music. The other key cities in jazz development were either spent forces in the evolutionary sense, or hadn't yet reached a stage where they were worth more that occasional coverage because of the limited time and facilities available to us, and it wasn't until the 1950's, when the focus shifted to L.A. for a while, that that changed in any appreciable way.

Walden didn't actually tell me that New York was out, but we both knew it. Thinking about it after I left him and went to catch up on some sleep, I could have wept. Because of what I saw as a piece of strictly fortuitous bad luck I'd been robbed of my dream, and there looked to be every possibility that I wouldn't get it back again. Even if they allowed me to carry on with survey duties, which looked to be very doubtful, it would almost certainly be somewhere where the chances of finding anything of real musical importance would be virtually nil. I was still brooding about it when I got to the accommodation quarters and went to bed, so I didn't sleep, just lay there, dozing occasionally and damning the man Salter, the police, the whole wretched mess, and I was at a really low ebb when I did eventually drop off for a while.

One of the things that had kept me awake was wondering how well I was going to handle the psych session, but in fact it went O.K., as far as I could tell. I was asked if what had happened had dampened my enthusiasm for what I was doing in any way, and I told them it hadn't, not at all; my only concern was how it might affect my position on future assignments. They seemed to accept that, and when I'd finished there I reported back to Walden, and he told me that he'd already talked to a couple of senior people but that no quick decision was going to be made, because the issues that it raised were too serious to be decided in a hurry. Although we were already more than halfway through the programme, which meant that the time left was becoming increasing precious, that was only one aspect of it, he said. Security had to be the first priority, and they had to be as sure as they could that if I was going to continue on survey duty it would be under circumstances where the risk factor was absolutely minimal. The situation was going to be gone into at a meeting that was scheduled for the following week, and in all probability a decision would be made then.

He finished up by saying that it was too bad I'd finally gotten around to shaving that morning, because if things worked out the way we hoped it would definitely involve a new identity, and a beard was the best natural disguise. It would be bound to age me to some extent, too, so I'd better quit shaving as from then, just in case.

8.

—

"Give it another couple weeks, and I'd say forty, forty-five," Walden said. "The grey certainly helps. The glasses, too. I don't think the draft people are going to be very interested, anyhow." He grinned. "How does it feel? I grew one once, and the damned thing itched all the time."

Lohmann scratched wryly at the stubble that shadowed his chin. "Right. I guess I'll get used to it, though. Do I take it that that means it's definite?"

Walden nodded. "Yes, but you're not going to be all that crazy about the actual detail. If we'd gone through ten years further back I'm sure you'd have been more than happy, but in this situation anything is better than nothing. My guess is that it'll only be temporary, anyway." He looked slightly apologetic. "You're going to carry on with what Cal Bush was doing in Kansas City. You can check out Missouri and Oklahoma as well if you like, but basically K.C. is it." He saw the anticipated disappointment in Lohmann's face.

There was a short silence, then Lohmann grimaced. "Actually, I'd already figured that that would probably be it. Cal tells me he didn't really draw anything such in the way of music while he was there, not as far as the locals were concerned, anyway. Basie played the Tower Theatre, but that was all the top level he caught. You want me to carry on with the interviewing principally, is that right?"

Walden nodded again. "There are still a lot of gaps on the historical side. Cal was only there for a couple of trips, after all. The only reason we pulled him out and put him on the road was because we decided that covering what's actually going down right now was more important. If we'd had the time and more survey people we'd have left him there at least a little while longer, but we had a re-think and that's the way we saw it. There's bound to be a lot of ground he didn't get the chance to cover, so there's no reason why you shouldn't keep busy." He studied Lohmann's still-sombre face sympathetically. "Look, I understand how you feel, but at least you've got somewhere to go. They were all for pulling you out permanently to start with, don't forget that. They felt you handled that business at the hotel pretty well, which certainly helped your case, but I've still had to do a lot of hard talking to swing even this much, believe me. It might only be for the one trip, anyway. We don't have so much time left that we can afford to waste it, and I'm going to get you back into the action if it's at all possible." He fiddled with a pen, and shrugged. "But New York is right out, you must understand that. We just don't dare take that kind of chance, and don't forget your neck would be right on the line if we did. You've got to stick to your own territory. No excursions beyond that, right?"

Lohmann nodded, reluctantly. "Right."

"It might not be so bad. Like you say, they get name outfits passing through, and it's still jamming territory, so I'm told. Not like it was, of course, but you might catch some good people taking the chance to stretch out while they're there. Bird might even show up occasionally, you never know. In any case, he's bound to have left some kind of mark, even if it was only a small one at that point in time. Anyway, I've got something else in mind for you for maybe your next-but-one trip, but that'd going to take a little more persuasion." He waved down Lohmann's enquiry. "Sorry, I shouldn't have said anything about that just now, but I wanted you to appreciate that I'm trying."

Lohmann nodded. "Thanks. I'm sure you'll do what you can."

"Don't put your shirt on it, but I think there's a reasonable chance," Walden said. "Meantime, dig out Cal's reports and see what looks like they might be reasonable leads. Well, I guess that's it." He rose, and stretched. "You know something? I'd give a couple years of my life to go through, even to Kansas City, but somebody's got to do this job. This is one of those times when I'd be more than glad to relinquish authority, believe me. So you're still the lucky one, remember that."

Lohmann smiled, absently. "Sure."

9.

—

During the 1930's Kansas City, Missouri, could safely lay claim to being one of the most progressive places in the country as far as jazz was concerned, a real melting-pot that had thrown up some of the genuine jazz giants at the time. There'd been various reasons why; its location, away from most of the pressures of the commercial music world, the political setup that'd made it a wide-open town, a partying town, things like that.

Prohibition hadn't really meant anything in K.C., of course; they'd simply ignored it, and during the Depression musicians and entertainers gravitated there like wasps round a honey jar. Pay wasn't necessarily all that good, not for a lot of the black musicians, anyway, but there was plenty of work, and when a job wasn't available there was always somewhere to jam. K.C. jam sessions became the real testing-ground around that time, clearly matching anything like it in New York, and the direct forerunners of what was happening in Harlem in '42; a put-up-or-shut-up scene, where a musician was only as good as his last solo. In that kind of atmosphere, where players were constantly being asked to prove themselves, it was inevitable that new things'd emerge and standards reach levels that were way above what they'd have been without that kind of stimulus.

But it didn't last, of course. When the clean-up people took over in K.C. in '38, everything quietened down. A lot of the places where the musicians worked closed or changed their policy, and most of the bands that hadn't already moved out either broke up or went out on the road, working the territory.

Like Walden said, if the hole had appeared a few years before it actually did, there was no place on Earth I would have rather gone to than Kansas City. By the early '40's, though, it'd virtually become a ghost town in any musical sense. After the Count Basie band began to make it in the late '30's the New York agencies moved in on K.C., skimming off all the musical cream and basing it in the east, so that by the end of the decade the talent had been thinned down to mostly second-raters. There were a few notable exceptions – Charlie Parker was the pick of that crop, by the way– but by the early '40's they'd left town, too, and that was it.

There's a museum now, housing plenty of memorabilia, and quite a few books have been published over the years, several histories and a handful of biographies and autobiographies, but it's not unreasonable to assume that they all contain inaccuracies and elements of hearsay and leave a lot of unanswered questions. So there was still a big gap there, but I really wasn't the person to try and fill it, that was obvious to me. Cal Bush was the gregarious type, ideal for that kind of job, whereas introverted would be a fair description in my own case. But bearing in mind the situation I was in, I was still obviously going to have to make a real effort to establish a toe-hold, aim for at least a reasonable degree of success, because if I simply marked time and came up more or less empty it could turn out to be a total waste of time; after all, whatever else it was that Walden had in mind for me there was no guarantee at all that it'd work out the way we both hoped it would, and I had to accept that there was a real and depressing possibility that K.C. would actually become my regular beat until the programme was wound down and the hole closed, presumably for good.

I spent most of my time at base checking out Cal's reports and mentally drafting a programme of research to try and fill the empty spaces I found, and he and I got together for a few hours just before I left. One aspect of the situation that made me uneasy as well as unhappy was the fact that I was going to be strictly on my own there; no local backup and no alternating shifts with anyone else. It'd been decided at the beginning that it simply didn't justify that amount of coverage, which underlined the relative value of the operation and did nothing at all to help cheer me up. The nearest backup was in St. Louis, I was told, but as long as I stuck to the book I should be O.K., so that amount of cover should be adequate.

I could think of several reasons why it might not be, but I decided it'd be politic not to argue about it; Cal had been working to that arrangement, and in any case my position was shaky enough without making it shakier. But I was still haunted by my memories of New York, desperately wanting to get back there while there was still time. What made it even more frustrating was the fact that by then I'd convinced myself that what was happening was probably unnecessary anyway, because after the business with the draft police the search for this Salter must have become top priority, which could have meant that they'd already caught up with him.

I put that to Walden, and he agreed it could have happened, but he pointed out that it wasn't going to be easy to check out unless it made the papers. And even if they had got him, he said, that wasn't necessarily the end of it as far as I was concerned, because he might be able to prove that he was nowhere near New York at the time of my own run-in with the authorities. Even so, he promised to instruct the New York-based people to keep their eyes open for any reference to it; if it did turn out that way then he reckoned that as long as I stuck with my new image – I'd been re-christened Gordon Perry then, by the way – there was at least an outside chance that I'd be allowed back on my original assignment.

Whether he meant it or not, I have no idea; probably not. But he was tactfully offering me a straw, and I grabbed at it, because that was how I wanted it to be, even though common sense told me that the armed forces weren't really likely to publicise the kind of unpatriotic reluctance this Salter was demonstrating. When you're desperate, though, reason tends to take a back seat, and at the time I was ready to kid myself that black was white if I thought it would have gotten me back to New York.

I went through the hole again the following Monday. It was a grey, miserable kind of day in 1942 Leyland, cold, too, with a lot of low cloud and a steady drizzle, a depressing kind of reception, especially in view of the way I was feeling. The cloud didn't really clear until the train was almost halfway across Illinois, and even though the sun came out I still saw the landscape as bleak and unwelcoming. The carriage I was in was full, too, and pretty noisy; quite a few service people and a lot of talk about the war, especially the way things were going in the Pacific. Guadalcanal had been featuring in the news, and there was a lot of speculation about what was happening there; Stalingrad was under siege, too, and there was concern about that as well, although understandably

Guadalcanal was the topic they worried at most. I kept quiet and pretended to read a book, but I got the same itch that I'd felt in New York, wanting to reassure them that it would all turn out all right, tell them that in the end they were going to make it, despite all the tragedies and hard times they were going to have to face during the next few years.

But needless to say, I didn't. The last thing I wanted was to draw any kind of attention to myself, even in the part of a nondescript greybeard who as far as they were concerned would be pegged as somewhere on the wrong side of rational if I started spouting stuff like that. So I just listened and turned a page occasionally and concentrated on re-acclimatising myself, trying to forget about New York and wondering just how much of a let-down Kansas City was going to be.

It was around then, when we were getting close to K.C., that I consciously started to think about Donna, in a more sustained and direct way than I had for a long time. She's never totally out of my mind; there's always some point in the day when she's there, even if it's only for a little while. Despite everything else that's happened since she died, she's always with me and always will be, I know, because quite apart from the ending any memory at all of her always plays havoc with my defences, and I remember the God-awful mess that we got ourselves into, and especially my part in getting us there.

Phyl, I've put this off until now for the simple reason that I haven't been able to get up enough nerve to talk about it until it became necessary. It might as well be now, though, because like I told you she does actually play a part in this business in a roundabout kind of way, and I'll be getting to that soon; besides, the longer I dither about it the harder it's going to be for me to tell it without dragging in excuses, and I mustn't do that.

It probably sounds as though I'm ignoring that already when I say that in our respective ways we were both at fault at the time, but that's simply how it was, you'll have to take my word for that. I'm not in any way attempting to apportion blame; as well as being pointless it would be totally unfair since she can't defend herself now, although to be as honest as I can the facts don't exactly flatter either of us. But there's no escaping that, and in any case my side of it's been poisoning my conscious for far too long. Maybe airing it now will at least neutralise it a little; I hope so, anyway.

I don't have any real reason to query the medical explanation of what happened, but what actually prompted the haemorrhage is something that only I know for sure, although I guess a few neighbours might be included in that as well. The fact is that less than two hours before she died we had another of our insane shouting matches, probably the worst as well as the last. I'm still too ashamed to tell you what it was about, because it was one of those unbelievably trivial things that gets blown up out of all proportion, when reason simply flies out the window. The subject isn't important, anyway – what does matter is that when she left to go to work she had a blinding headache, and there's no way that the two things can't be connected.

So even though there can never be any kind of conclusive proof, I'm sure that I'm at least fifty percent responsible for what happened to her. I've carried the guilt for it ever since, and it's no exaggeration to say that it's changed me as a person; for the better in some ways, maybe, but the cost has been almost unbearable at times.

At least it's made me honest enough to face the fact that selfishness was what ruined us, most of it on my part, although I think it's fair to say that it was pretty mutual. We both tended to concern ourselves too much with our own interests, shutting each other out a lot of the time. I guess the truth is that being the people we were it was an idiotic thing to do, jump into a high-risk commitment like marriage, even though it felt right at the time. But whatever the rights and wrongs and whoever was most at fault, I do know that in part at least I killed her.

It sickens me to tell you even that much, but you had to know, and not because confession is good for the soul; that part of it's only a side-issue when it's weighed against the rest of this. I had to tell you so that you understand at least the things I've done that relate to her, and I hope that by the time I finish you see me in a kinder light than you have done up until now, and certainly more favourably than you must do at this moment. I'm not asking for your forgiveness, because it could be that I was always going to do it anyway; you'll understand what I mean by that a bit later on. But I'd like to think that my conscience and my real feelings for Donna had at least some influence on events, and even if they didn't that what I've done will eventually go some way towards compensating her for my own contribution to the wrecking of our relationship and what it eventually led to.

So there it is. Those are the facts, and in some ways at least I'm glad that they're finally out in the open. To be honest, if things hadn't followed the pattern that they have it's more than likely that I'd have kept them to myself, but they've become relevant so they had to be told. I know only too well what a sad and sorry commentary they are on my own behaviour, and despite anything I may have achieved in the way of atonement I know too that I'll never completely escape them, especially in my dreams. But I deserve that at the very least.

It never occurred to me at the time just why I should have focussed on Donna like I did; in a vague kind of way I assumed that it was because of the things that had recently happened to me, the fact that I was feeling something of a failure again, quite unreasonably, because what had finished New York for me had been purely fortuitous, at least that's what I believed at the time. Now, though, I'm not so sure. In one sense at least what's happened to me very recently's given me a much clearer picture of what we're involved with, but it's still left a lot of uncertainties, and that's one that I can't imagine we'll ever know the answer to.

I know you've been to Kansas City a few times; there were those business administration courses a few years back, so you've got a rough idea of the central layout at least, although inevitably there've been a lot of changes since 1942. My own one and only visit was a twenty-four-hour stopover on my way to the west coast a couple of years ago; I spent most of that time in the jazz foundation annexe of the museum, though, so I hadn't had time to cover much territory. This time there was a room booked for me at a hotel located just off Paseo, near the centre of town, so I went there and registered, then took a stroll uptown to where the jazz scene used to be mostly concentrated. The sky was clear and it was quite warm, nice conditions for walking. There were a lot of people on the streets and a general feeling of hustle, although nothing like as extreme as I'd found it in New York.

The hotel was at 39th and Paseo, so it was a fair haul to the area where the real action had been a few years before. At that time there'd been around fifty clubs and cabarets rubbing shoulders in the six blocks between 12th and 18th Streets, maybe the biggest concentration of its kind in the whole history of the music, but that had been during the Pendergast era, before K.C. had the plug pulled on it by the reform lobby in the late 1930's.

If you want to look at it from the point of view of civic responsibility and morality in general, it was something that'd been long overdue. I'm sure you know the basic facts, so I won't dwell on them, but before the clean-up the administration there simply ignored government legislation that it considered inconvenient and gave virtually free-rein to anybody who was prepared to pay kick-backs. There was a huge gambling empire, rampant prostitution, racketeers, gangsters and all the interests that you'd automatically associate with them. Most of the clubs had gangland connections of one sort or another, a lot of them owned outright by people who were firmly established on the wrong side of the law. But despite that it was a situation with one positive aspect, because as far as the musicians and a lot of their employers were concerned it was a live-and-let-live relationship, with a minimum of interference with respect to what actually went on up on the bandstand. 'Play what you like, and keep your noses out of things that don't concern you' – that was the arrangement that they mutually existed by.

There's no denying that in some respects it was a pretty chilling kind of symbiosis, and I'm quite sure that the majority of the club owners didn't give a thought to the creative aspect of the licence they were permitting. But they did understand the musicians at least well enough to know that that kind of freedom was what they really wanted, even more than money and the things it could get them, and they were shrewd enough to exploit that. Playing jazz *was* freedom as far as most of the musicians were concerned; an irresistible outlet for the rhythm and melodies and personal feelings that they carried around inside them. As long as they had enough money for what they regarded as the necessities of life, they were prepared to settle for that. Besides, no other town offered the sheer scale of opportunities for jamming, not even New York, the chance to try out their ideas and hone their musicianship, do nightly battle with their peers and sometimes visiting celebrities. So they accepted the generally lousy pay that was offered, and the kitty handouts that helped to pad that out a little, and honoured their part of the deal by turning a blind eye, because that was the only price that was acceptable to the people in charge.

It's extraordinary, isn't it, just how often beauty has been propagated by ugliness, right the way through history? In a lot of ways that's how it was in much of the jazz world then, as well as before and after, certainly in Kansas City at that time. It's something that I've thought about a lot over the years, especially since finding myself faced with this particular reality. But apart from the question of the amount of time I have left to finish this, I see no real point in going into the rights and wrongs of that, either. Maybe our concepts of morality are simply inadequate when they're applied to such insoluble mysteries as the creative processes and the conditions that they flourish in; they frequently sit uneasily in one another's company, so that has to be at least partially true. Life's a muddle of ambiguities at the best of times, and there aren't a whole lot of answers that don't invite at least some dispute.

Anyway, wandering around between 12th and 18th Streets was a pretty depressing experience, as I'd guessed it would be. There were still a few places left that carried familiar names, but it was a shadow of what it must have once been. The sunshine that had cheered me up a little earlier didn't help, either. As far as I was concerned jazz has always been more comfortable after dark; night music, a sound for recreation and recuperation. All that brightness just emphasised the neutrality of what I was faced with; a bunch of drably anonymous streets where it was difficult to imagine that you could detect even the faintest echo of the magical sounds that had filled them only a few years before.

I'm not going to waste time detailing what happened during the next couple of weeks; it's enough to say that I was as disappointed with the live music side as I'd expected to be. The musicianship rarely rose above second-rate, and when it did it still fell a long way short of the best stuff that I'd grown accustomed to listening to during the preceding few months. Just occasionally I caught a faint acknowledgement of the changes that were surfacing in New York, but most of what I heard had a well-worn, second-hand quality to it, and it wasn't simply a question of over-familiarity with the formula as a result of all my years of listening to recordings of the time and my knowledge of just how far things had already developed elsewhere.

Apart from buying drinks for some of the people I heard and encouraging them to reminisce during the breaks they took, the most productive thing at that time was a conversation I had with one of the bartenders in a club I visited during the first week. As well as having a fund of stories that I knew I was going to find useful, he was one of the first to voice something that I was going to hear in a lot of places; a lament for the good old days, when it had been Tom's town; not really a lot of money unless you were on the inside, but always a job and always great music to be found, a real fun town. He told me he'd worked at several of the famous clubs during the 1930's and that he'd known a lot of the musicians who'd played them, including some who'd gone on to become big names, so I earmarked him for future consultation.

But that was it. By the end of the first week I'd still found nothing worthwhile, so I went to Oklahoma City for a couple days, stopping over at Wichita on the way back to K.C., but I didn't find anything to induce me to hang around in either of them. Maybe I didn't give them a fair shake, but I was still too restless to do more than give them a pretty cursory once-over, all the time convinced that I wasn't going unearth anything really worth bothering with anyway. By the end of the second week I'd covered virtually all the recommended places and people in K.C., and in terms of recorded evidence I had next to nothing that I felt was going to add anything meaningful to the existing records. I'd had faint hopes of a couple of after-hour sessions that had started off promisingly, but as they went on it became obvious that nobody there was really capable of extending themselves significantly beyond the standard of playing that they'd demonstrated at the beginning; if anything, the chance to stretch out only emphasised their limitations. It gave the whole business a rather sad and embarrassing feel, rather like well-meaning salutes to an heroic tradition that had no hope of actually emulating it or doing it justice, because the spirit and circumstances that had been largely responsible for its creation had changed and simply couldn't be repeated.

On the Monday of the third week I decided to give the whole thing a rest; I was still picking up bits of information that were going to be useful on the history side, but the lack of real enterprise in the music was beginning to make me very tense, even irritable. I went to the cinema that afternoon, and when I came out I was feeling stiff and stale; two weeks of sitting in movie houses and restaurants and dives is no way to stay fit, that I can guarantee.

It was a warmish day with no breeze to speak of and only a few clouds high up, and walking seemed like a good idea.

I washed and changed at the hotel, and then headed uptown, then west, along Armour Boulevard. I hadn't been that way before; I'd been told that there were one or two places in that general direction that might be worth checking out, but I wasn't in the mood anyway, so I wasn't really looking for anywhere specific. After a while I turned right and headed north again, just drifting around, glad of the change of scene and the chance to stretch my legs and get the kinks out generally. The temperature gradually dropped and the street lights came on, and after I'd been walking an hour or so a wind got up and it began to feel quite a bit colder.

I'd only had a light lunch, and I hadn't eaten since then; I'd simply figured on dropping into some restaurant or other when I worked up an appetite and saw somewhere I liked the look of, but although I was pretty hungry by then I hadn't seen anywhere that grabbed my fancy for a while. I had no idea where I was; I'd forgotten to bring the street map that I'd bought along with me, and I'd changed direction so many times by then that I wasn't even sure which way I was headed. I decided the best thing to do would be to find a cab and head on back to Paseo; there were a couple of decent places near the hotel where the food was O.K., which meant I wouldn't be taking a chance, and I was ready to quit by then, anyway.

The street I was in was pretty quiet; I'd passed a bar back on the corner, but most of the buildings were residential and there weren't many people about. I hadn't seen any cabs for a while, either, so I decided my best move would be to ask somebody the way back to Paseo where I'd be more likely to find one.

I'd slowed down while I was deciding what to do, and while I was dawdling I heard someone coming up behind me, a woman's footsteps by the sound of them, moving quite fast. I stopped and turned around, and I saw her about a dozen or so yards away. The wind had gotten pretty squally by then, and she was leaning into it with her head down, holding her hat on with one hand. There was a street light some way beyond her, so she was almost a silhouette, just a shape without any real detail.

I didn't experience anything unusual, no hint of premonition, anything like that. She was just someone who was heading in the same direction as me, a possible informant as far as what I needed to know was concerned, and it wasn't until she was only two or three yards away and suddenly turned her head towards me that I saw her face. She didn't really know I was there, not immediately, because her eyes were almost closed against a particularly fierce tug of wind. But for a few seconds I could see her clearly, and it was just as though I'd suddenly been encased in a block of ice.

I've always been plagued by dreams. There isn't a night that passes without me finding myself in some situation that I often know can't be true but which somehow carries its own illogical conviction. As often as not Donna's in there somewhere, usually reproving me in a sad kind of way. But in all the dreams of her that I've suffered since she died, I've never before encountered her windswept ghost, blindly approaching me in a dimly lighted street in a strange town in a time before either of us was born.

10.

Thinking about it later, she decided that she probably wouldn't have noticed the man at all if the wind hadn't gusted sharply just before she passed him. She turned her head away as it struck her, holding her hat on with one hand and half-closing her eyes against the accompanying shower of dust particles.

She opened them again as the wind subsided, and then she saw him. He was standing at the back of the pavement, staring at her, his mouth slightly open. There was no suggestion of threat about him, nothing to frighten her that she could see. He looked shocked, almost as though the sight of her had transfixed him for some inexplicable reason.

Then she was past him, hurrying on. There were other people approaching in the near-distance, and she felt no real sense of alarm, just brief disquiet at his strange reaction to her presence. She listened carefully, but there were no footsteps behind her as far as she could detect against the sound of the wind, no indication of pursuit. She glanced back as she crossed the street, and saw him still standing where she'd passed him, staring after her, his expression indistinguishable in the half-light.

The last thing she wanted right then, she told herself, was to have to discourage some interested party. She was a little late, and although Mr. Williams seemed friendly and easy-going, she didn't want to take any chances as far as the job was concerned. She thought about Foster, experiencing a now familiar flush of excitement. She wondered if he ever thought about her at all, as an individual, of if he simply saw her as somebody who worked at the same place as he did, no-one of any real identity. He'd smiled at her a couple of times, but he'd never seemed inclined to take it beyond that.

Nobody said much when she got there; there was a good-naturedly caustic remark from one of the other waitresses, but that was all. She hurried into her uniform, straightened her hair, and went out into the restaurant.

It was less than a quarter full, and the only one of her tables that was occupied was by a couple that were just in the process of seating themselves. She took their order, and went back to the kitchen. A minute or so later she went back out again with their entrée. There was someone else sitting at another table by then, in the rear corner of the room. It was only as she approached the table, taking her order-pad from her apron pocket, that she recognised him.

It was the man who'd stared at her as she'd been on the way there, she was sure of it. Although her sight of him had been brief, she'd seen him clearly in the light of an adjacent street lamp. It was an easily recognised face, made distinguishable by the beard and glasses. She'd realised that he was white, but now his paleness seemed particularly marked; an unhealthy pallor that shone dully in the subdued lighting.

He was gripping the menu tightly with both hands, staring down at it with fixed intensity as she approached. She halted beside the table. She felt nervous now, a little irritated. Was she really going to have to fend off a pass, right here in the restaurant? She was half-relieved that the place was as empty as it was and the table relatively isolated.

Looking down at the man, she was suddenly aware of the movements that were afflicting him. Although his pose was one of stillness, it was being disrupted by ague-like tremors. He looks sick, she thought. She said, shyly, "What can I get you?"

The man looked up at her. Behind the beard, his face was bleached and drained. He opened his mouth as though to speak, and then there was an abrupt, spastic movement as one hand jerked itself free from the menu-holder and the folder catapulted from the table.

He bent to retrieve it. He was still groping for it as he slid from his chair and struck the floor at her feet. He lay on his side, breathing shallow, rapid breaths, his mouth open and his eyes closed.

11.

———

The first thing I was conscious of when I started to come round was hearing somebody talking; not directly to me, just a voice, some distance away. I was laying on something soft and there was a cushion or pillow under my head.

Things were pretty blurred at first when I opened my eyes, but after a little while I got some idea of where I was. It was a small room, an office, with a desk and a couple of filing-cabinets opposite where I was laying. There were a lot of photos on the walls, black and white show-biz style glossies for the most part, and there was a big, black, almost bald middle-aged guy sitting behind the desk. He was wearing a tuxedo and tinted spectacles, and he was talking on the telephone. When he saw me looking at him he said he had to go, and then he put the phone down and asked me how I was feeling.

I didn't really feel nauseous any more and my breathing was more or less normal, but I was still a little groggy. I told him so, and he said I should just stay there until the doctor he'd sent for came; he'd only just finished saying it when the doctor arrived, a little guy in a houndstooth suit and a sporty vest. He was black, too, and very cheerful. He took my pulse and sounded my chest and asked me if I'd been ill recently. Although I was still fuzzy I had enough sense to tell him I'd had food-poisoning a few days before; that I still didn't have much of an appetite and I hadn't been eating regularly. I'd just been going to order my first meal of the day when I'd keeled over, I told him.

He asked me who my doctor was, and I told him I wasn't local and in any case I didn't have a regular one any more because I moved around a lot. I'd been in St. Louis staying with friends when I'd been taken sick, I said, and I couldn't remember the name of the doctor they'd called in. He didn't press it, just wrote out a prescription, told me I needed food more than anything else, and that I should take it easy for a few days. He could recommend the food right there, he said; he ate it himself and it didn't seem to have done him any harm so far.

The big man went out with him, both of them laughing. I'd already figured out that I was still in the restaurant; there was a hint of cigar smoke in the room, but I'd smelled cooking as well when the doctor had come in and gone out again. After a minute or so the big man came back and perched on the desk and asked me what I wanted to do. I could stay there as long as I wanted, he said; rest up until I felt fit enough to move, or he could have some food brought in if I felt like eating something, it was up to me.

I said I'd just like to stay there for a little while – it was a sofa I was laid on – see how I felt, then decide. I said I was sorry for all the trouble I was causing, and asked him how much the doctor had charged. No charge, he said; he was a friend, and they did each other occasional favours, whatever that meant. He said I still looked a little beat, and maybe I should sleep for a while. I was still groggy, a bit light-headed, so I didn't argue. He said he'd leave me to it; he had a couple things to attend to, and he'd see me again in a while.

I settled down again and closed my eyes and began to think about how I'd ended up there, the crazy encounter out on the street and what it had led to. It didn't seem to make any kind of sense, because whichever way I looked at it I couldn't see how the girl out there in the restaurant could possibly be Donna. When I'd seen her close to, even though the lighting had been subdued the resemblance had still been quite remarkable, enough to tip me over the edge and react in the ridiculously humiliating way that I had. Even the voice had been similar; there'd been a slight regional inflection, but apart from that the tonal quality had been very much the same.

Thinking about it then, though, I recalled one or two dissimilarities as well; the nose was maybe a shade wider, the cheekbones less pronounced, the chin not quite the same, a little shorter, things like that. At the time I'd put them down to the age difference, because she was obviously pretty young, certainly younger than Donna had been when we'd met. By then, though, I wasn't so sure. After I'd thought about it for a while I decided that there was only one possible answer that made any real sense; that since she was so like her, there had to be a family link of some kind. I remembered how I started to think about Donna on the train going there, and then things started to click into place. You'll have figured it out already, I expect. It hadn't occurred to me then that your people came from Kansas City and that you and Donna still had relatives there, mostly people she'd either lost touch with or hadn't actually known. In a subconscious way I must have recalled that as we were approaching K.C. and that's what had triggered my thinking just then.

I began to feel a bit better about it all after that; disappointed as well, I admit, in a wry kind of way, but mostly relieved that I wasn't becoming deranged, starting to see things. It had simply been a coincidence, I decided; an incredible long-shot, but even so that was what it clearly had been. I still had to face the fact that I'd made a complete fool of myself when I'd actually been confronted by her, whoever she was, but I was pretty sure that nothing like it would happen again, now that I'd had time to work out a rational explanation.

I dropped off again after that, but I don't think it was for long. When I woke the second time, I heard somebody warming up on a saxophone, a tenor, running scales and arpeggios and holding a few long notes. It was coming from the other side of the wall that the sofa was up against. Although it was pretty muffled I could tell that whoever it was had a pretty good sound, nice and full without giving the impression of pushing it very hard. I heard some talk that I couldn't decipher, too, and a couple of people laughing.

I got up and wandered around the room and took a look at the photos on the walls. They were mostly of well-known musicians and singers; a lot of studio portraits and some showing groups of people, all of them decorated with pen-written signatures. I spotted the big guy in some of them; in one he had his arm around Jimmy Rushing's shoulders. Rushing you wouldn't know, but he was a celebrity at the time, one of the great jazz singers. One of the pictures was in a frame and hung beside the desk; it showed a seven-piece band, with what looked like a younger and lighter version of the big guy in the front line, holding an alto saxophone.

He came back in just then, and I told him I was feeling better, which was true; I even had the beginnings of an appetite again.

He asked me if I'd like to eat there, in the office, and I told him no thanks, I'd go back into the restaurant. I had to test myself again sometime, and I'd already decided that it would be best if it was sooner rather than later. The saxophone player had quit his exercises while I'd been looking at the pictures, but I could hear occasional talk from the next room. I said I took it they had a band on the premises; I'd seen the dance-floor and stage while I'd been in the restaurant, and I'd heard somebody warming up while he'd been away; had it been him?

He laughed, a little pleased, I think, and said no, it hadn't; he'd given up playing a few years ago. They had a nice little outfit there, though, he said, five pieces. They played for dancing a few hours each evening and backed a cabaret routine on weekends as well. He asked me if I liked music, if I played myself.

I've never thought of my piano playing as anything to shout about; I played pretty regularly with other people during my student days, and I've worked with amateur and semi-professional groups fairly frequently since then, but that's been the limit of my band experience. I've used it for demonstration purposes during my lectures, and technically I'm quite sound, but my work has exposed me to so much music that exists on another creative plane altogether that I've never thought of myself as more than adequate.

So I told him yes, I played a little piano, but strictly for myself now; I'd never tried for it professionally, anyway. I told him who and what I was supposed to be, too; it seemed like a good time to establish my credentials, because he'd obviously been around the music scene and looked as though he might be another useful source of information. He said he was Porter Williams and that he owned and managed the place; we shook hands, and he said he was pleased to know me and that he'd be glad to help me on my research if he could.

I'm pretty sure his initial idea was that I was probably just a reasonably well-heeled crank, some kind of dilettante with academic pretensions who was indulging in a little artistic slumming, but that was O.K. as far as I was concerned, because in a way it would have helped my cover. I told him I'd been pretty disappointed in what I'd heard since I'd been in town; that K.C. music was a particular interest of mine, but that it really did look as though the cream had been skimmed off since the heyday of the '30's. I named a few of the places I'd visited and some of the musicians I'd heard and told him that with very few exceptions it hadn't been a very rewarding experience.

I think that sent me up a notch or two in his estimation, the fact that I seemed to know enough to be able to make that kind of judgement, and he agreed that the local action was very quiet compared to the old days. As I thought, he'd been around the scene for quite a few years and had worked the territory during his playing days; he'd even made it as far as California a couple times, he told me. There were still a few good players around, he said, but there was a lot of movement just then. The draft was pulling people in all the time, and a lot of them preferred to stay on the road where it wasn't so easy to catch up with them. They came back to town occasionally, but they didn't stick around for long; even so, they usually got into the after-hours action while they were there. He told me he'd keep his ears open and let me knew if anything promising turned up.

I was pleased about that, because it meant that he'd decided that I could be trusted. After all, he only had my word for it that I was what I'd told him I was, and at that time the draft authority managed to snag quite a few people who were trying to duck enlistment by approaching them in a roundabout way, sneaking up on them and acting friendly while they made sure they had the right party. For all he knew I could have been someone like that, sniffing around to see if I could pick up any leads, but he obviously decided that I wasn't. There was nothing naïve about him, either, I can tell you; it was a face that had been around and knew a lot about people; a pretty wise bird that wouldn't fool easily.

I asked him about the band he had there, just how good he thought they were, and he said they were O.K.; a dance outfit, basically, but they were all capable of playing above that if they wanted to, especially the leader, the tenor guy, Dan Foster. He said the best thing I could do would be to judge for myself; they'd be on in a few minutes, and if I still felt like eating I could catch them at the same time. He gave me back my spectacles before I left the office – I'd totally forgotten the damn things – and I put them on, and we left the office and went back to the restaurant. The door of the room next to the office, where the saxophone practising and the voices had come from was closed, so I didn't see anybody as we were going past.

The restaurant had filled up quite a bit while I'd been away; about three-quarters of the tables were occupied and there were more people coming in as we went inside, most of them black, although I did see a few white faces. It was mostly the after-theatre crowd, Williams told me; that was their clientele, them and people from a couple of the dance halls. He found me a small table near the stage and said he'd get somebody to fix me up right away; he was going to be busy for a while, but he'd check back and make sure they were looking after me.

12.

___

He was still pale, but she decided that was probably how he normally looked; an indoor complexion, emphasised by the darkness of the beard.

He raised head as she stopped at the table, looking up at her with a kind of wary intentness the reminded her of her first sight of him and later embarrassment when she'd recognised him in the restaurant.

She said, awkwardly, "Mr. Williams said you'd like to eat now." She wished he'd told one of the other girls to see to him, she thought. And did he _have_ to stare at her like that? "Would you like to order?"

His eyes were suddenly shy behind the horn-rimmed glasses.

"Yes. Yes, I guess I would." He blinked. "Actually, I'm still not really all that hungry." He moistened his lips. "Would it be O.K. if I had a couple of bread rolls and some butter and cheese?"

"Surely." She wrote it down, avoiding his gaze. "Anything to drink?"

He hesitated. "Coffee, please. No milk, no sugar." He lifted a hand in a nervous gesture. "Look, I hope you haven't got the wrong idea about why I've been – looking at you, or why I'm here. The fact is, I saw you a little earlier, out on the street, and you reminded me very much of someone I used to know." His eyelids continued their restless movement. "Actually, I knew that there was no way that you could have been her, but I wondered if you were related. I didn't like the idea of speaking to you then, so I followed you here. I hope you don't mind."

So that was it, she thought, relieved. He didn't really look like the usual kind of chaser, although it wasn't always easy to tell. But it seemed like a reasonable enough explanation.

She smiled. "No, of course not. What's her name?"

He hesitated again. "Waters. Donna Waters." He seemed to grimace, very slightly.

She shook her head. "I know some people called Waters, but they're no relation. My name's Thelma Woods, and my mother's name was Culley."

He nodded, and shrugged. "That's it, then. To tell you the truth, now that I've see you close to, you're not really all that much like her. You'd a lot younger, too. How old; eighteen, nineteen?"

She smiled again. "Eighteen." He was at least forty, she decided, certainly old enough to be her father.

"Maybe I need a change of glasses. It could have been because it was pretty dark, I suppose. It's not always easy to recognise people in that kind of light."

She agreed, and went back to the kitchen. He seemed nice enough, she thought, not at all what she'd expected. Anyway, it was a relief to know that she wasn't going to have to fend him off after all.

She got his order and took it out to him. As she was putting it on the table, she said, "Are you all right now? Mr. Williams said you'd been sick and not eating."

He smiled a small, rather wry smile. "I'm fine, thanks. I hope I didn't alarm you too much when I keeled over like that. I don't normally make that kind of fool of myself." His smile widened, a little shyly. "Just as well it happened before I'd eaten. I wouldn't have wanted the other customers to get the wrong idea."

She laughed. "You'd have been the first since I've been here."

13.

——

I watched her go, feeling pretty pleased with myself, the way I'd handled it. What I'd told her about the lack of resemblance had seemed the sensible thing to do, a way of putting her at ease by implying a lack of interest after all, and my adaptation of the doctor's line about the food had helped, too, making a joke out of what had been a horribly embarrassing situation.

Even so, there was still this thing nibbling away at the back of my mind; a completely irrational feeling of disappointment that she was who she was, and that a miracle hadn't happened and she wasn't Donna after all. Completely crazy, of course, but it was there, and there was no way I could kid myself that it wasn't. Commonsense told me that even if she had been Donna, who'd somehow been re-located in that time, it would have been a pointless encounter as far as I was concerned anyway, despite all the lessons I'd learned since she died. She would have been a Donna who was still not much more than an adolescent, while I was a thirty-five-year-old who looked maybe ten years older than that, someone who couldn't even survive for more than three weeks at a time at that point in the past and whose total time there was inescapably limited by events that were completely beyond my control. But I still had to acknowledge that it was there, underneath all the rationalisation and my acceptance of her real identity; a sad, silly twinge of the sense of loss that I'd been carrying around with me for the last four years, which never really went away and in all probability never will.

The band had been drifting onto the stage while we were talking; bassist, drummer, pianist, and a guy with a trumpet, all of them in dark crimson band jackets and black trousers and shoes. The last one to come on was wearing a white jacket, identifying him as the leader; he had a clarinet in one hand and a tenor-saxophone hooked across his shoulder. He was medium height and slim, and his skin was lighter than the others. There was a slightly Oriental touch about his features, and he had a general air of self-confidence that could have been just this side of complacency. But he looked pleasant enough; neat, well-groomed, rather good-looking, a little more refined than the others.

He parked the clarinet and hooked the sax onto his sling, then checked the microphone and said good evening into it; welcomed everybody to Porter Williams' Grill and Music Place, and told us that for the rest of the evening they'd be playing for our listening and dancing pleasure.

They kicked off with some medium-tempo thing, I can't remember what. It was all very neat and smooth; fairly subdued and not really very interesting, a straightish reading of the melody that alternated between unison passages and some very basic harmony. They all soloed, except the drummer. The trumpet was O.K. but very conservative, playing what sounded like something he'd more or less worked out beforehand, and the pianist was no more than fair; competent, but a bit mechanical. The saxophone player was the most interesting; a nicely rounded sound and good technical control, but even though his solo was better structured than the others it still wasn't all that much, really, a pretty dispassionate sort of exercise that stayed comfortably inside the proscribed harmonies. The bass and drums were adequate, quite light and springy, suitable for the kind of group that they obviously were.

I decided very quickly that Williams had been right; they were basically a nice little dance outfit, pleasant enough in their over-polite way, but as far as I was concerned containing nothing of any real interest. I nibbled at the food, but I found I still wasn't very hungry. The place was pretty busy by then; people out on the dance floor, cigarette and cigar smoke and a lot of talk, some of it fairly raucous. I stuck around for a little while, but although the band did loosen up a little the music stayed more or less predictable, and after maybe three-quarters of an hour I decided I'd had enough. I got my check and told the Woods girl that I'd decided I needed rest more than I needed food, and then I went, glad to be out in the fresh air, away from the smoke and chatter and uninspired playing and the regular glimpses of her that I'd caught during my time there.

It turned out that the place was just off Troost Avenue, only a few blocks from Paseo. I found a cab and went back the hotel, telling myself that an early night would be a sensible move, the best way to re-charge my batteries, which were definitely a little flat by then. I was feeling jaded and depressed again, pretty much deflated by things in general and particularly by the events of the evening; the shock of seeing of Thelma Woods, the confusion and tension that had resulted from it, the fainting business – even after all this time I still feel a fool when I think about that – the anti-climax of finding out who she really was, the non-event of listening to the restaurant band. It had been one of the those occasions when I'd allowed pointless hope to over-rule commonsense, despite all the logic I'd talked to myself at the time. Feelings nearly always win out in the end as far as I'm concerned, and the truth was that I'd known all along what I was really wanting from it all, however insane the whole idea had been.

The early night was another failure. I've never been able to sleep if I go too bed too early, and I must have been laying there a couple hours at least before I dropped off, and then I had my usual quota of bleak dreams. The last one had me walking along a street that was totally dark except for very clearly defined pools of light that occurred at regular intervals; there were no street lamps that I could see, simply these circles of light punctuating the darkness and stretching out into what as far as I knew could have been infinity.

The only way I knew it was a street was because of the echoing sound of footsteps; there was no traffic, no visible buildings, just this sound, bouncing back off a lot of hard, hidden surfaces. Thelma Woods – or maybe it was Donna, I had no real way of telling – kept appearing in these circles of light and then moving on, with me following her, only by the time I got to where I'd last seen her the light that had been there was gone, as though her passing had somehow tripped a switch to some kind of temporary illumination that had only been there to draw me on. After a while the lights that were still ahead of me suddenly all went out, and at the same time her footsteps faded and then died away altogether. All that was left was total darkness, like solidified tar, and I was locked inside it, barely able to breathe, and then I realised that I was going to be there forever, eternally smothered by the darkness and tortured by a terrible sense of loss that I knew couldn't be consoled.

There's sometimes a point in nightmares when you get kicked awake by sheer unbearable terror, and that's what happened then. Even though the relief was overwhelming, the dream was still there, surrounding me like some irremovable black cloud, and although I went back to sleep eventually and didn't dream it again it was still hanging around me for the rest of the following day. I spent a lot of time brooding about it, thinking about all the things that had happened on the previous evening, and reluctantly accepting that something that dug that deeply into my feelings of guilt and loss wasn't likely to go away in a hurry, maybe not ever, and that in fact might turn out to be a recurring dream from then on, a nightly ordeal that I was only safe from as long as I awake.

So in the end I decided that there was only answer; it had to be exorcised, and the only way to do that was to tackle it head-on. I had to make myself accept the realities of the situation, *really* accept them, make myself believe beyond any shadow of doubt that Thelma Woods was who she said she was. The logical explanation for the similarity had to be that she was a distant ancestor of Donna's, but the only way to really prove that would be if I was able to dig up evidence from some kind of family record of the period when I went back to base.

I wondered whether to hurry it up by cutting the trip short, going back straight away and telling them that I'd been feeling under the weather for a couple of days, and since there had to be a chance that the medication had kicked in early again I'd decided to play it safe. Even if I said I was O.K. by then, though, that it must have been a false alarm, if they thought my health was in any way suspect it could mean that I'd be withdrawn from survey duty altogether, and I didn't dare risk that. In the end I decided that what I had to do was go back to the restaurant, face Thelma Woods again, and somehow get to know her better, find out things about her life, her family background, the sort of things that would help my research when the trip was over.

It's more than probable that you've concluded that what I was really doing was kidding myself about all of this; that because of her resemblance to Donna and despite the absurdity of such an idea, I was actually beginning to think about her in some crazily impractical romantic way. If that's so, Phyl, you couldn't be more wrong. After my initial reaction, it was never like that. The age and time difference and the temporary access and the responsibilities that I'd accepted as part of my being there at all weren't the reasons, either. Donna was Donna and Thelma Woods was Thelma Woods, and physical similarity is nothing more than surface detail, a fraction of the whole person. In any case, I've never been inclined to fall in love in a hurry, and my failure when I did certainly hasn't ever encouraged me to risk repeating my mistakes, believe me, even on a short-term basis; despite the things I'd learned from it, I still somehow suspect that it really was once-in-a-lifetime experience as far as I'm concerned. Even so, I was beginning to think of Thelma in a special way, and in that sense it didn't really matter to me anymore that she wasn't Donna. I was already convinced in my own mind that the family link was there, and because of that I'd somehow begun to get the feeling that it was important that I demonstrated the better side of myself to her; that even though she could only ever be a kind of two-dimensional reminder of Donna and my behaviour towards her could never be more than a token gesture, I'd still be offering a sort of apology for all the errors of judgement and cruelties that I'd subjected Donna to during our relationship.

It didn't really make any kind of sense to me, even then, and I told myself that it had to be because I was as screwed up over Donna as I was, ready to grasp at the flimsiest of straws in an attempt to ease my conscience. In fact, it was the beginning of something that was going to become very important to both of us eventually. But at the time I simply saw it as a purely one- sided things, for my benefit only; the necessity to gain her esteem, even her affection in a strictly platonic kind of way. I had no idea if anything like that was even going to be a possibility beyond the next few days; after all, Walden had told me that there was a reasonable chance that it was going to be my one and only trip to K.C.. But I could see that while I was there the sensible thing to do would be to lay the groundwork for such a relationship, because if I didn't do that and subsequently found myself back there I'd have wasted what I was beginning to believe could turn out to be a unique opportunity to at least partially straighten myself out.

So I went back to the restaurant that evening, lateish, around nine o'clock. Again, it wasn't all that full, although there were probably more people than there had been when I'd first gone in on the previous day. Thelma saw me come in, and we smiled at one another, and I went to the same table that I'd sat at before. The stage was still empty, just the music stands and drum kit and piano up there, and the double bass, laying on its side by the rear wall.

I hadn't eaten much during the day, so I was pretty hungry. After a couple of minutes she came over, and we said hello, and I told her that I'd decided that one way or another I hadn't given the food a fair shake the day before so I was there to put that right. She said she was sure I wouldn't be disappointed, something inconsequential like that, and she took my order and went out again. It was all relaxed and easy, no strain of any kind, and I gave myself a mental pat on the back at how sensible I was being and sure I was doing the right thing.

She must have seen Williams and told him I was there, because after a few minutes he came in from the back and straight to my table. He said it was nice to see me there again, and hoped I was O.K., and I said I was fine; I'd gotten up late morning, which was more or less true, and that the doctor's prescription seemed to be helping, too, which was a downright lie because I still had it my wallet. But I felt it was the tactful thing to say; after all, he'd gone to the trouble of getting him there for me.

I asked him if he'd heard of anything promising in the meantime, any news about bands heading into town, and he said there was nothing really special coming in off the road that he'd heard about, but he thought I might be interested to know that there was going to be a session later that night, a couple of blocks from there. It was going to be in a lodge building that was occasionally used for that kind of thing, and a few of the better local people usually showed. Some of the guys in the house band would be there, and it would give me a chance to hear what they could really do. The saxophone player and the pianist would definitely be going, and maybe the bassist, too.

I thanked him, but it wasn't news that excited me in any way; nothing I'd heard on the previous evening had even hinted that his own people were likely to produce anything really worthwhile. There was no fair way of pre-judging anybody else who might be there, of course, but going by what I'd found up until then I didn't see any reason to feel optimistic. I had the recorder with me, but it wasn't because I expected to use it, simply that I'd decided that it would be safer to take it with me than leave it back at the hotel the way I had the previous evening.

He was obviously trying to be helpful and it would have been churlish of me to say that I wasn't interested, especially as I'd already told him that I was feeling O.K., so I said yes, fine, I'd go along for a while, see how I felt, if I could stand the pace and so forth. I asked him if he was going himself, and he said he would be, although he was going to have to quit early; he had a business appointment in the morning, and he'd reached an age when he needed his sleep more than he did the music. But he'd be happy to take me, he said, introduce me to a few people and see if he could pick up on anything else that might interest me.

So that was it, and it could have been worse, because if he was only going to be there for a little while he wouldn't be put out if I left soon after he did. He invited me to join him in the office after I'd eaten; he'd buy me a drink, he said, and we could talk and maybe he'd be able to help out with the kind of information I was looking for.

That actually sounded more promising than the music, so I said I'd be glad to, and just after he'd gone Thelma came back with the first lot of food. As she was putting it on the table, she told me that she'd spoken with her mother and asked if there was anybody in the family called Waters, maybe some distant relative that she didn't know about who looked a bit like her. While this was happening the band had come onto the stage, and although she carried on talking I could see that her attention had already wandered away from me, because she started looking in that direction. I glanced that way, too, just in time to see Foster, the saxophone player, came on, and when I looked back at Thelma I saw this little hint of excitement in her expression.

I wasn't really upset by it. Who she liked was her business, and Foster was a good-looking boy in his way, so her obvious interest in him was perfectly understandable. But I guess I was just a little annoyed that something was disrupting our conversation, just as I'd been offered the ideal opening to start what I was after from her. So, in what I suppose was a mildly ironic way, I asked her if she liked music.

The irony sailed right past her, thankfully. She said yes, she did, she liked music, and she liked dancing, too. Mr. Williams had told her that I was some kind of music researcher, she said.

How did I like the band they had there at the restaurant? Was it the kind of thing I was looking for?

I could have kicked myself, because I'd walked right into it. Instead of thinking about how she might react, I'd stupidly let my instincts dictate what I'd said, and it had landed me in a situation where I was going to have to take some kind of stance over the band. Whether she really thought they were good or not there was no way of knowing, but she plainly liked Foster, and I could see that I was going to have to tread pretty carefully just then if I was going to make any kind of progress as far as my own interests were concerned.

So, picking my words very carefully, I said that from what I'd heard of them on the previous evening, they did a good, professional job; that they were all competent musicians, but to be perfectly honest they weren't really the kind of thing I was looking for. I was in K.C. to research the jazz scene, I told her, the really creative side of things, and while the people in the band were all very capable, their working set-up inhibited them too much to allow them any real freedom, the chance to demonstrate what they could really do in that direction.

It was close enough to the truth for me not to feel that I'd allowed myself to be pushed into telling an outright lie, and tactfully put, too, I thought. But she didn't like it at all, that was clear straight away. Her mouth went a little stubborn and her eyes weren't really friendly any more. She said she didn't actually understand music, not in any technical sense, but they sounded good to her, as good as anyone else local she'd heard. She obviously didn't know exactly what I was looking for, she admitted, but she was sure that given the chance they could play as well as anybody else in town.

It wasn't a rational statement by any stretch of the imagination, but I could see that there'd be no point in arguing with her about it. Because I'd spoken without thinking, the opposite of what I wanted happening was happening, and the whole thing was turning sour before it had even gotten off the ground. For a few seconds I didn't know what to say, because I had to wriggle out of it somehow, come up with something that would cool the whole thing down again and re-establish friendly relations. And then I saw the answer, because it was already there, set up and waiting, and I'd just been getting too panicky to see it straight away.

I asked her if she knew about the session that would be taking place later that evening, at some local lodge, and she said no, she didn't. The saxophone player and the pianist and quite possibly one or two of the other people in the band would be playing, I told her; Mr. Williams was going to take me, so why didn't she come along as well? It was going to be a blowing thing, a free-for-all, and it would give the people in the band the chance to stretch out, show what they could really do. Maybe she'd be proved right, I said, and in any case it would be interesting to find out. Her whole expression changed, and she looked shy and excited all at the same time. She said she'd have to call her mother and let her know that she'd be back late, but yes, she'd like to come if that was really O.K.. So I said I'd tell Williams when I saw him and we'd let her know when we were ready to go. The band kicked off their opening number just as she started to walk away, almost like a celebratory fanfare, it seemed, and we smiled at one another and she went back to the kitchen.

I relaxed again, and made a start on the food she'd brought. It had been tricky for a minute or two, but I told myself it had only been a temporary hiccup, nothing to be discouraged by. The important thing was that she still saw me as a friendly character, somebody who was prepared to be sociable and helpful in what she probably thought was an unwitting way. Depending on how she really felt about Foster, it was even possible that she saw me as a kind of Cupid, which would be bound to strengthen my position in the long term. The fact that she was interested in him didn't necessarily mean that it was at all reciprocal, of course; the chances were that it was a one-sided infatuation, the kind of thing that would soon fizzle if it was left to work itself out. I told myself that it was none of my business anyway, and that what I had to do was concentrate on making sure that our relationship stayed on an even keel so that it had the chance to work the kind of therapy that I was hoping I'd get from it.

I went back to Williams' office after I'd finished eating, and it turned out that she'd already told him about my invitation. He'd had a word with her mother, telling her that he'd be there and that he'd see that she got home O.K. afterwards, so that was all squared away. Then he poured us a couple drinks, and we spent most of the next hour or two chatting, with me asking the questions and him providing the answers and anything else relevant that he was reminded of. He was a good, interesting talker, full of the kind of reminiscences that I was looking for, and I kicked myself afterwards for not setting up the recorder until about halfway through the conversation, when I took a couple pictures of him. But my memory's always been good when it's taking in something that really interests me, and I was pretty sure that I'd remember most of the early details afterwards. In fact, what happened later that evening knocked just about everything else out of my head completely for a while, although I did recall most of it when I was back at base and able to concentrate on thinking back to then.

He left me for a half-hour or so while he supervised the clearing-up, and then he came back with Thelma. She'd freshened her makeup, and she really did look pretty nice; obviously excited, and trying hard not to show it.

It was just after 1 a.m. when we left and headed for the place where the session was going to be.

14.

___

It was a big room, its dingily tobacco-yellowed walls supporting a high, shadowed ceiling and decorated with a trio of fringed banners hung at its far end, behind where the musicians were loosely grouped on the shallow stage there. The only lighting in use was concentrated directly over them, now slightly diffused by an uneven veil of smoke. A long table with chairs stacked on it had been pushed against the rear wall, and the rest of the chairs were loosely grouped in front of the lighted area. Folding card tables were scattered among the audience, all of them carrying bottles and glasses.

She sat at one of these, Williams on one side of her and the man Perry on the other, the ever-present camera around his neck. There hadn't been much conversation for a while now; Perry's attention had been focused more or less exclusively on the music and Williams circulated a lot of the time, talking to people in other parts of the room. She didn't mind, though. She was quite content to sit there, nursing her watered-down drink and watching and listening to Foster.

He occupied a chair in the middle of the row that faced them, sitting with his legs crossed and his saxophone resting diagonally across them as he played, a studiedly casual pose that she found exciting. He was flanked by an assortment of musicians; two other saxophonists, two trumpet players, a trombonist, and a man playing amplified guitar, with the rhythm section grouped to the left of the line.

The music made her want to dance, but no-one else seemed to share her inclination. Feet tapped and heads nodded, but for then at least that was the only visible physical reaction among the rest of the audience. They were obviously happy to just sit and listen, she decided, even the other women there, the kind of people who'd probably think her own response naïve. She liked what was being played, but the truth was that it was beyond her capacity to really appreciate what they were doing. But it was clever, she could tell that; patterns of melody and harmony and rhythm that miraculously blended in instantaneous fusion, collective spontaneity that she found quite dazzling.

During a pause between numbers, Perry stirred himself. Although he'd seemed absorbed in the music she thought she detected a little boredom in his expression now. She felt herself stiffen slightly as he asked Williams about Foster, what he knew about his background, his musical history.

She listened intently to Williams' reply, absorbing the information hungrily, feeling a kind of pride by proxy in Foster's record of achievements. He'd led a high-school band when he was fifteen, Williams said; he'd been a precocious player, an obvious natural, and after he'd finished school he'd turned professional straight away, spending the next eighteen months with a couple of territory bands. He'd been on the road with them on several occasions, but the novelty had quickly palled; the generally poor food and accommodation hadn't suited him at all, so both times he'd quit soon afterwards; he came from a comfortable home and he'd been glad to get back there and gig around in local outfits for a while. He'd put the current band together about a year ago, and they'd been resident at the restaurant for the past six months or so. He was an easy-going kid, Williams said; knew his instruments and was probably as good a player as there was locally just then. He'd had a couple of offers from semi-name outfits when they'd been passing though town, but he hadn't been interested because of the pressure and hassle of touring, preferring to stick with the comforts of his own back yard.

Perry nodded. "It fits. Too bad, really. He's got the equipment to go further than he has, technically, anyway. Wrong temperament, though, I guess." He stared around the room. "There's nobody here to really push him, of course. He'd need to try New York if he wanted to see if he's really got what it takes. I think he'd find it very different – " He broke off, glancing quickly at her, then shrugged and smiled, suddenly embarrassed. "Of course, that's his business."

It sure isn't _yours_, she thought, resentfully. His remarks in the restaurant when she'd asked him what he thought of the band had irritated her, but his obvious desire not to give offence had softened her reaction then. What did he really know, anyway? He was probably one of those people who appointed themselves experts, claimed a degree of knowledge and discernment that it was impossible for someone like her to refute.

She wanted to speak out, challenge him, but she didn't really know how. The chances were that she'd simply make a fool of herself, she knew that. She wondered if Williams and Perry had detected her interest in Foster, if her presence there was a subject of unspoken amusement. They'd given no sign of the kind, but that might simply have been good manners on their part.

She glanced at Williams, silently urging him to take up the cudgels on Foster's behalf, but he just ducked his head non-committally and said that it was hard to tell. Local competition had become pretty limited, he said; there were still some pretty good people around, but it had to be accepted that K.C. simply wasn't the testing ground it had been a few years before.

The music started up again as he finished speaking. Annoyed at this refusal to take a more defensive stance over Foster and still smouldering resentfully at Perry's comments, she re-directed her gaze back towards the line of musicians, and was startled to see Foster approaching their table.

He pulled up a chair, sat down and said, "Hi." He grinned at her, and exchanged nods with Williams and Perry. She softened again, the resentment melting away in his unexpected presence.

Williams said to him, "This is Mr. Perry, the gentleman I told you about." Foster and Perry shook hands. Foster said, "Nice to meet you. I hear you're doing some research, for a book or something. That's why you're here, I guess." He smiled. "How do we rate so far?"

She felt herself stiffen during the brief pause that followed.

Perry's smile was a little awkward, patently uncomfortable. "Fine. That was a nice bridge in your second chorus on the last thing."

Foster laughed. "Thanks. How about the rest of it?"

Again, a pause, longer this time. Something snapped inside her head. She heard herself say, "He didn't think—" She broke off, appalled, wanting to vanish into thin air.

There was a sudden stillness at the table. Foster looked at her, his head tilted to one side and his eyebrows raised. The smile remained on his face, but it was a little cool now. He glanced back at Perry. "What was it you didn't think?"

Perry's face was flushed. He tried another smile of his own, a rictus that contained more embarrassment than humour. "Actually, I'm a little in the dark here. I don't really know what – " He looked at her, his eyes nervously pleading. "I think there must have been some kind of misunderstanding."

She said, sullenly, "You said he'd have to go to New York if he wanted to see if he's really got what it takes." She immediately berated herself again, damning her seeming inability to keep her mouth shut, stay out of something she didn't really understand.

Foster's cool smile appeared unruffled. "So you think its necessary to go to New York to become a good musician?"

Perry's embarrassment continued, but there was something else in his expression now, a shadow that could have been obstinacy.

"That's not quite how I meant it, but it is a fact that nobody ever knows what they're really capable of until they find themselves really stretched, and you're not going to get that around here, not any more. New York's been the principle testing ground for quite some time now, of course, but some of the things that are happening there are making even a lot of the top people realise that they've got a lot of work to do if they're going to stand a chance of cutting it in that kind of situation."

Foster shrugged. "Technique's no problem if you're prepared to work at it. You don't have to go to New York for that. You can woodshed anywhere."

Perry shook his head. "I didn't mean technique as such, instrumental control. I'm talking about harmony, principally; augmented chords, different changes to the usual stuff. The rhythmic side's changing as well, though. The whole thing is becoming a lot more demanding now, opening right out. Technique's not your problem anyway. You know your instrument, but there doesn't seem to be anybody local who could really push you in that way."

Foster's smile was still coolly dismissive. "We've got people around here who fool with screwy chords sometimes. If that's what they want to do, that's up to them. It's not going to get them any place, though. Nobody's ever going to really buy that kind of thing." It was his turn to look a little bored.

Perry said, after a moment, "I wouldn't count on that. But it's your choice, of course. If you're happy doing what you're doing, then that's fine. It all comes down to what we want for ourselves, I guess."

There was a brief, uncomfortable pause.

Foster shifted slightly in his chair. "You figure I couldn't handle that kind of thing, is that what you're saying?"

Perry flushed again. "I don't really know. Unless I actually heard you in that kind of setting it isn't possible to say. Have you worked on harmony much?"

"I know as much as I need to know. I've got a pretty good ear, anyway."

Perry nodded. "Yes, you have. That might not be enough, though. I still think you'd find it tough going if you don't know really know much about extended chords."

The question that had been fretting for release at the front of her mind abruptly surfaced.

"You're saying that these people are making music more complicated, is that right? Why should they do that? I don't see how—"

Foster cut in on her. "No, he's right. Part right, anyway. We're supposed to be looking for new stuff all the time." To Perry, he said curiously, "You play anything yourself?"

There was another pause, that lasted several seconds. "A little piano."

"Yeah? How little? Can you play augmented chords, those kinds of changes?"

Perry's hesitation was longer this time. She looked at him, and saw that his eyes suddenly contained a hunted look, a trace of furtive uncertainty. 'Well, yes. Yes, I can."

"You don't sound so sure."

Perry looked down at the table top. He moistened his lips. "I wouldn't ever claim to be a real musician. My fingering isn't all that fast, but I do know something about chords."

Foster nodded towards the corner of the room where the piano was located. "How about laying some of it down now? 'Lady be good' in G, that O.K.?"

Still watching Perry, she saw something else appear on his face, a flicker of what could have been shocked excitement.

15.

It couldn't have been more that a few seconds, but it felt like an eternity before I heard myself say yes, sure, if that's what he'd like me to do.

It wasn't simply a straightforward question of allowing myself to be provoked into accepting his challenge, either. Despite the pressure of the situation I'd managed to stay clear-headed enough to realise that there was only one possible way of hanging onto what little credit I had left with Thelma, and because of what that might mean as far as my own salvation was concerned it'd suddenly become more important to me that any of the rest of it; the programme, the music, everything.

If I lost her respect completely, backed off and automatically labelled myself a phoney, than that'd be it, the end of whatever chance I had. Equally, if I played and made a monkey out of Foster in the process, that'd be bound to do it, too. So I had to play, I realised that, but in a way that wouldn't foul him up and still preserved my credibility, that was the only realistic option. I wasn't in any way oblivious to what it'd mean in broader terms, either, but in that situation I had to make a snap decision, and right then my emotional concerns dictated which way I jumped, whatever the consequences turned out to be.

I'm sure you view all of this as total irresponsibility on my part, Phyl, and to be honest at that stage in the proceedings at least part of my brain was telling me the same thing. It wasn't enough to deter me in any way, though, because the emotional pressure I'd lived with since Donna died had soured my life for far too long for me to have thrown away the one slim chance I'd ever found that looked as though it might ease it a little. If you can understand that, then maybe you won't continue to see it as the kind of reprehensible act that it must look to your right now; in any case, what's happened since has put the whole thing into perspective, but for a while at least I admit I was scared rigid by the implications of what I'd done and what I was going to do.

It wasn't simply the irresponsibility aspect that bothered me, either, because during training we'd been told that every so often members of the survey staff would be selected to take a lie-detector test, an extra piece of insurance against deviations from official procedure, and although so far none of our people had been chosen I knew it happened in other sections. None of them had resulted in anybody being withdrawn from field-duty, though, and they didn't occur all that often; the controllers obviously felt that just an occasional one, combined with the chance of being selected, would be enough of a deterrent to anyone who was tempted to stray out of line, and it looked to be a policy that normally worked. I realised the fact of accepting Foster's challenge was going to make the possibility of me being chosen a particularly weighty addition to the worries that I normally carted around with me while I was there, but I'd committed myself, so I was obviously just going to have to keep my fingers crossed real tight and hope that it didn't happen.

Anyway, my agreeing to play seemed to have jarred him quite a bit. He thought he'd had me backed up in a corner, and suddenly I was there, out in the open and at least putting in a show of not being intimidated by the prospect. He nodded a very wooden acknowledgement and said he'd fix it so that we went on when they finished the number they were playing, and then everybody at the table just sat there not saying anything, avoiding one another's eyes and concentrating on the music, ostensibly at least.

It gave me a chance to consider the whole picture, and it was a singularly sobering one, of course, because as well as the lie-detection angle there was the question of just how much it was going to disturb the existing pattern of events and what came afterwards. The fundamental rule we'd been had drummed into us was as specific as it could've been under the circumstances; except in cases of extreme emergency there was to be no participation whatsoever beyond the minimal demands of any situation that we found ourselves in, and on the face of it was a perfectly reasonable restriction. The planners accepted that even though it was limited the fact of our being there at all meant that we were bound to be involved to some extent with what was happening at the time, and of course the emergency proviso covered what had happened with the draft police in New York.

Kicking the rules into touch for purely personal reasons, though, was something else, and it really did worry me, initially at least. Even though I intended to go easy on Foster, there still had to be chance that I'd dent his complacency enough for him to take a complete change of musical direction, the kind of disruption that might alter the whole shape of his life. And not just him; after all, there were other musicians there who might be affected by what I was going to do, too. In any event, whichever way it went it meant that the immediate future was going to contain a very special irony, I could see at least that much very clearly; a middle-aged white man with the incalculable advantage of foreknowledge giving a bunch of young Aframs a glimpse of the direction the music was going to take in the near future, a role reversal that'd make it a uniquely sardonic piece of deceit.

In that situation it was inevitable that I'd try to justify what I was doing, and it wasn't long before I was asking myself if I actually was likely to do serious damage by involving myself in such a relatively innocuous way. As long as the things that any of us did while we were there remained low-key, I could see no *real* reason to take it for granted that far-reaching changes would definitely result. They might, of course, I accepted that, but not necessarily, and in any case it was perfectly reasonable to query whether or not the planners were really right as far as the participation parameters were concerned. When you're dealing with unknown quantities, with no yardstick or rule book to guide you, caution's understandable, but it could leave you way short of the real possibilities. I was going to be stretching the rules by played, admittedly, but since some kind of provision obviously existed to accommodate our temporary presence I couldn't see any logical reason to assume that I'd be disrupting the pattern in any meaningful way, if such a thing was even possible.

I mentally fiddled around with the pros and cons for a while, but the more I thought about it the more convinced I became the it really did make sense, whether it involved my personal circumstances or not. Looking back now, I don't recall any real twinges of guilt or uncertainty, either, although whether I truly believed I'd gotten it right I still don't know, and I guess there's no way that I ever shall. Self-deception's something we all practice to one degree or another, especially when it involves something we want very badly, and that certainly applied to what I was hoping to get from Thelma.

But at least I seemed to believe it, and that was all that mattered to me at the time. One thing that helped me get there was the fact that I was as certain as I could be that Foster never actually impressed himself on the music scene to the extent that he'd entered the written records. Although I had no way of checking it at the time, I do have a pretty encyclopedic memory for that kind of detail, and I was at least 99% sure that he wasn't there, even as a footnote. The very least that that implied was that he'd stayed what he was right then; a competent second-rater who lacked the initiative and musical curiosity that might lead him to leaving some kind of lasting mark behind him.

I decided that what I'd heard so far that evening made it look as though the same thing probably applied to the other people who were playing there, too. Even if any of them did develop into real contributors there was no discernible evidence at that stage, and the premature hint that I'd be dropping would be hardly enough to steer any of them in a really creative direction, anyway. Certainly nothing musically significant was likely to result from what Foster at least did in the future, and ever since I'd had time to consider the likely outcome I couldn't seriously imagine him changing his fundamental life-style, either. He'd already demonstrated that he was a stay-at-home by nature, happy to settle for a comfortable, easy-going existence. If I was right about his failure to make the record books, too, then whatever happened afterwards it looked as though my playing was going to be no more than a brief, harmless excursion that'd be absorbed and neutralised and at the same time provided me with a memory that I'd treasure for the rest of my life.

The number that they were playing finished, and Foster got up and went to the piano and spoke to the guy there, and then to a couple of people in the front line. There was some conversation and a few glances in my direction, and after a while the front-line people parked their instruments on the chairs they'd been sitting on and drifted over to where the tables were, still eyeing me occasionally.

Foster came back, and told me we were on. There'd be just us and the bass and drums, he said; would that be O.K. with me? Strictly speaking it wasn't at all, because it meant that I was going to be a lot more exposed that I'd anticipated, but it was too late to argue the point. Besides, I wasn't really scared about the prospect of playing, not in the way I would've been if I'd felt I was taking on something that I wasn't really sure I could cope with. None of my experience of group playing has been at anything like top level in any sense, but the overall standard hasn't been bad, and at least it meant that I'd learned how to back other people.

In any case, I've always played, ever since grade school. I haven't just fooled around, either, neglected fundamentals; quite a lot of the time I've practised in a fairly organised way, and I've worked at harmony long enough to be able to handle more or less anything, as long as the modulations and tempos and timing don't become too rough, anyway. What he'd proposed certainly wasn't likely to pose any kind of problem; it was a jamming favourite from way back that I'd played on lots of occasions, and the standard chord structure wasn't at all demanding.

Foster headed back to the stage, and I took a couple of mental deep breaths and got up to follow him. I glanced at Thelma as I was leaving the table, but she was still making a point of not catching my eye, so I just winked at Williams, more of a nervous tic than a real wink, and then went over to the piano, switching the recorder on while I was on my way there. I stuck it on an unoccupied chair, and sat down and tested the keyboard action; it was pretty loose, and there were a few dead keys, but I've played on far worse in my time.

16.

——

Now that his initial irritation had abated, he was coolly amused by the situation, the way the kid had leapt to his defence, confirming what he'd disinterestedly suspected. He eyed her across the room as he hooked the saxophone back onto its sling. She was pretty cute at that, he decided. O.K., baby, this one'll be for you.

He blew a few octave-distanced notes, followed by a fast exercise that covered the whole instrument. The reed responded without protest, vibrating lightly against his lower lip, producing a warmly rounded sound.

He was unconcerned by the prospect of what was going to happen, secure in the knowledge of his capabilities. Even if this Perry had picked up on extended chords a little he'd already confessed to technical limitations that were bound to restrict him to some extent, making it improbable that he'd present any real challenge. Maybe the guy couldn't even swing, Foster thought; after all, the woods were full of triers who never really got up off the ground. He sure didn't look the part at all; the greying beard, the glasses, the tweedily academic suit. He looked across to where he was settling himself at the piano, quietly testing its response.

He went over to him. "Four bars hi-hat, then we make it, right?" He looked at the drummer, silently mouthed the count-in, and cymbals snapped into life. He lifted the saxophone to his mouth, and at the start of the fourth bar ran a spiral of quavers down the instrument before launching into the chorus. It was a deliberately early entry calculated to catch Perry off-balance, but he still came in on cue, working to the fundamental changes, discreetly punctuating the saxophone's line.

O.K., sweetheart, Foster thought. *We've got lots of time.* He closed out his paraphrase of the tune's first eight bars, then began to relaxedly weave his way around the familiar harmonic foundation.

17.

___

I didn't try anything remotely fancy to start with, just laid down the basic chords and kept an ear on what Foster was doing. The fact that I was actually up there in front of what constituted a pretty knowledgeable audience and playing with musicians who were competent professionals even if they weren't exactly top-grade made me a little more nervous than I'd hoped I was going to be, but the backing was nice and steady, and every so often the drummer responded to something I put down, an answering punctuation that showed that he was listening to me as well as Foster, and I began to relax, really savour what was happening.

I waited until we got to the second chorus before I gradually started to amend things slightly, augment some of the standard chords and occasionally substitute others. I began to change the rhythmic emphasise as well, sometimes playing between the beats or accentuating or anticipating the on-beat; nothing really complicated, just enough to demonstrate what I'd been talking about and to show Foster that what I'd claimed hadn't been empty talk.

Initially, he ignored what I was doing, sticking to the kind of pleasant but not particularly adventurous stuff that he'd kicked off with, regularly inserting licks that were common currency in the jazz vocabulary of the time, but it wasn't long before his line started to fragment a little, lose some of its continuity. When he'd invited me to play he'd made it clear that he didn't seriously expect me to come up with anything he wouldn't be able to wing his way through without any real difficulty, but his hesitation was an obvious hint that he was finding the mix he was being fed a bit richer than he'd anticipated.

The truth is that it was a bit richer than *I'd* anticipated, because by then the backing wasn't altogether being dictated by just me any more. After I'd started to tinker with the rhythmic side the drummer had very quickly fallen into line, clearly in sympathy with the kinds of things I was doing, answering me with off-centre fills and even prompting little variations of his own on a couple of occasions, and the unexpected support that I was getting from him could have been the extra nudge that triggered Foster's eventual reaction, convinced him that he had to demonstrate that he hadn't been just mouthing off either.

Thinking about it all now, I still can't altogether understand how I could have been so incredibly stupid. Anticipating events is always a high-risk game, of course, and I suppose I do at least have the excuse that the circumstances that had pushed me into what I was doing had given me a hell of a lot of things to consider at the time. But whether that's a justifiable argument or not I have admit that what was happening right then was a possibility that simply hadn't occurred to me when I'd agreed to play. It's hard to believe now, but I'd actually been naïve enough to take it for granted that after I'd made my point in a tactfully low-key kind of way, doing my best to make sure that what I did didn't openly clash with his normal style of playing, Foster would be smart enough to accept the situation and then we'd just carry on to a conclusion that wouldn't seriously embarrass either of us.

Although I'd realised that he had a sizeable ego, I'd still badly underestimated just how big it obviously was. There'd been no way that I could've anticipated the drummer's support, of course, but even without that I guess Foster's vanity would still have been more than likely spurred him into responding, because he was the one who'd issued the challenge, and since he was already stuck out on a limb he'd clearly decided that his only option was to show me that his own claims were no less valid than mine.

At least he had the sense to try and adjust his rhythmic concept first, match his phrasing to the kind of background the drummer and I were laying down by then. He plainly wasn't comfortable with it, though; his attempts were pretty hit and miss, and it wasn't long before the rest of his playing began to be affected. The hesitations became more frequent, and when he added to his problems by trying to pick up on the amended harmonies I was dropping in as well there were some teeth-grindingly obvious collisions. His tone changed gradually, too. Normally it was full and fairly soft-edged, but by the time he finally quit, after what felt like an eternity, it'd become almost raucous, like a muffled snarl of frustration, which of course is exactly what it was.

I still cringe when I think about it, remember how I tried to persuade myself that there'd simply been no need for it to happen, that if he hadn't stuck his neck out the way he had everything would have been O.K., but even then I knew it was just a feeble lie, an attempt to justify what I'd done. I'd cast the bait and he hadn't been able to resist rising to it, and it quickly became horrendously obvious that he simply wasn't equipped to handle anything like that right then. I felt as though I'd been floating along inside a kind of bubble of self-delusion that I'd inflated around myself and suddenly had reality sink its teeth into it, exploding all my nonsensical reasoning about his technique and his youth into pathetic fragments. Not only that, I also had to face the fact that the business of Thelma and me hadn't been the only consideration. Even though I'd been pushed into doing it, the truth is that I'd wanted to play, and it was because I had that he'd eventually been humiliated by what had turned into the progressively cruel exposure of his limitations.

I felt physically sick by then, very close to actually vomiting. I didn't dare look at him, just fixed my eyes on the keyboard and tried to focus on shaping some kind of coherent solo, at the same time wishing myself a million miles away, even back in my own time. I don't recall actually thinking about Thelma at all at that point, the affect it must have been having on my relationship with her, but I was in such a sweat by then that I had to concentrate as hard as I could on what I was doing, try not to make any blunders of my own while the spotlight was on me.

There was only one feasible thing to do in that situation, so I did it; moderated my playing as imperceptibly as possible, very gradually smoothed things out again as I worked through a couple of choruses, steering the music back to ground that I knew he'd be more comfortable on when he decided to close the number out. The drummer caught on and pulled in his horns, too, so by the time the bass player had walked through a chorus of his own we were more or less back where we started, in territory where Foster wasn't likely to encounter any real problems.

I'm sure the change in musical climate was very obvious, but there'd been no way round that. When he came back in after the bass player's bit he pointedly rejected the opportunity to redeem himself, just played a single pretty perfunctory chorus, and that was it. At least it was over, and I exchanged nods and smiles with the bassist and drummer; Foster was half-turned away, making a pretence of checking his instrument, so before anybody had a chance to say anything much I got up and said a general 'thanks' and headed back to where Thelma and Williams were. I figured that a tactful withdrawal would be the sensible thing to do; I'd plead unexpected tiredness, say that I obviously hadn't completely gotten over the food-poisoning episode, and then take off to save further embarrassment. One guy held my arm and said I'd going good before I ran out of gas, and while I was standing there I got some grins and nods from a few other people, too.

I didn't really pay any attention to what he else he said, and I honestly couldn't even tell you what kind of applause we got in the finish, because by then the sheer enormity of what I'd done was all I could think about. I don't mean the participation aspect of it all, I mean on the personal level. Looking at the situation as objectively as I could, I decided that whether my theorising about how much leeway we had was right or wrong, what I'd actually achieved was the total obliteration of any chance I might have had of getting what I wanted from Thelma; that from then on she'd simply think of me as a spoiler, someone who'd deliberately and maybe even maliciously deflated Foster, in some destructive way that was beyond her musical comprehension made a fool of him in front of the audience and his peers.

As well as feeling nauseous, I was utterly depressed as well by then. Even before I got to the table I sensed the chill there; not from Williams, who had a faint grin in his face, but Thelma was hating me down to the soles of my shoes, showing a stony profile and completely ignoring me when I arrived.

I mumbled my exit lines, and Williams said that he had to get going, too, obviously deciding like me that the sensible thing to do would be to cut the proceedings as short as possible, but the embarrassment didn't quite finish there. Thelma didn't get up when Williams did; she was staying, she said, and she'd make her own way home when she was ready. Williams hesitated for a second or two, but then shrugged and said O.K., if that was what she wanted to do. He had his meeting in the morning, he said, and was ready for bed, not as young as he used to be, and so on.

I dithered, but not for long, because for the life of me I didn't see what I could say that would be acceptable in that situation, so I said goodnight and followed Williams out. As I went through the door, I looked back to where the musicians were congregating again and saw Foster watching me go before he turned away and continued fiddling with his saxophone, a sullen show of indifference that wouldn't have fooled a two-year old, not even at that distance and in the uneven light.

18.

Nothing was said as they got back in the car and headed downtown. They'd gone several blocks before Williams let the grin break through. He glanced sideways at Perry, intrigued by his silence.

"You don't seem too happy. If I was in your shoes, I'd be feeling kind of pleased with myself. You did all right back there. Some of it wasn't really my kind of thing, but you sounded like you knew what you were doing."

Perry shifted in his seat. He looked forlorn, a little fretful. "I didn't really mean it to turn out that way. I hope I didn't cause any real bad feeling."

Williams laughed. "It won't kill him. I guess he asked for it, anyway. He's not a bad kid, but he's got a pretty good opinion of himself, you know." He glanced at Perry again, amused by his still glum expression. "You don't want to take it too serious. What you said about him not being stretched was right, you know that. If he's ever going to make the most of what he's got, he needs that kind of shove."

"Aren't you worried you might lose him?"

Williams shrugged. "He's not going to stay at my place for ever. If he doesn't hit the road soon the draft is going to catch up with him, so maybe he ought to make a move. There's plenty of people around who could handle a gig like mine."

They rode in silence for a while, then Perry said, "Your girl didn't seem too happy about it, either."

Williams laughed again. "She'll get over it. Everybody at the place knows she's got eyes for him. She's a nice kid, though, so they don't rib her too much. It's a one-sided thing, anyway. She's not his type. He likes them out of the line, strictly casual."

95

Perry cleared his throat. "She was a bit upset when we left. Maybe we should have tried harder to persuade her to come along."

Williams shook his head. "That was the way she wanted it." Why should you worry, anyway?, *he thought.* You got eyes for her yourself? *He said, "She's not really a kid, you know. She only lives about a mile from there, anyway. If she sticks around 'til the finish somebody'll probably give her a ride home."*

Perry didn't say anything. A funny kind of guy, Williams thought; the nervy type, a worrier. Pleasant enough, though; just a little green around the edges, despite his age and background. But there was more there than he'd figured. What had happened back at the lodge had been quite an eye-opener in its way, a genuine surprise.

Hidden depths, he thought. Maybe he's carrying a few more aces up his sleeve, too. He grinned again as he pulled the car up outside the hotel.

19.

___

I've experienced plenty of anti-climaxes during my lifetime, but none of them matched what I went through during the next few days. I was right back where I'd been before I'd known of Thelma's existence, only worse; horribly depressed, almost unbearably restless; sick with self-disgust, too, because by then I'd really come clean with myself.

The truth was that the drummer's obvious approval of what I was doing had eventually persuaded me to grandstand a little, demonstrate my relative musical sophistication to a totally unnecessary degree. Despite the business with Thelma I'd idiotically let my own ego surface, and in the process apparently killed stone-dead whatever slight chance there might have been of getting what I hoped to get from her. I saw it as a temporary burst of insanity that I was never going to forgive myself for; a once-in-a-lifetime chance of salvation that I'd thoughtlessly thrown away through sheer vanity. All I wanted right then was to get out of there and find that Walden had been successful in reassigning me again, and then try to forget the whole God-awful mess, not that there'd be a hope in hell of that, of course.

Apart from all this maundering, the only thing that I clearly remember from that time is a conversation I had with the bartender who'd been helpful at the start of the trip. I'd dropped into where he was working one evening, more to get my mind off things by just talking to someone than anything else, and while we were chatting I mentioned Williams's place. He knew him, he said; a nice guy in his opinion; smart, too, a good business head. According to the bartender he'd successfully walked a fine line in the old days, and was still a useful person to know; lots of contacts, that sort of thing. It was a conversation that I've to come value since, more than I can say, but I'll be telling you about that later, when it slots into all of this.

I stayed away from the restaurant until Thursday, my last night there. It was only intended to be a courtesy call, anyway, because it was at least possible that it would be my last chance to see Williams and thank him for his kindness. I considered 'phoning instead of actually going there, but in the end I went, I wasn't really sure why. I told myself it was because I shouldn't be chicken about it, that I mustn't let my mistakes dictate my actions to that extent, but the probable truth is that I wanted a last glimpse of Thelma, even though I was convinced that seeing her again would be totally pointless, simply twisting the knife in the wound.

When I got there, she was almost the first person I saw, serving a table near the door. She saw me come in, so there was no chance of retreating until she'd gone back to the kitchen, but as soon as she recognised me, to my total amazement she gave me her normal shy smile, not a trace of animosity about her that I could detect, and said that if I was looking for Mr. Williams he was in the kitchen just then.

And that was it. I thanked her, and went out back and stuck my head through the kitchen door, and Williams saw me, signalled that he'd be right out, and I stayed there in the corridor, feeling a surge of relief that was like a tidal wave racing around inside me. I had no idea at all what had squared me with Thelma, but right then I was just too relieved to try and figure it out; I'd obviously been reprieved, and that was all that mattered. I felt like leaping about and whooping and hollering, but of course I didn't, I just paced around until Williams came out and took me into the office.

Things were a bit hectic just then, he told me; if I liked to wait a little while, though, he'd join me for a meal, but I'd already decided not to stay. What I needed more than anything else just then was to keep moving, burn off some of the sudden excess energy that was making me want to jump and shout, and sitting at a table eating wasn't going to do that.

So I thanked him for the invitation, but told him that I wouldn't be stopping; I had to make an early start the next day, and I'd just looked in to thank him for all his help and assure him that what had happened at the lodge session didn't have anything to do with my not going there during the week, I'd simply been too busy checking out other venues and people. In any case, I said, I'd just seen Thelma, and she seemed friendly enough, no problem there that I could see, and he grinned and said that was because she'd ended up with what she'd really wanted that evening. Foster had taken her home afterwards, and she must have played her cards right because since then he'd carried on doing it when the restaurant put up the shutters each evening.

Actually, it didn't come as a total surprise, not quite. At one point during my fretting something like that vaguely crossed my mind, but then I'd remembered what Williams had told me about Foster's taste in female company and decided I was simply grasping at a particularly flimsy straw and promptly forgot about it. In any case, I hadn't considered it as something that would necessarily help my own situation, because I didn't see that it would automatically soften Thelma's view of me in any way.

Judging from her response when I'd turned up that evening, though, that was exactly what had happened. I hadn't been a spoiler at all, I actually had been a kind of Cupid, and that meant that instead of wrecking my chances I'd actually been laying the foundations of what I wanted from her. Of course, that meant that I did an immediate about-face on the re-assignment question, and I fervently hoped that Walden hadn't been working on it too hard. It put the music back into second-place, too, at least for the time-being. It wasn't any less important to me than it had been before, it was simply a case of my personal affairs taking precedence, at least until I'd had time to find out whether this idea of mine about possible emotional rehabilitation was just a pipe-dream or something more.

I realised that Thelma's change of attitude had no real bearing on Foster's feelings towards me. His professional pride had been damaged, I had no idea how badly, and that made what was between him and me a totally different issue. From his point of view, I'd certainly done him no favour in that direction. So I told Williams that I was glad that Thelma at least wasn't continuing to bear a grudge, and then I asked him if Foster had said anything at all about had happened at the lodge. Not to him, he said; he'd maybe been a bit quiet since then, not exactly conversational, but he was never a great talker, anyway.

He asked me when I'd be back in town, and I told him it was possible that I'd be there again towards the end of the following month. If I was, I'd probably be around for three weeks or so, I said, and he said that'd be good timing, because he'd been told that the Benny Valentine band was going to be starting a week's residency at the El Torrean ballroom five weeks from then. He had some good people right then, he said, several of them from K.C., and it was certain that the jamming scene would be pretty lively while they were there.

It was a piece of news that was definitely welcome if I *was* still going to be stuck with the Kansas City assignment, but there was something there that held me back from embracing the prospect whole-heartedly, for a moment or two I wasn't sure what. Then I realised what it was, and a chill hit me, because it re-awakened something that I'd more or less pushed to the back of my mind by then, especially during the last few days.

Valentine was out of Oklahoma City, an arranger and occasional trombone-player who'd led a medium-sized territory band for a few years until he upped it to fourteen or fifteen pieces and began to make it nationally. He was never really big in the commercial sense, one moderate hit and a couple of near-misses recorded just before the ban came into force, but several people who went on to become biggish names passed through that band, and somebody who could and should have gone on to be one of the biggest was Buddy Henry.

Do you know who I'm talking about? He was the trumpet-player that I'd caught that night at Minton's in New York, the one the audience hadn't taken a lot of notice of until Ben Webster appeared and took the session by the scruff of the neck. He'd joined Valentine a couple months after that, and it was while they were on tour that he died, exactly when and where I couldn't recall just then. But it was to be some time in the near future, I did know that, and it was that realisation that had put the chill in my bones.

It occurred to me that it could mean that I'd get a second chance to record him, of course, reinforce what I'd already caught, but it was a prospect that didn't really lighten the situation in any way; until I got back to base and checked I couldn't be sure whether or not he'd died before the band reached K.C., anyway. So I told myself to forget it, for the time being at least. Whichever way it turned out there was nothing I could do about it, because it was there in the records, indelible and inescapable, and there was obviously no point at all in dwelling on it.

I didn't let any of this show, not as far as I could tell. I told Williams I looked forward to it and that I'd be seeing him again soon, and then I left and walked back to the hotel, not quite as full of fizz as I had been earlier, but still restless enough not to want to ride there. I did manage to get my mind off Henry, though, for a while at least, because I began to think about Thelma again, her relationship with Foster.

I wondered how seriously he was taking what had apparently gotten started between them. I had no way of knowing just how far her feelings for him went, but I sensed that it wouldn't be the sort of thing that she'd approach light-heartedly. There was a touch of Donna's seriousness about her, maybe the one thing that strengthened the similarity beyond the purely physical side.

When I'd considered all the circumstances, it seemed to me at least possible that it'd develop into a long-term thing. After all, Foster was a stay-at-home, which implied that he'd settle down eventually, probably get married, start a family, take on the usual commitments. He seemed happy enough at Williams' place, which made it likely that he'd stay there until the draft caught up with him, always assuming it did, and that'd allow time for the relationship to grow, really establish itself. Something else that occurred to me, of course, was that if it did end in marriage it could mean that Foster was related to Donna, too; I still didn't know for sure that there was a family link between her and Thelma, but I was already convinced that the connection existed.

If I dreamed at all that night I couldn't remember it the next day, the first time that'd happened in God knows how long. So despite the Henry thing and the fact that there could be a couple of hurdles for me to get over back at base, on the whole I was feeling pretty good when I headed back to Leyland. My principal concern was the relocation business, of course, whether or not Walden had had any success in that direction. If he hadn't been able to win over the people in charge, then the whole thing was already settled and there was no problem. But if he had, then I obviously had to offer him something persuasive enough to convince him that I ought to continue with what I was doing, and I'd only been able to come up with one answer that looked as though it might stand a real chance of swinging it.

Since this is all in the way of a confession I might as well own up to something else I know you've always at least suspected, that I'm a congenital and usually plausible liar. It isn't something I'm proud of, exactly, and all I can do is plead the shy person's excuse of using it mostly as a defensive device, but whether you accept that as sufficient justification or not, in this situation where pretence is essential it's a skill that's been absolutely invaluable, a real blessing in its way.

Anyway, my solution demanded a very convincing example of it, and although I was normally pretty sure-footed as long as the circumstances aren't openly threatening like the draft police incident had been, I knew that I was still going to have to put on one of my best performances. Frankly, that was my only real concern, because I'd given it a lot of thought and I couldn't see that any obvious harm was likely to result. Even if I'd decided that there was risk of damage, I'm pretty sure I'd still have used it; a damning admission in some ways, I suppose, but I simply can't picture myself passing up what I saw as probably the one chance of appeasing Donna's spirit that I was ever likely to find. I'm quite sure I can predict your reactions at this point, Phyl, and of course you'd have to be me, actually in my situation, to really appreciate just how desperate I was for relief by then, but I hope you can stretch your imagination enough not to be too judgmental.

I spent a lot of the trip polishing the details of my lie and rehearsing it in my mind, and I had it pretty straight by the time I got to Leyland. It was fairly late and I was feeling very tired by the time medical had finished with me; Walden and the psych people had quit for the day, so I turned in, but although I was really beat I had a restless night, which wasn't altogether surprising. As well as the possibility of having to use my lie, I still had the pysch session to get through, and despite all the rationalising and self-justification I'd dug up at the lodge session I was still feeling edgily guilty about flaunting procedure the way I had. I guess I must have got some sleep, though, because when I woke in the morning I was relieved to find that I'd calmed down quite a bit. I really had been pretty close to exhaustion when I'd hit the sheets, but I imagine it was emotional as much as physical. Tiredness often make things look bleaker than they do when we're rested, of course, and I was feeling a lot more relaxed than I'd expected to be when I went for the psych de-briefing as soon as I'd finished breakfast.

I got through it O.K., no problems. I wasn't asked any awkward questions and there were no stumbles on my part as far as I could tell, although I doubt that I'd have had that easy a passage if I'd shown the kind of nervousness I was feeling the previous evening. Anyway, my confidence got a real boost from the way it all went, but that only lasted until I got to Walden's office.

He was there when I arrived, and as soon as he saw me, he grinned and nodded in a way that sent my heart diving like a lead weight, because I knew what he was telling me. He didn't even ask me how things had gone, any of that, just told me that he had some great news. He said that while I'd been away he'd managed to persuade the brass that as far as my situation was concerned invaluable time was being wasted, and that there really would be no risk of me being picked up by the police if I was put on the road, covering the tour that the newly-formed Tommy Eden band was due to start a couple of weeks from then. The chances of me being recognised really would be minimal, he'd reasoned, because I'd be nowhere near New York at any time, and in any case I'd be on the move every day or couple of days. They'd been reluctant to go along with at first, he said, but he'd persisted and in the end they'd agreed.

If I'd been told that a week before I'd have been up off the ground with relief and excitement. Eden was a white saxophone player who'd come up through some of the best white swing bands; he wasn't truly a great player himself, but he always kept his ears open, and his outfit had several young guys in it that were destined to feature with some of the really progressive outfits later in the decade and through the 1950's. It was very much a musicians' band; the book was pretty uncompromising and the whole project commercially shaky from the off, only due to last a few months, with just a handful of poorly recorded titles as aural evidence of its existence.

It was something of a minor legend in jazz history, and in any other circumstances I'd have been jumping for joy, really feeling that I'd been let off the hook. But instead all I had was a terrible sinking feeling, because I knew that my lie was the only thing that could possibly salvage the situation and that I had to use it right then, because if it I hesitated at all it might plant a seed of doubt in Walden's mind that could lose me everything; my one chance of reprieve, maybe even my place in the programme.

20.
——

It certainly hadn't provoked the response he thought it would, Walden reflected. Surely he hadn't seriously expected it to be New York again?

He spread his hands, and shrugged, feeling a slight twinge of irritation. "Well? What do you say?"

Lohmann said, wryly, "You've beaten me to the punch. I've got something for you, too, and it could make a difference. The fact it, I've hit on somebody that I really think we should follow up." He produced a recording cartridge, and slotted in into the player on Walden's desk. "I caught him on my last night. He isn't the greatest pianist I've ever heard, but he's still way out in front with some of his ideas, even more than Monk and the New York bunch. The people he's playing with are so-so, but the drummer's beginning to catch on." He activated the machine. "See what you think."

Several minutes later, he switched the player off again. Walden sat with a hand over his mouth, trying to come to terms with what he'd just heard and the implications that it had posed. He felt disorientated, a little dazed. The music still rang disturbingly inside his head, teasing him with contradictions, a totally unanticipated assault on the common beliefs that he's shared until then.

He roused himself. "Is that it?"

Lohmann nodded. "That's it. He turned up at this session I got myself invited to, sat in for one number, then took off immediately after that. You can tell the tenor player wasn't too happy with what he was laying down behind him, and apart from the drummer and a few people in the audience, nobody else seemed to dig what he was doing, either. A little too soon for them, I guess."

"Who is he?"

"The bass player told me afterwards that his name's Shaddick, or Shaddock, he wasn't sure which; Joe whatever-it-is. He played a one-nighter with him in some scratch outfit a few months before that, he said. It was a stopover on his way back to K.C., after the band he was with folded out on the road. He can't even remember where it was for sure; somewhere in Iowa, anyway, some small town. This guy was fooling around with chords a little on the gig, apparently; nothing like as advanced as this stuff, he said, but still kind of weird. I gathered that hadn't been all that impressed himself."

Walden checked a further flicker of irritation. "Why didn't you corner him yourself, check him out? Jesus, we might not be able to find him again."

Lohmann ducked his head, slightly embarrassed. "I did goof there, I admit. I didn't realise he was cutting out completely when he quit playing. I meant to get to him later, when the thing folded, but he was gone by then. I know where to find him, though. He told the bass player he was working with the relief outfit at the Roseland. He started there a couple of weeks ago, but it's turned into a real drag already, he said. That's why he showed up at the session, hoping he was going to chance to stretch out, let off a little steam." He shrugged. "It didn't work out too well, though, not as far as most people there were concerned, anyway. It's obvious they still prefer their music Southwestern style."

Walden sighed, relieved. "Well, that's something. At least we've got a lead on him." He frowned. "Shaddick, Shaddock. It's a new one on me." He punched into his desktop console for a while, studying the screen, then sat back, shaking his head. "Nothing at all. I guess he can't have been around long enough to have registered. You'd have thought there'd at least have been a whisper about him, even if nobody was sure of his name."

Lohmann nodded. "It's a puzzler, all right. Maybe he just became disillusioned, tired of people putting him down. He might have quit the jazz scene, even got out of music altogether; anything, really."

Walden pinched his lower lip. "I wonder if he and Dameron ever got together? Is Dameron still around K.C.? Didn't he go to Chicago round about that time?"

"He worked there in a factory for a while. I think it was about then. He doesn't seem to be around, anyway. I suppose they could have met somewhere along the line."

Walden thought hard for a while. Eventually, he said, "O.K., forget about Eden. I'll try to fit that in somewhere else. It would be a pity to miss out on him, but it's more important that you get what you can on this guy while there's still time. I think we've hit pay-dirt, and we're not likely to get a second chance at it, at least that's how it looks. Even if he did get out of music, whatever, what he's doing now must be having some effect, maybe even on guys in name bands, that kind of thing." He tapped his desk repeatedly with both hands, unable to contain his excitement. "Do you realise just how significant this could be? He might even have been an influence on Bird or Diz, any of them." He shook his head. "I really would give a lot to know what happened there."

21.

———

Like I said just now, my skill at lying isn't something that I'm actually proud of, but right then I was just thankful that it'd gotten me through the situation as smoothly as it had.

It wasn't the sole reason I was going to get the chance I wanted, of course. The recording was obviously the principal selling-point, but if I hadn't been able to put over my backing story persuasively as well I somehow don't think he'd have gone along with it all as readily as he did. In fact, I can see now that I should have had a lot more faith in what I'd presented him with, because there's nothing more seductive that the imagination, and I could tell from his expression that his had been stimulated to the extent that he was already picturing himself helping to nudge aside accepted beliefs and re-write the text-books, that kind of thing.

Even though what I'd told him had been pure fiction, jazz lore's always been peppered with stories of the great unsung, shadowy figures of legendary repute who usually preserved their reputations by staying put in some musical backwater, although once in a while one would eventually emerge onto the wider public stage, sometimes denting the legend in the process, but sometimes confirming or even enhancing it. Buddy Henry was already in the second category, but it was obvious that as far as Walden was concerned 'Joe Shaddick/Shaddock' looked as though he could be an even bigger find, a total unknown whose unexpected discovery could lead to dramatically revising an important chapter in the music's evolution, a prospect that he'd have had to be exceptionally tough-minded to resist.

In the event, I wouldn't be too surprised if he saw a welcome boost to his professional prestige coming out of it, and if that sounds like an implied put-down, it isn't, not really, because if 'Shaddick/Shaddock' had been the genuine article I'd been looking forward to some more kudos myself, to add to the ones I'd already picked up over Henry. The truth is that I didn't enjoy fooling him at all, and I'm still not happy about it; he's been very helpful right through this whole business, and I've learned to really respect him, but I've simply had to accept it as a regrettable necessity, along with a lot of the other lies I've had to tell.

Anyway, he wanted to know about photos, which was O.K. because I'd covered myself there. I'd taken a few shots at the session before taking over from the restaurant pianist, and I was sure there'd be very little danger of someone who was obviously destined to remain a total nonentity being identified when his picture went on file. I realised that there had to be a possibility that Cal Bush had run across him during his time in K.C., but that was an outside chance at best; in any case, if I hadn't been able to produce so-called visual evidence it could seriously have weakened my story, and there was no way I could afford to take the risk.

After a while I steered the conversation onto the pending visit of the Valentine band and the Buddy Henry link, and reminded him of the way that was going to end. That brought him back down to earth with a bit of a jolt, but after pondering on it he said that still gave me a couple of weeks to concentrate on 'Shaddick/ Shaddock', so I should have plenty of material there by the time Valentine hit town. He felt I should continue to keep an eye on "Shaddick/Shaddock", but then split my time between them when Henry showed; in any case, he said, since they were clearly kindred musical spirits there was always going to be the chance that they'd meet up, actually jam together and create a fitting epitaph as far as Henry was concerned, place him in a setting that'd really stretch him while there was still time.

He began to get quite excited about that, even speculated that I might be part of it, the catalytic factor that brought them together, but after a bit he quietened down again and told me I mustn't go out of my way to make it happen, deliberately force the issue in any way, and I agreed that I obviously had to avoid any suggestion of direct involvement, make sure that I didn't contravene the regulations by actually initiating an event of that kind. It was a ludicrous conversation, needless to say, with him taking it all extremely seriously and me going along with everything he said, because I had to reinforce it all, make sure he was hooked as firmly as possible, so I just carried on trotting out the kind of responses that I knew he wanted to hear, selling him on the whole thing as convincingly as I could.

His suggestion that Henry and 'Shaddick/Shaddock' might actually meet up and play together was intriguing, of course, but I hadn't let it get to me too much. When I'd played at the lodge that had been in response to a challenge that had a direct bearing in my own situation, but that no longer applied. I'd achieved my aim, so I didn't have that excuse any more, and the idea of deliberately contriving another public performance instead of being pushed into it by circumstances simply didn't seem right, despite what I believed about the probable degree of flexibility as far as events were concerned.

That was something I had plenty of time to consider, though, so I didn't think too much about it then. We carried on talking for a while, and then I left, my dream still intact. There was no way of guaranteeing that it'd turn out the way I hoped it would, I realised that, because I still had to find verification of a family link between Donna and Thelma Woods, but at least I still had a chance there, and for the time being that satisfied me.

The first thing I did after that was check the files on the question of Henry's death, and they confirmed what I'd broadly remembered, and in a particularly chilling way. He'd died on December 15th, 1942; the place was the Morrison Hotel, Kansas City, Missouri, and the 15th was five weeks and six days from then, the Saturday of the week that the Valentine band played its residency at the El Torrean.

I read it I don't know how many times, feeling more and more helpless and depressed because it was telling me that someone who'd been gifted with a unique and beautiful talent was very soon going to die a dreadful death, and that even though I was going to be there, in the same town and at the same time, there was nothing at all I could do to prevent it. The only thing I could do was what Walden and I had agreed; I had to shadow him as closely as I possibly could and try to record every single note he played during that time so that his swan-song would at least be preserved. It was a prospect that sickened me more than anything else, but he deserved his special niche in history and I was the only person in a position to ensure that that happened.

Although it bothered me a lot it was still secondary to the reason for my lie, but I'd given that a lot of thought by then and I'd remembered something that I decided might very easily provide me with the information I was after. I could have looked for it in the national register of births and deaths, of course, but what was happening collectively had made me more restless than I usually was during my spells at base, and following up what I'd remembered would mean that I'd be getting away from there for a day or so.

That was an unusually attractive prospect right then, so as soon as I'd finished the stuff I had to do I went down to Pittsburgh. Apart from Donna your Aunt Clara's the only member of your family I ever felt really comfortable with, probably because she isn't as fearsomely bright as the rest of you; a little over-sentimental at times, too, maybe, but a nice person. She was actually glad to see me, which made me feel pretty ashamed, because I hadn't contacted her since the funeral, but for what I'm sure are very obvious reasons now after that it had very quickly become a habit to try and shut out as many reminders of Donna as possible.

22.

___

She hadn't recognised him when she'd answered the door-chime. The beard had been the principal reason, but he was wearing his hair differently, too; it was a lot shaggier now, and there were grey streaks that she was sure hadn't been there before. Of course, it was nearly five years since Donna had died, and they were both that much older, she reminded herself. But, even so, he'd aged a lot more than she would have expected him to.

He drank the tea and ate one of the biscuits that she insisted on getting for him, but he didn't really seem hungry. She wondered how well he took care of himself, eating, and things like that. She'd always liked him; he was quiet and polite, although Phylicia had told her that he and Donna fought a lot of the time. But he hadn't re-married or anything, she gathered, and that told her how he really felt.

It had been kind of him to look her up, take time off from his business visit, she thought. He told her he was very busy; a government research programme of some kind, although he didn't say exactly what. She told him about the way things were with her, how busy they were at the day-centre, inundated with the seemingly ever-increasing problems that people brought there. It was like the world in microcosm, really, she told him; things never seemed to get any better, just more and more pressures and less time and facilities to deal with them.

He agreed with her, and she saw a distant look on his face, as though he was thinking about something very far away. He was remembering Donna, she decided, and she busied herself with taking the cups and saucers and plates out to the kitchen because she didn't want to embarrass and upset him by letting the tears show.

He was standing by the bookcase when she went back. He'd taken down one of the photo-albums and was leafing through it, studying the pictures very carefully. She remembered showing the albums to him when he and Donna had visited the first time, when they told her that they were getting married. He'd been polite about it then, but he hadn't seemed very interested, which had been understandable, really. Now, though, he looked totally absorbed, his face serious and thoughtful.

"Those old pictures," she said. She clucked. "Well, nobody else in the family ever seemed to care about that kind of thing, not to look after them properly, anyway. They were glad to let me do it for them, I think." She sat on the sofa, and patted it. "Come and sit here, and we'll look at them together."

He sat beside her, and she told him who was who, elaborating on details that she'd written underneath them. He was very patient as she worked her way through from the beginning. The earliest pictures were over a hundred years old, six generations of family ago; some of them were very faded and a few were still badly creased, despite her attempts to iron them flat again before mounting them.

They were about a quarter of the way through when she felt him suddenly stiffen, become very still, and then she realised why. She found herself close to tears again, knowing what he must have been feeling.

"No, no," she said. She shook her head. "That isn't Donna. She did look quite a lot like her, though. That was her great great grandma Fry. The big boy's great uncle James, and the little one's great uncle Samuel. The girl was great aunt Ernestine." She tried to smile. "Lots of people have said how much like her Donna was."

He nodded, seeming to relax again. "There is quite a resemblance. It's funny how that kind of thing can happen, generations later. Dormant gene patterns, or something like that, I guess." He locked his hands between his knees. "What was her maiden name?"

She had to cudgel her memory for a moment or two.

"Woods, I think. Yes, that was it. Thelma Woods. She married a railroad man, John Fry. He was a church deacon, too. That's him, there." The adjacent portrait showed a stiffly posed, unsmiling figure wearing a hard-collared shirt and dark suit, a bible clenched against his midriff. "She died quite young, poor thing. A kidney complaint, I think it was. There were so many things like that they didn't know how to treat back then." She clucked again, sadly, and turned the page, tactfully obliterating this unfortunate reminder. "It's not all that

different now, I suppose, not really. There's always something new coming along, so we never really catch up, do we?"

He excused himself soon after that. He had to meet some people, he told her, the real reason for his being in Pittsburgh. He wasn't sure when he'd be seeing her again, but he'd try and make it, sometime. She saw him to the door, then watched him from the window as he crossed the street and walked away, not looking back.

He'd been more upset by seeing great great grandma Fry's picture than he'd pretended to be, she told herself. Well, it had been inevitable, really. The whole visit must have been disturbing for him, and it had to mean that he was still missing Donna very badly. But it had been nice to see him, in a sad kind of way, good of him to find the time.

She put the album back in the bookcase, wondering if she would ever actually see him again.

23.

___

I hadn't liked doing it, using her in that way, but the albums were the obvious place to check, so that was another instance where I didn't have any real choice. It wasn't a question of remembering the picture from that first time, either; as I recall it, we only looked at relatively recent stuff then. But it was there, the proof that I wanted, confirmation that the link existed and that what I was hoping for at least had its roots in reality.

Learning about Thelma's early death shook me, of course, because it was almost like an echo of what had happened to Donna. I wasn't all that surprised to learn that she'd married someone other than Foster, though; despite my speculating that it might turn out to be something that actually might develop with time, I'd never really convinced myself that it was a realistic possibility. It obviously had been a one-sided thing after all, and I decided that the only reason it got started in the first place was because she'd openly sided with him at the lodge before I'd played, and very likely taken the opportunity to reinforce that after Williams and I left. Foster would have welcomed the salve for his ego, but despite the fact that he'd continued to take her home from the restaurant after that evening I'd never really seen it as a liaison with any kind of long-term future.

Thinking about it then, I did feel a twinge of responsibility; after all, it had been my actions that had created the situation. I just hoped she wasn't going to be too badly hurt by it, and that her marriage to the man Fry was a good one for as long as it lasted. The photo was pretty faded, but she looked reasonably happy; older, of course maybe thirty or so, but she hadn't really changed.

So even though there was this undercurrent of despondency when I went back through the hole, I still felt a real surge of relief when I got off the train at K.C.. There was no way I could have explained it in strictly rational terms just then, but I suddenly felt as though I really was back home; not necessarily just the town, but the era, the whole thing, and that whatever happened in the future, when time ran out and the programme ended and I was forced back into what I still reluctantly accepted was my own period of history, I'd still think of it as where I really belonged.

I went back to the restaurant that night, wondering what sort of reception I was going to get. I told myself to take it easy, not expect too much, that it wouldn't be anything special. Despite the things that had happened and the fact that Williams seemed to have taken something of a shine to me, I was still basically just a customer after all, and a white one at that, a stranger who didn't really belong, in either K.C. or that particular segment of society.

But when I got there, things simply carried on the way I'd hoped they would. The place was quite full; the band was playing, and I got a pretty straight-faced look from Foster as I caught his eye, but Williams and Thelma both seemed quite pleased to see me. Williams was talking to some people who were just on their way out, and when they'd left he came over and shook hands. He told me he hadn't eaten yet and repeated his invitation to join him for a meal, and I said I'd be glad to. We both ordered what we wanted, then we went into the office and talked while they fixed the food.

I told him some more lies; that I still hadn't felt one hundred percent when I'd left last time, so I'd spent a while with friends, just taking it easy and writing up what I'd found during that first trip. I'd been in New York for a couple days immediately prior to coming to K.C., I said, checking things out there; in fact, what I told him about my supposed visit was simply a repetition of what Artie Mastin had told me while were back at base together.

After a while we got the nod that our orders were ready, and we went out into the restaurant and sat down at a table in a rear corner. Thelma served us, and we exchanged a couple of pleasantries, everything very affable, a kind of final reassurance that we were back on good terms, and I felt the last traces of uncertainty lift and leave me feeling completely relaxed, as near to being contented as I had been for a very, very long time.

Williams and I started to eat, still talking occasionally but mostly concentrating on the food. I wasn't particularly conscious of the music, partly because of where we were in the room, with a barricade of general chatter between us and it, and partly because I wasn't very interested anyway, but I suddenly caught myself looking over towards the stage, because I heard something unusual happening there.

I can't remember now what they were playing; some medium-tempoed thing, not that it really matters. Foster was soloing, and it was what he was doing that had grabbed my attention. It still wasn't all that far removed from the written harmonies, but some of his phrases were uncharacteristically angular, nothing at all like the kind if thing that he normally played. The overall effect wasn't all that happy, but that wasn't altogether his fault; the pianist was still laying down a very basic backing and the two elements weren't really meshing, which made the whole thing almost a bizarre reversal of had happened at the lodge session. I saw the pianist glance over his shoulder a couple of times, grimacing in a not very amused way, but he still stuck to what he'd been doing all along, consistently emphasising the bar divisions and playing song-copy chords.

When Foster wound up his solo and turned away from the microphone, his face didn't show any of his customary equanimity; his expression was wooden, echoing the look he'd given me when I'd arrived, and I got the feeling that he was consciously not looking in my direction. I did catch Williams' eye, though, and he grinned and shrugged, but didn't say anything, just carried on eating. I grinned back, but it was an uncomfortable moment, and I didn't say anything either, because I was feeling unsure of my ground again. Nothing else like that happened while we were finishing the meal; the music went back to its usual undemanding formula, and when Foster soloed it was more or less the kind of stuff I'd come to expect from him; smoothly played, melodic, swinging in a fairly predictable way. But just occasionally I detected one or two other things as well; a hint of real indifference, and maybe a touch of sourness, too, an implication of discontent that hadn't been there before.

The place was full by the time we finished the meal, and there were people waiting for tables. Williams invited me back to the office for a drink, and after we'd been chatting there for a few minutes I casually remarked on Foster's slightly aberrant solo, saying that I'd found it a little out of character. Williams agreed, and said that he'd been doing that kind of thing occasionally during the preceding couple of weeks, sticking his neck out to some extent. In his opinion it wasn't altogether working out as far as the overall result was concerned, but it wasn't something that happened all the time. Some evenings he stayed more or less in his normal groove, he said, but every now and then he'd still pull things around a little, try stuff that was unusual for him.

Again, I wasn't really sure how to respond, because I was already quite certain in my own mind that I was personally responsible for the change. From what I'd heard out there in the restaurant it seemed glaringly obvious to me that when I'd played with him at the lodge session I'd done exactly what I didn't want to do, disturbed his complacency to the extent that he'd begun to try and stretch the musical boundaries that up to then he'd been perfectly content to be confined by. What he'd played just then had been structurally uneven, a little clumsy, but it had been a genuine attempt at originality and by no means a total failure. I really had detected the seeds of an authentically creative statement, and that had to mean that the dissatisfaction was there, tempting him into musical waters that he'd previously had no interest in exploring.

Right then I didn't think too much about the deeper implications; my immediate reaction was that I didn't like the idea of what was happening creating any awkwardness between Williams and me. An element of unrest had entered the situation, and despite his professed attitude to such things, from a business point of view I could hardly expect him to like it. So I looked him in the eye and asked him what he thought; did he feel that I'd influenced Foster; that what had happened when we'd played together had actually affected his attitude to that extent, prompted the change that I'd heard just then?

He laughed, and said he was sure it had, but there was no hint of resentment that I could detect, and I really don't think he was feeling anything of the kind. He told me that I wasn't to feel embarrassed about it, and that he considered himself lucky to have kept Foster there as long as he had. Although he hadn't actually said anything about quitting, if he was ready to move on that was O.K. with him. The job didn't really call for that class of player anyway, he said, and we both knew that he was largely wasting his talent by not aiming higher than he had. The truth was that the majority of the restaurant's customers wouldn't really notice if he had to bring somebody else in, not from a musical point of view, and despite the inroads the draft was making there were still plenty of competent people around.

It was a relief to find him taking it like that, but I should have expected it, really. I'd temporarily forgotten that he'd been a musician himself and obviously understood the frequent frustrations and generally fluid nature of the game. People were always moving around then, trading chairs in different outfits, going for jobs that paid better or where the musical opportunities looked more interesting, a whole range of reasons.

None of that had anything to do with Foster's obvious restlessness, of course. But even though I knew for a cast-iron certainty that the responsibility was mine, I found that in the event I wasn't anything like as concerned as I'd originally imagined I'd be. For one thing, I'd had time to think about the lodge session and what it could lead to by then, and I'd already decided that even allowing for his apparently conservative nature the truth was that the same thing would almost certainly have happened to him eventually, without any prompting from me.

The only difference would have been in the timing. The kind of changes that I'd introduced him to were already beginning to filter into the musical climate, and they'd have been bound to touch someone of his generation sooner or later, even if it turned out to be just a temporary distraction. One of the things I'd done during my last period back at base had been to check out whether or not his name showed up in any future records and discographical data, and there'd been nothing at all, so even though I had caused a premature disruption to his thinking the obvious assumption had to be that that nothing of real significance was going to come out of it anyway, musically at least.

Of course, there were other considerations stemming from his situation and how he got there. The obvious ones were his relationship with Thelma, and how my playing might have affected the other musicians at the lodge session, but those were only the inner ripples of what was bound to be an ever-expanding series of them, because in effect I'd lobbed a stone into the surface of a dozen or so lives, and the changes that that could provoke were potentially limitless.

But I found that I wasn't seriously concerned about any of that, either, which may simply have been irresponsibility or apathy on my part, although in view of what's happened recently I'm less inclined to see it that way now than I have been on occasion. I'm not going to confuse things by explaining that right now, but a lot more questions have been thrown up since that time, and although I can't claim to know the answers to all of them, at least some have been resolved, and that's been enough to reassure me that in fact there never was any real reason for me to have felt concern over that particular issue.

Anyway, Williams and I sat and talked about other things for a while, had a couple more drinks, and then I took myself off and headed back to the hotel. The visit had been just a scouting mission to reassure myself that the lines of communication were still in good shape, and all in all I felt it had gone pretty well; Thelma and I were still O.K., and I had three weeks to build on that. Before I went, Williams reminded me about the Benny Valentine visit; he knew Valentine, he said, and he'd introduce me when they got into town; it'd help to establish my credentials, and then I could take it from there.

I visited the restaurant for a late meal every two or three days during the next couple of weeks, and each time I was there I could clearly detect the changes that were gradually appearing in Foster's playing. It wasn't simply a matter of his attempting to broaden what he did in a harmonic sense, his tone and time were being affected, too, his whole musical concept. The laid-back quality that had sometimes verged on indolence was being replaced by an element of tension, the uncertainty of someone who wasn't altogether sure which route to take because he was suddenly finding himself faced with options that he'd never really considered before.

It wasn't like that all the time. He usually kicked off his solos in his normal, smoothly relaxed style, using the kind of phrases that obviously fitted comfortably under his fingers and required no real mental effort to string together. But it rarely stayed that way for long. After a while he'd start worrying at the harmonies and phrasing again, sometimes coming up with things that were reasonably effective, other times just sounding uncertain and fretful, even a little angry. During those couple of weeks we never actually engaged in conversation; we exchanged greetings of a kind, but they were restricted to poker-faced nods and one grudging spoken hello on his side, an acknowledgement that he obviously regretted as soon as he offered it. He looked sullen a lot of the time, as well; not really overtly, but it was there in the line of his mouth when he wasn't blowing.

As far as Thelma was concerned, I became more or less one of her regular customers; I always made sure to eat at one of her tables and we'd have the usual basically meaningless conversational exchanges between customer and whoever's looking after them. It didn't get beyond that, partly because after my first night back, although she was still friendly enough she was a little abstracted most of the time, too; thoughtful and noticeably quieter that usual.

I realised that the most likely reason was that things were already cooling between her and Foster, and I wondered how much that had to do with the fact that I was around again, because it was obvious that my presence was reminding him of what had happened that night at the lodge. It was equally obvious that he was very moody just then, and his attitude toward me and the things that were happening to his playing had to mean that his mind was very much on the music, probably to the exclusion of virtually everything else. It made for a slightly uncomfortable atmosphere, but I decided that in the long term it was probably for the best anyway; the sooner it was over between them the sooner she'd settle again, and maybe it would be my shoulder that she'd cry on until she did.

That was another turning-point, because it was a possibility that made me consider the situation in a far less one-sided way, start to see it as maybe much more than something that was just for my benefit, the way I'd thought of it up until then. I began to wonder if in fact it was going to be mutually beneficial in some way, a kind of necessity as far as both of us were concerned. There was still no question whatever of it taking the form of some unrealistic romantic attachment; that never entered my mind at any time, believe me. But I was beginning to feel as though the reason for our relationship existing at all wasn't quite the way I'd been viewing it, that in fact I might be there to give as well as take, and that what I had to do was bide my time and wait until the picture became clear and maybe showed me what my own role was going to be.

Something else that I had to take care of while I was on that trip, of course, was my official reason for being there at all, the 'Joe Shaddick/Shaddock' business. Despite my reasoning, the change in Foster's playing had reinforced my feeling about actually performing again, and that decided me. 'Shaddick/Shaddock' had taken off before I got back, I'd say; he'd quit the Roseland job and left town, nobody knew exactly where to, but he'd told a couple of people he'd back in K.C. in the near future, a matter of weeks. It would be enough to sustain Walden's interest, I knew that, maybe even increase it, and at least the Buddy Henry material that I'd be taking back with me would confirm that it hadn't simply been wasted time on my part.

Williams took me across to the El Torrean the night the Valentine band opened. He knew Valentine pretty well, and he introduced me and told him what I supposed to be doing. Valentine was pleasant, very friendly, a little amused at the idea of being the subject of academic interest, I think. He said he hoped I got what I wanted, that he had a few good guys in the band just then that I'd probably find it worth my while tailing, anything he could do to help, etc., and that was my entrée to that particular scene. I introduced myself to Henry as well during the first interval; I button-holed him when he came off the stand and told him about seeing him at Minton's; he was ostensibly off-hand about it, but obviously rather pleased that I remembered him and that I was being complimentary about what I'd heard.

I bought him a drink, and we talked until he had to go back on. He was on the quiet side at first, a little guarded, but he gradually loosened up. That had been the first time he played at Minton's, he told me; he'd been in town visiting relatives for a few days, and he'd taken the opportunity to exercise his lip and sound out the things that he'd heard were happening there. The reason he'd cut out so early was because he'd had a cold coming on, he said; playing had started to become uncomfortable, and he hadn't fancied being blown away by the kind of fire-power he'd have been working alongside if he'd stayed. It sounded like a genuine excuse to me, not an expedient get-out because he'd actually been afraid to compete at that level, hadn't really been sure that he could cut it. In fact, he exuded a kind of quiet self-confidence, the air of someone who believed in his own capabilities and wasn't likely to be easily demoralised in that sort of situation.

His solo opportunities with Valentine turned out to be pretty limited; most of the trumpet spots were handled by a louder and in some ways technically more solid guy, a relative nobody who was better suited to that kind of hard-swinging outfit. Although his sound had clearly filled out a little since Minton's, Henry's playing was still altogether more thoughtful and restrained, which meant that it demanded a much more intimate setting, a backing that would be sympathetic to what he was doing and wouldn't swamp him with heavy section figures and loud drumming, all the normal big-band trimmings.

He didn't go anywhere to blow after the gig; when we'd talked earlier he'd told me that he was pretty beat, that they'd travelled almost five hundred miles that day and that he was going to hit the sack as soon as they'd finished. It was a disappointment, but understandable; they'd been playing one-nighters for almost a month, and he didn't look to be physically strong, anyway; although he was medium height, he couldn't have weighed more than a hundred pounds or so. In fact, the El Torrean job must have been a blessed relief from the customary one-night grind for all of them. Apart from actually playing the job and travelling, their normal life consisted largely of cat-naps and snatched meals in diners and hash-houses, and to settle for six whole days in a town where a lot of them had friends and in some cases family must have been like a holiday as far as they were concerned.

I established a new routine after that. Each evening I had a lateish dinner, more often than not at Williams' place, took in the last set at the El Torrean, and then tailed Henry until the early hours, usually around six or seven in the morning. Although he had no way of knowing what I was really doing, after a day or so he seemed to be acknowledging me as a kind or barometer; every so often I'd see him glancing at me while he was playing, usually when he'd just produced a particularly felicitous bit of phrasing, as though he was checking my reaction.

His playing wasn't totally consistent, of course, no-one's is. But at every session, it didn't really matter what the setting was or what kind of musical company he was keeping at the time, there would always be something of his personal poetry for me to relish and preserve. To some extent it was still a style in embryo, still being put together and refined, but every time he soloed I could detect touches that clearly spelled out the fact that his contribution to the new music would have been a major one, and despite the macabre aspect of what was happening I was glad I was there, surreptitiously helping him to achieve at least some of the recognition that was going to be denied in his own time.

Not all the Valentine musicians made a nightly thing of it. Like most bands of the period it had a core of seasoned professionals, older guys that the draft wouldn't be likely to reach for a while and who as often as not chose to conserve their energies, with the balance made up of youngsters, several of them not even at a draftable age, who were prepared to ball all night or at least until a worn-out lip or exhaustion forced them to quit. Henry was a kind of in-between; he was twenty-two then, but he had a bum ear-drum that had kept him out of the services, he told me. Despite that and his frail-looking physique, after that first evening he really was one of the night-people, always ready to blow and always the one to produce the most interesting music. I wasn't his only supporter by any means; several other members of the band, usually the younger ones, were always ready to applaud him, and some of the other people who attended the sessions as well. So he actually was beginning to make his mark, and that was what made the situation particularly tragic and why I made sure I got down everything that he played.

Williams was at a couple of the sessions, although he never stayed the course. I didn't see Foster much at all that week, not until my last night there; the fact that I ate a little earlier than usual so that I could make it across to the El Torrean for the closing set usually meant that I was out of the restaurant before the band came on, and because I was concentrating on Henry I hadn't really given him much thought anyway.

But I had really begun to worry about Thelma. She'd gone quiet to the point of not really talking at all, no more than was absolutely necessary. I tried to make conversation while she was taking and delivering my orders, but it was a total waste of breath. I really did get the feeling that she barely recognised me some of the time, that her mind was so fixed on something else that she was going through the motions of the job without really thinking about it at all. Twice, she brought me things I hadn't ordered, and on one occasion she was bawled out by a women with a loud voice because she did the same thing to her. She just stood there, not saying anything until the woman finally shut up, and then she told her she was sorry and took the offending whatever it was back into the kitchen.

Even then I got the feeling that she was so far removed from what was actually happening that the woman's tirade had affected her as much as water does a duck's feathers. It wasn't rudeness or indifference like the noisy woman obviously thought, it was simply that she was buried so deep in her own thoughts that she barely knew what was going on around her. My protective feeling had grown to the extent that I really wanted to intervene, tell the woman to take it easy, that getting a wrong dish was no reason to humiliate someone that way, but I didn't. I don't think it was cowardice; Thelma looked to be approaching some sort of crisis, and I decided that it would probably be then that I'd assume the responsibility that was going to be my contribution to the relationship, and that to openly take up cudgels on her behalf right then might even precipitate that. In the event I got it right, but I was still furious for her at the time, hating the woman and her raucous complaining with a degree of intensity that I hadn't felt for a long time.

Several of the after-hours things were a place on 14th Street, the back room of a joint called the Basement Club, and that's where we were on Thursday, my last night in town. Thelma was with Foster when he came in, sometime after 1 a.m., and right away I could see it was virtually over between them, that what I was witnessing was the terminal stage of something that never been more than a temporary expedience as far as he was concerned.

24.
____

She was sure that he'd meant to go without her that evening. He'd denied it, but he'd been on his way to the rear entrance, dressed for the street and carrying his instrument case when she'd come out of the kitchen and almost collided with him.

He'd been going to put his saxophone in the car, he said, then come back and collect her. It was a lie, she knew, plainly visible in the sullen evasiveness of his expression. He'd been like a little boy who'd been caught sneaking cookies, she thought; guilty and resentful, stubborn with his denial.

She didn't want to fight, so she'd fetched her coat and gone with him. She hadn't wanted to, really. The growing strain that she was under meant that she tired easily, and she know that it was likely to be very late before he was ready to take her home. But she wanted to be close to him, in case she got up the courage to tell him what had happened. She still probably wouldn't get the chance to do that, she realised; if he decided to play a lot while they were there it was more than likely that she'd lose her nerve again, postpone it to another time.

She wasn't even sure she loved him any more. Maybe she never had, really. For the first few weeks she'd been sure that she did, happy to be with him even when he was quiet and not all that attentive, but he said very little at all now. She still clung to a fraying shred of hope that this withdrawal was temporary, that he'd eventually approach her again with something like his initial need for consolation, but she didn't really believe that that would happen. In a way, she didn't even want it to. When she'd given herself she'd known that he didn't really feel the same way about her as she did about him; she'd simply hoped that it would grow from that.

But it hadn't, and she knew deep down that it was never likely to now. His attempt to sneak off that evening had been a shabby pointer to the truth; that as far as he was concerned she'd already become an embarrassment, an encumbrance that he was anxious to rid himself of.

It wasn't that easy, though, she told herself. Maybe it was for him, but not for her. Whether he liked it or not, he had a responsibility to share, and he had to be told about it, accept his part in what happened. She could have told him in the car on the way there, she supposed, but somehow it hadn't felt the right time.

Maybe a little later, she thought. Maybe we can find a corner to sit in for a while, have a drink and talk. He might be a bit more relaxed, not so sulky, if he had a drink first.

She followed him into the building and down the stairs, flinching at the wall of smoke and the welter of music and voices that greeted them as he opened the door at the end of the corridor and went inside.

25.

⸻

By pure chance I was looking in the direction of the entrance just then, and I saw them come it. Foster was carrying his saxophone case; Thelma was a few paces behind him, so anyone who hadn't known about the relationship wouldn't necessarily have deduced that they were actually together. But even though I did know about it, the whole picture implied that there was more than just physical distance between them, that what closeness there had been was already on the wane and that Thelma was simply struggling in his wake, unable to keep up with him and losing ground the whole time.

It was sad to see, and it put another damper on the proceedings, because I was already in a pretty ambiguous mood. The session had been going well, and that only heightened its tragic aspect; Henry was in great form, less vulnerable to technical lapses than he sometimes was, and some of the other people there had turned in creditable solos as well. The drummer was the young guy who'd played at the lodge session, and whenever Henry soloed he was showing the same kind of understanding and willingness to respond that he'd shown behind me then, so the backing to what I was thinking of as his swan song was in part at least worthy of him.

Foster and Thelma had been there a few minutes when I saw him staring at me. Thelma had already faded away to a corner of the room, nursing a drink and still obviously immersed in her personal concerns, and he was talking to some people by the bar when I saw his eyes were fixed on me. I nodded, and although he didn't openly respond I detected a change in his face, a hardening around his mouth; not the sullen look I'd become accustomed to, more a kind of bleak determination.

He carried on talking for a couple minutes, then he came over and said hello. It wasn't in any way friendly, just a terse dismissal of customary formalities, a clearing of the ground. He asked if I'd played that evening, and I said, no, I hadn't. Was I going to?, he wanted to know.

His question didn't surprise me at all. It had been obvious from his behaviour at the restaurant that our encounter at the lodge session had never really left his mind, and that what had happened had been eating at him ever since. Now it was right out in the open, and I could see the scale of it clearly for the first time; he was still bitterly resentful, it was there in his face and the tone of his voice. He wanted a second chance to prove himself, put the record straight, and he was challenging me to supply it.

Of course, I'd already decided not play again on that trip, partly because of Foster's change of direction, and in any case all my musical interest was focussed on Henry. But now this was happening, and I guess that subconsciously I'd always known it would. I felt that in a way it was right that it should, too; it was my playing before that had been one of the reasons, maybe the major one, why Foster and Thelma had gotten together, and during that time he'd demonstrated what kind of person he was. My first impression of him had been right; he was spoiled, selfish and vain, somebody that Thelma would be better off without. Despite her obvious unhappiness, I realised that she probably didn't see it that way at all. Love, or infatuation, whatever you like to call that kind of attraction, has a bad habit of blinkering us against the truth, and the fact that she was there that evening must have meant that she was still clinging to some remnant of hope that things would still work out the way she wanted them to.

They wouldn't, of course, and it was obvious that the best possible thing as far as she was concerned would be to have the blinkers ripped off so that she could see Foster as he really was, realise that she'd been wasting her affection on somebody who didn't deserve it. She'd be hurt, of course, but like always in that kind of situation it would be better to do it then than let it drag on and hurt her more in the future. I decided that for me to play again might be the only real way of achieving that; that by leading Foster a dance that his musical instincts and limitations simply wouldn't allow him to follow to his satisfaction, his self-absorbtion and petulance would surface to an extent that even Thelma wouldn't be able to ignore.

There was a risk of jeopardising my own situation, of course, the possibility that for whatever reason she'd decide to revert to the stance she'd taken at the end of the lodge session and blot me out of her considerations as well. But even though I realised that, I felt that I had no real choice. I'd helped create the circumstances that had led her to where she was right then, so it was up to me to try and remedy that, even though it could mean chancing my own position again. I told myself that this was probably the part that I was destined to play in our relationship, the contribution that I'd anticipated without knowing exactly what it was going to be. If it was, I could see that it had a singular irony to it, because Cupid was about to become the spoiler after all, a transformation that looked as though it had become a regrettable necessity.

So I said, sure, I'd play if it could be arranged, if that was what he wanted. He nodded, and went across to the piano and spoke to the guy there. The pianist didn't look particularly happy about it, but there was an urgency about Foster that must have persuaded him. Foster came back and said we'd be on after they finished the number they were playing, and then he went away and unpacked his instrument and assembled it, not looking at me at all while he was doing it; very deadpan, obviously tense and trying not to show it.

The number finished, and I went over and exchanged hello's with the departing pianist – he looked a little bemused when he saw who was replacing him, which I guess wasn't surprising – then I put the recorder on an empty chair beside the piano seat and sat down and tried a few chords. I wasn't really thinking about what I played, all I was doing was checking out the piano's action, but then I turned and saw that Henry was staring at me with his eyebrows raised, grinning with what looked like a mixture of curiosity and approval.

Despite the real reason for my being there, for just those few minutes since Foster had challenged me, I hadn't really consciously thought about Henry at all, and the fact that I accepted meant that I'd actually be playing with him after all simply hadn't occurred to me; I guess the potential importance of what I was going to do, the effect it might have on my relationship with Thelma, had just blocked it out of my mind for the time being.

But again I got the feeling of rightness about what was happening, because in a sense he was about to repay the service that I was doing him by strengthening my case for being allowed to stick with the K.C. assignment. 'Joe Shaddick/Shaddock' had surfaced again and was going to meet Buddy Henry after all, an irresistible encounter as far as Walden would be concerned, and the fact that only a few hours from then Henry would be dead made it all the more fitting somehow. I was the person who was ensuring his immortality, and it simply seemed right that we should converse in the special intimacy of the jazz language before it happened, create an appropriate coda to it all.

Foster came and stood beside the piano, and I tuned him in until he was satisfied, and then he went along the front line, said hi to the people there, and sat down at the far end, not speaking after that. Two guys who'd been playing trombone and tenor had just taken a break, and the front line consisted of Henry, Foster, another trumpet-player, a local I'd seen before, and an altoist from the Valentine band. The bass player was Valentine's man, too, and the drummer was still the young guy from the lodge session. He'd seemed pleased to see me, greeted me as 'doc', which again was understandable. The beard and glasses and my generally conservative look must have presented a ludicrously anomalous picture; a middle-aged white academic among a bunch of sharply dresses young Aframs, a sore thumb to beat all sore thumbs.

But I didn't feel uncomfortable or out of place; rather the reverse, if anything. Because I knew what I knew and despite my musical limitations, I actually felt that in a way I was in charge; that I was the tutor and they were the students, there to benefit from that foreknowledge, be guided by me. The responsibility and guilt thing didn't enter into it all, either, because as well as the question of Thelma I saw it as a chance to help Henry achieve just a little more of his potential in the time that he did have left, make an even more positive mark than he already had done.

Henry and the altoist had been debating what to play next; in the event it was a blues, but they wanted to do it in Db, which was pretty unusual at the time. I said that would be fine, and Foster and the local trumpet-player O.K.'d it as well, although the trumpet-player didn't look too crazy about the idea. Medium-fast, Henry said; two choruses of piano, then they'd riff a couple before soloing down the line from left to right. He blew a little figure, and the others echoed him, the altoist playing it as a harmony line. Henry counted us in, and we were away.

The moment we started moving, it was as though something else had somehow clicked into place; not a piece of a jigsaw, exactly, more like a cog or some other essential machine part, and there was touch of déjà vu about it, too. But whatever it all added up to, I felt that I belonged there, at that time and place and doing what I was doing, *really* felt that, and in the whole of my life I've never been more relaxed or sure of myself, ready to handle anything at all that the situation threw at me.

The altoist and the local trumpet blew a handful of choruses each; neither of them was what could be called inspired, but there were no real lulls and an occasional nice turn of phrase, but then Henry took over, and from the moment he did there was a wholeness to what was happening, as though an entity had suddenly been achieved. Without even consciously thinking about it, I found I was augmenting chords and slipping in substitutions and varying the placement of the beat, echoing characteristics that I'd detected in his playing, establishing foundations I knew he'd respond to, and he did, and it was like – I guess organic growth's the nearest I can get to it, because what I was doing and what he was doing meant that we were feeding off each other in a way that I could never truly adequately describe, because there's simply no way. It was a meeting of minds, a moment of total truth that was like nothing I'd ever experienced before, my foreknowledge and his imagination combining to create something very, very special, and right then it was as though I was finding a part of myself that I'd always hoped was there without ever really believing that it existed.

Does that make sense to you, Phyl? I can't imagine it does, and that's no reflection on your own sensibilities. Why try to describe the indescribable, anyway? Whatever it was, it happened, you have my word on that. Between us we were constructing something that had its own unique validity as a creative statement, my contribution the underpinning and his structural beauty that rose above it. It was extraordinary and deeply moving and telling you about it now's bringing back at least some of the feeling I had at the time.

I don't remember how many choruses Henry played; seven, eight, maybe more, but it was while he was blowing, close to the end of his solo, that I glanced in his direction and saw Foster's face just beyond him. The aggression had gone from it completely; instead he looked dazed. There were other things there as well; awe, fear, a kind of naked hunger. For the first time since we'd met I felt pity for him, because the was his moment of truth as well, when he encountered something that reached way past the limits that he'd cocooned himself in and shown him another plane of musical existence. What I'd done at the lodge session had only hinted at what was there, but right then he was hearing it open out before him, a dimension of what must've sounded like infinite possibilities that cried out to be entered and explored.

There was a lot of shouting and whooping and whistling when Henry eventually finished. I hadn't really been conscious of it at the time, but listening to the playback later the gradual dwindling of chatter while he was playing was very evident. I looked across at him, and he was looking back at me, laughing and nodding, holding his trumpet vertically with the bell pointed at the ceiling, like some triumphantly held trophy. But I knew it wasn't just for himself. He was acknowledging me and my part, too, and despite everything that's happened since then it's still a kind of pinnacle that's never really far from my mind.

It was only when the applause began to fade that I realised that Foster had started to play. He was in the chair beyond Henry, largely masked by him and the others, and after that one glance he'd simply slipped from my mind while I savoured the moment, totally forgetting that he'd be soloing when Henry finished. In fact, I'd carried on playing, just dropping in occasional chords to stay with the bass and drums, but it was purely a reflex kind of thing, not a conscious backing for him.

But then I heard him, and straight away I realised that he was working around what I was doing; only in a muted, hesitant way, but I could still tell that for the moment at least he was being guided by me. His phrasing was very tentative, almost as though he was waiting for my instructions before committing himself to anything more positive.

What was happening was a submission, nothing less. Something traumatic had happened to him when Henry and I were playing, and it wasn't just to do with his attitude towards the music. I think that in a way he'd been purged, that his ego had been deflated to the extent that temporarily at least he'd been humbled into accepting that he was considerably less than he'd thought he was, and that right then he was involved in a situation that he couldn't handle without help, if at all.

I'd grown to dislike him, but that was mostly on a personal level, because of what he was doing to Thelma. Musically, if anything I felt sorry for him, seeing his attitude as an impediment to his obvious talent, something to be pitied because of what it denied him. But what he was doing at that moment was offering a kind of confession, an open acknowledgement of deficiency. Right then the music was the important thing for both of us, and he was asking me to help him, show him a way that he could at least follow without completely humiliating himself in the process.

So that's what I did. I modified what I'd been doing, not too much, certainly not to the extent I did the first time, but I adjusted the rhythmic placement a little and made the harmonies a shade more basic, taking them close to the kind of thing he was used to, trying not to be too obvious about any of it. His playing gradually became a little more relaxed, but he refused to retreat back to ground where he'd have been completely comfortable, still occasionally employing intervals that echoed the deviations that that I'd been hearing from him at the restaurant. I paced him for a couple of choruses, then I started to move back towards what I'd been doing before, coaxing him to go with me, and he did; a little awkwardly at first, but very gradually getting the feel of what was happening.

It was a little bit like someone easing himself into a new suit of clothes that desperately wanted to wear, but wasn't altogether sure was going to fit him. Even so, his solo had shape to it, an occasionally rough-edged sense of form. When he finished he got a pretty good hand, about right for what he'd done. Henry apart, there was no question that he'd outplayed the other people there, especially the local trumpet man; he hadn't been as polished as Valentine's altoist, but from the point of view of invention he'd headed him by a fair margin. I saw Henry talking to him while the bassist worked through a couple of choruses, and again I saw something on his face I hadn't seen before, an eager look, maybe even a touch of shyness, very different to the initial blandness and eventual sulkiness that I'd come to expect.

When the bassist finished they all traded fours for a while and then riffed it on out. There was a lot of applause, and I sat there, wondering what to do, hating the idea of quitting, but thinking that perhaps I should. 'Joe Shaddick/Shaddock' had re-emerged and had his say with Henry, and as far as Foster was concerned I'd proved my point and accepted his admission of error. It was a kind of 'let's-cut-out-while-we're-ahead' moment, but it didn't last long. The pianist I'd taken over from didn't reappear and Henry was already demonstrating a variation on a standard to the others. Although it was ostensibly a free-for-all he'd stamped his mark on the proceedings to the extent that he was being tacitly accepted as the one who should call the shots, and that was fine by me. Although I still felt that I was in a position to steer things more or less the way I wanted, I didn't really like the idea of being too prominent, a real focus of attention. I decided that as long as Henry continued to play it would be O.K. for me to carry on, still doing what I had been, but in the background, organising the engine-room and leaving the real exposure to the up-front people.

There'd be no real point in going into details as far as the rest of the session was concerned; I'm not too sure that I could, anyway. In a sense what was happening was unreal, because it was the realisation of a dream. Whenever Henry soloed it was as though he and I were somehow detached from everything else that was going on around us, sometimes reaching levels of rapport that had something that was – again, I doubt that I could ever describe it adequately. In a way I suppose it could've been compared to a spiritual experience, because there was something a little unearthly about it; a kind of controlled ecstasy where I was free of normal restraints, but still able to think clearly, create a lucid platform for him to build on. After a while, the local trumpet-player quit, then the altoist; other people sat in and played for a while before cutting out again, but the nucleus was Henry and the drummer and me, with Foster doggedly staying with us, trailing all the time but playing with a stubborn determination that occasionally resulted in a touch of genuine creativity.

It was past 7:30 a.m. when we finished. Henry's lips had started to go a while before that, but he'd hung on until he really couldn't make it any more. Foster and the drummer had held on, too;

there'd been a couple of changes of bassist, but apart from that the group had stayed the same for the last hour or so that we played.

It really was like waking up, surfacing from a deep sleep, reluctantly coming back to another, altogether colder and dingier world. Apart from us the room was almost empty; there were a few people who'd stayed around to the finish, one guy asleep in a chair, but there was no sign at all of Thelma. The air was thick with smoke, not all of it legal by any means and rapidly turning stale. It had been making me light-headed for a while, but that suddenly went and I felt a rush of almost total exhaustion; not just physical, in every way.

Henry came over and sat down beside me; apart from calling tunes and brief discussions between us about keys and tempos it was the first time we'd talked during the whole thing. He began asking questions; where I was actually from, what was my musical background, had I ever played professionally?

I kept my answers as short as I could, partly because I really was exhausted and partly because the feeling of let-down I was experiencing wasn't simply to do with the fact that we'd quit playing. My total absorption in what I'd been doing had even temporarily pushed Henry's situation to the back of my mind, the fact that those were the closing hours of his life. That could be interpreted as a comment on my depth of feeling, I suppose, maybe an indication of just how far my recently acquired ruthlessly selfish streak had developed, but whether it was or not I've pretty much given up on sitting in judgement on myself as far as most of this is concerned.

The exact time of his death wasn't stated in the records; the day was given, but not the hour. Sitting there, looking at him while he talked and trying to push back the fog that was filling my head, I had this terrible chilling vision of him back in his hotel room, probably only a short while from then, suffocating and blinded by smoke and frantically struggling to escape the blazing nightmare that surrounded him when what was happening eventually forced him awake.

But I told myself that he wouldn't, that that was the way it was going to be and that there was no way at all of preventing it, because at a given point in time he was destined to die, in a situation that would be gruesomely similar to the one I was picturing. It might even be caused by his own carelessness, falling asleep with a lighted cigarette in his hand, something like that, but the cause would be irrelevant, anyway; however it came about it was pre-ordained, and even if I totally disregarded the rule-book and tried to save him circumstances would still ensure that it happened when the moment arrived. It was suddenly all too much, past the limit of what I could take right then, so I cut in on his questions and told him I was leaving town that morning and had a train to make very soon but I was sure that I'd be seeing him again some time, and then I said so long and headed for the door. Foster had stayed in his chair, not saying anything while Henry and I had been talking, drying out his saxophone and taking it apart; I passed him on the way out, and said, 'nice going' I think it was, and he nodded and said, thanks. He looked dog-weary, too; drawn and stubbled, nothing at all like his usual rather svelte image. But I could detect a touch of serenity about him as well; not the old self-satisfaction, though, more the look of someone who'd been tested and found not altogether wanting and was comforted by that knowledge.

And that was it. I went back to the hotel, collected my stuff, and caught the first available train. Like always it was almost full, but I managed to find a seat in the day coach, and then I semi-dozed for a lot of the journey back to Leyland. There were the usual unscheduled stops en route, something else I was used to by then, so again I got back to base too late to check in with psych or Walden; I hadn't really slept at all, either, and I was totally drained. After going through medical I turned in, but despite my exhaustion I still found it hard to sleep, because my mind kept drifting back to the same images of Henry I'd had during our last conversation, and I just lay there tossing and turning and wondering if I should have at least made some kind of attempt to save him, despite the fact that it would have been utterly pointless. I told myself that I had to forget it and get some sleep because whatever I'd tried would have been futile, but it wasn't until daylight that I managed to drop off for a few hours, and I felt like a squeezed-out dishrag when I eventually got up, some time in the middle of the morning.

I was still feeling very low, so I was pretty uneasy about how well I was going to cope with the psych session, but ironically enough it actually worked to my advantage. The guy who was handling the de-briefing told me that the depression I was obviously feeling was simply end-of-programme blues; most of the field operatives were feeling down, he said, suffering from a species of withdrawal symptoms now that were about to be deprived of what had been feeding our individual addictions. It wasn't a total mis-analysis, but in any case it gave me an easy out, so I said I guessed he was right which seemed to keep him happy and helped make the rest of it go smoothly enough as far as I could tell.

When it was over, I headed for the section office, wondering how Walden was going to react to the recordings of the Basement Club session. I hadn't checked it out at all, but I remembered that the cartridge I'd been using had reached saturation point before it had finished; I'd been so wrapped up in what was happening that I'd simply forgotten to take a break and change it, which meant that I'd lost about an hour of music, but actually that wasn't the disaster it could have been, and in one way that had worked in my favour, too. The magic had begun to fade a little during the final stages anyway, and at least it had meant that there'd been no space left on it for a post-session interview that I'd have expected to engineer with 'Shaddick/Shaddock'. I'd goofed again, was what I decided to tell Walden, left the replacement cartridge at the hotel when I'd gone out that evening, and then I'd feed him a supposed conversation that I was pretty sure would placate him, especially after he'd heard the music.

He was on the 'phone when I walked into his office, looking and sounding very serious, but he closed the call as soon as he saw me, told whoever it was that he'd get back to them.

26.

The nurse had been on her own in the ward for five minutes when the man in bed 27 knocked over the water carafe and tumbler. The sound was loud and startling in the near-darkness, prompting muttered protests and general restlessness in the other beds.

She went to him, finding him struggling with the covers, trying to sit up.

"Now, then," she said. Glass crunched underneath her feet. "You're awake, are you? Do you want to do something?"

The man continued to tug feebly at the covers. His stubbled face, more grey now than black, still contrasted darkly with the bandages that covered the top of his head, and sweat was sharpening the shadows around his eyes and nose and mouth. He said nothing for a moment, still hauling with weak desperation at the bedding. After a few seconds, he lay back, staring at her, his eyes bright and feverish.

"How long — been here?"

"Eight days," the nurse said. She began to tidy the bedding. "You came in last Tuesday. You had an accident, remember?"

There was a brief pause, then the man said, "Escalator." He closed his eyes. "Oh, God." He opened them again, and his tongue appeared, moistening his lips. "What's the date?"

"Date?" the nurse echoed. He looks scared out of his wits, she thought. "It's the fifteenth."

He rocked his head on the pillow, his face strained and sweating. "What year?"

The nurse smiled. "You've only been here eight days, sweetheart. It's the same as it was then." The man began to prise himself into a sitting position again, his face glistening with effort. "Now, look," the nurse said. "You're not going any place. Can't you see you've got a broken leg?" She patted the bedding, soothingly. "You stay right there, and I'll fetch sister."

She went back to the staff office where sister had ostensibly gone to check some records, although it was well-known that that was frequently the excuse she used when she wanted a smoke during the late shift. Sister was stubbing her cigarette out and dispersing the smoke with her hand as she went in, warned by her approaching footsteps. "Is Margolies back yet?"

"Not yet," the nurse said. "It's 27. He's come round, and he's trying to get out of bed."

"You shouldn't have left him, then," the sister said. "I was just coming." She led the way back to the ward. The man had thrown the covers off, but was laying down again, panting with exhaustion. "Now, then," the sister said. "What do you think you're doing? You won't be walking on that leg of yours for a while yet." She checked that the drip was still connected, then began to rearrange the covers. "How are you feeling?"

After a moment, the man said, faintly, "Sick." He closed his eyes. "Weak."

"I'm not surprised, " the sister said. "You lost a lot of blood, and you had a nasty crack on the head as well." She rested her palm on his forehead. "You've still got a fever, too." She frowned, fumbling for her thermometer.

The man opened his eyes again. "What happened, exactly? I remember somebody knocking into me…" His voiced tailed away.

"Some stupid man tripped you on an escalator in the subway," the sister said. "Running to catch a train. There's too many impatient people in the world. I hope you're not one of them, because you're going to be with us for a while, you might as well know that now." She stuck the thermometer into a corner of his mouth, then began to check his pulse. She wondered how well his leg was mending. It had been a particularly ugly break, the bone severing the main artery before it emerged through the flesh. Bleeding had been excessive, and they'd only just got him there in time. She smiled down at him. "You're lucky to be alive, do you know that?"

The man offered no sign of acknowledgement, staring past her towards the darkness of the ceiling with terrified eyes.

27.

———

I'd anticipated a cheerful reception from Walden, eager enquiries, that kind of thing. But he was looking reluctant and awkward, fretful even. He told me to sit down, because he had some bad news that was going to hit me pretty hard. So I sat down, and then he told me that Artie Mastin was missing.

I just stared at him, not knowing what to say and feeling as if a large chunk of lead had suddenly materialised in my stomach. He was six days overdue, he said, and it had to be assumed that circumstances beyond his control had prevented him from making it back before his time allocation ran out; whatever the cause had been, it was officially accepted that he was dead. He knew that we'd been friends for a long time, he said, and he could understand how I was feeling.

He didn't really understand, of course, especially one part of it, because there was no way that he could have. Against his own wishes he'd been stuck there at base, so he had no real knowledge of what it was like to be relocated in time, the utterly unique sense of isolation that it'd induced initially and which'd only very recently disappeared as far as I was concerned. Despite that, and the feeling of belonging that had gradually replaced it in my own case, there was still no way of overcoming the permanent underlying fear of things going irretrievably wrong, the way they must have done for Artie.

To live there, to actually be able to survive and somehow make a place for myself, that was something I'd gladly have given a dozen years of my life for. Dying there, though, that was different, because it was bound to be a singularly lonely end, in a place of strangers who it would be impossible to confide in, tell them the truth without being thought delirious or deranged. I'd actually experienced that fear in its most concentrated form that last night in New York, and the memory of it made me hope fervently that whatever it was that had happened to Artie had meant a mercifully quick finish, that it hadn't been some injury or illness that would've dragged the whole terrifying business out, with him caught there like a doomed animal in a trap, knowing that escape was impossible.

It seemed patently obvious to me that my finding Thelma and all the things that had developed from it made my own situation very much one of a kind, because even though it would only be a temporary association I was totally convinced by then that an essential element of my own future was there in the past. But Artie had no such hang-ups, I was pretty certain of that. Like the rest of us, he was single, but in his case it had been a matter of choice. He'd always led an active social life and he obviously liked women; it was simply that he was one of nature's bachelors, someone who apparently lacked any kind of domestic streak, the desire for a family of his own, even for a long-term romantic attachment. He'd known Donna and he was genuinely sympathetic about what had happened to her, and although we'd normally only seen one another two or three times a year since our college days, some years less than that, I'd always considered him to be one of my few close friends. But right then I had to accept that our collective nightmare had caught up with him, and that I wouldn't see him again, ever.

My interludes at base always had me fretting to some extent, but that was the worst one by a very long stretch. Because of what I knew about Thelma and Buddy Henry the situation already had tragic overtones, and the empty feeling I'd come back with was magnified by what Walden told me and made it almost impossibly difficult to keep my mind on the things I had to do there. Everybody was shaken up over Artie, but after a couple of days we didn't talk about it much, kept our feelings to ourselves. Ironically, I was bolstered a little by the general reaction to the Henry/'Shaddick' recording; I told Walden I'd checked it out and that was how it was spelt. Foster's playing generated a few mild compliments as well, and it was agreed that he was promising and that it was a pity he obviously hadn't gone far enough to make his mark, for whatever reason.

I wondered what had happened to Thelma that last night, and afterwards. I decided that the most likely thing was that she really had given up on Foster, that her disappearance from the session meant that she'd finally walked out on him, humiliated by the fact that he'd deserted her to play for virtually the whole of his time there, totally immersing himself in the music, maybe even to the extent of forgetting that she was present.

Although I'd developed an element of respect for Foster, I hoped that was what had happened, and that in a roundabout way my plan had worked, whether it had damaged my own situation or not. When they'd gotten together in the first place he'd been far too self-regarding to have treated someone like her with the kind of consideration that she deserved. As a result of what happened on that last night, he'd changed, but I doubted that it was totally for the better, because if I'd read him right it had left him with a new committment, a real sense of purpose, and even if it turned out to be short-lived, for the time being at least it would still leave him just as selfish, maybe even more so. Either way she'd be better off without him, I was certain of that, free to find herself again and wait for the man called Fry, the one she'd eventually marry.

Because of the recordings my next trip had received whole-hearted official blessing, which was another irony of course. I really was Walden's boy by then, because I was responsible for what he saw as the section's biggest coup, and he was embarrassingly open with his enthusiasm over my 'discovery' and what it had led to.

I should have felt like a total fraud, I suppose, but to be honest I didn't, not at all. My own playing had spurred Henry to a level of performance that had already confirmed his rightful place in the annals of the music, and I felt pride in that, not shame. It wasn't the pride of personal achievement, because virtually everything I'd contributed had been second-hand. It was more the fact that fate had selected me for that part, put me in that place at that time and allowed me to participate in a creative act of that quality. I guess that in some ways it really was the high-point of my life, because I find it hard to believe that my future holds anything that'll match it. But even if that's true, I have the memory, and that's something that's always going to warm me in its own very singular way.

When I went to the restaurant on my first night back in K.C., there were two more shocks waiting for me. The first one wasn't

altogether a surprise, because after the Basement Club session
I'd found it hard to picture Foster continuing to settle for the
limitations of the job at Williams' place. The band was on-stage
when I went in, but the tenor player was somebody that I'd never
seen before; an older, square-built character with a rather heavy
tone and a more or less on-the-beat sense of swing. The second
surprise didn't hit me straight away; I looked for Thelma, but the
fact that I didn't see her didn't disturb me at all; she could have
been out in the kitchen, or maybe taking the night off. There was
a young girl working her usual tables, another new face as far as
I was concerned.

I checked with her if Williams was on the premises, and I
was told he was in his office. I went back there, and after we'd
gone through the usual exchanges I asked him about Foster. He
grinned, just a little wryly, and told me that he'd left town with
the Valentine band. Valentine hadn't been at the sessions, but some
of his people who were had told him about Foster afterwards, he
said. He had an empty saxophone chair, because one of the people
he'd brought with him was a K.C. boy who'd decided to get off
the road for a while, and Foster was his replacement.

So that was it. He'd gone, fired by his re-ignited hunger
for musical adventure, ready at last to take on the frustrations
of touring; the long hours and back-break journeys, the greasy
spoons and poor accommodation. But he'd learn, because in effect
he'd gone back to school. There'd be after-hours sessions on the
road, when he'd have to take on the best local talent, periods
in New York when he could really test himself at Minton's and
Monroe's and other places. He's suffer in the process, but he'd
learn from it, and it would leave him a better musician, maybe
even a better person in some ways, because he had a sense of
purpose that hadn't been there before.

I told myself it was a shame that ultimately he was going to fail
to climb any appreciable way up the professional tree, far enough
to achieve some kind of recognition. The personnel turnover
in bands was particularly erratic just then, and because of the
recording ban it had been impossible to check it out, but I knew
for sure that he wasn't listed when Valentine eventually recorded
again, or anywhere else that I'd been able to trace. As I saw it then,
there were plenty of possible reasons; another tragedy in the offing
as a result of the draft, or finding that he couldn't really cut it in

the kind of company he'd be mixing in, or maybe simply that he
eventually decided that life on the road really was too big a price
to pay after all and faded back into provincial obscurity. But at
least what he was doing right then was bound to benefit him in a
musical sense, because it would place him in situations where he'd
have to employ his skills in a genuinely creative way, not waste
them on the comfortable coasting he'd settled for up until then.

Then I got my second shock. I asked after Thelma, and
Williams told me that she'd gone, too. Just for a second I had
this picture of her, still with Foster but out there on the road,
desperately trying to salvage the relationship at the cost off her
own humiliation, but Williams went on to tell me that she'd quit
a week after Foster had left town. She was still around, though,
he'd been told; one of the other girls still saw her occasionally, but
she'd left home and was living in a rooming-house not far from
the other girl's place. She didn't appear to be working, the girl
thought, but she didn't know for sure.

I asked him why she'd left; had it been because Foster wasn't
there any more? It was a stupid question, really; she'd hardly have
confided anything like that to Williams, but he was polite about
it, just shrugged and said he didn't really know; she'd 'phoned in
one day and told him that she wouldn't be coming in any more,
and that had been it. But he was obviously being cautious, refusing
to commit himself to speculation, playing his usual diplomatic
game. Was she in trouble? I asked him, and he shrugged again,
and said maybe.

That was as much as he needed to say, and I knew then that
that was the time I'd been waiting for, when I had to meet my
obligation to her, and that my playing with Foster that second
time had only been the preface to it after all. Something else that
I could see, all too clearly, was the degree of responsibility that
rested with me, because it had been my actions that had triggered
the sequence of events that had led to her present situation.

But even then I still felt no guilt, just a kind of tired resignation,
a feeling that regret would be totally pointless, despite recognising
my role in all of it. I asked Williams which of the waitresses had
told him about Thelma, and he said he thought that I'd be smart
to keep out of it; she wasn't my responsibility, after all. I told him
that I didn't agree; in some respects she was, because it had been
me that had created the circumstances where she and Foster got

together. He didn't say anything for a while, and then he shook his head and took me into the restaurant and pointed the girl out. I'm still not altogether sure how he viewed me at that moment, whether he thought I was simply a complete fool who should save himself trouble by keeping out of other people's business, or somebody with a conscience that went a long way past what he considered to be reasonable bounds.

I didn't care what he thought, because the whole game had changed into something far more important than the one I'd thought I was playing. I was beginning to see a whole series of links that stretched right out into the future, links that were going to affect Thelma and Donna and myself and probably countless others as well, some of them people I would never actually know about because there was no possible way that I could.

I got Thelma's address from the girl, and then I went straight over there. It was just around a corner off 10th Street, a two-storey place that badly needed a new coat of paint and had a ROOMS TO LET sign over the porch. The woman that answered the door looked at me a bit suspiciously when I asked for Thelma, but then she took me upstairs and knocked on the door of a back bedroom.

It took a minute or so for Thelma to answer it, and when she did I was shocked to see the way she looked. It was obvious that she'd just gotten out of bed; she was wearing bedroom slippers and had a coat pulled around her. But there was a generally bedraggled look that wasn't simply to with that and the absence of make-up and untidy hair. In uniform or out of it, she'd always struck me as somebody who cared about her appearance, who liked to be neat and nicely groomed. Right then she looked as though she didn't care at all about such things, or anything else much for that matter. Her face was dull and empty, and she just stood there, not saying anything, just staring at me blankly while the woman hovered at my elbow and fidgeted in a disapproving kind of way.

I told Thelma I wanted to talk to her, but before she could answer the woman chipped in and said I'd have to come back another time. She didn't allow men in the girls' rooms, anyway, she said, and besides it was late and she wanted to lock up. I didn't want to embarrass Thelma by getting into an arguement about it, so I asked her if there was somewhere we could meet the next day. I told her it was important, and after hesitating she said, all right; there was a place just down the road, a park; she'd be there next morning, around 10.30.

28.

Perry was already there, sitting on a bench just inside the entrance when she arrived. It was a cold, dry morning, with a thin layer of cloud obscuring the sun. A man and a woman were walking a dog some distance away, but apart from them and Perry and herself the small park was deserted.

He got up as she approached. She returned his smile and greeting, then they both sat down. She'd been too tired and confused to think clearly when they'd made their arrangement on the previous evening, and when she'd woken that morning she'd almost made up her mind not to go, horrified by the broad implications of his visit. He must have been to the restaurant and talked to people there, she realised, found out about her quitting and moving to her new address. She couldn't imagine why he'd sought her out like he had, though. He'd always been pleasant to her, and it had been stupid of her to get angry at him when he'd played the piano that first time, but even though that was over they weren't really friends, anything like that.

He asked her how she was, and she said, fine. He stared at the ground for several seconds, nodding, then took a deep breath, almost like a sigh.

"I want to ask you something, and please don't be offended by it, because it's important to me that I know." He hesitated, then raised his head and looked at her. "Are you pregnant?"

It hit her like a sudden deluge of cold water. After a while, she began to shake. Then the tears came. She turned her head away, trying to hold them back, but feeling them well up uncontrollably.

He said nothing as she wept, offered no comment or gesture of consolation. When the crying eased, he began to talk, very quietly. He told her that in a sense he considered himself to blame for what had happened. If he hadn't played at the lodge that time, he said, discomfitted Foster the way he had, then he and she might never have begun their relationship. Because of that he felt a degree of responsibility towards her and wanted to help in any way that he could. He'd gathered from the fact that she'd left home and moved to where she was that her parents weren't likely to sympathise with her situation. Had she decided what she was going to do? Was she going to have the baby, or was she going to try and arrange an abortion? And did Foster know about it?

He fell silent, and she stared across the park, not saying anything, feeling cold and ashamed. How had he known?, she wondered. She hadn't told Mr. Williams why she was leaving when she'd 'phoned, and she hadn't confided in anybody else at the restaurant, either. He was right about her parents, too. They didn't know about it, although they might have suspected something of the sort when she'd told them that she was leaving, getting a place of her own. She saw her father's mottled, furiously injured face, and heard her mother's anguished voice. She hadn't wanted to hurt them like that, she thought, sadly. She'd fought with them a lot of the time, but she hadn't wanted that to happen.

The man and the woman with the dog had gone, she didn't know when. She began to talk, still staring blankly across the park, empty now except for themselves.

She told him that Foster didn't know, and that she didn't want him to. As far as having the baby was concerned, she hadn't decided. She wanted to keep it, but she didn't see how she could. She had a little over fifty dollars, but when that was gone she wouldn't have anything. A friend knew of a woman who did that kind of thing, got rid of unwanted babies; she charged twenty-five dollars, and the way she looked at it it seemed sensible to get it done while she still had the money. But she didn't want to do it, because it would be like killing somebody who was innocent of any crime.

The she cried again, and this time Perry put his arm around her shoulders. She experienced no instinctive desire to retreat, no alarm of any kind. She leaned against him, letting the tears exhaust themselves, leaving her drained and very tired. When she quietened again, Perry told her that she wasn't to worry about money, that if she wanted to have the baby he'd take care of that side of things until it came and she was able to get back to work, support it herself.

She felt unease at that point. She sat up and moved away from him, staring at him curiously.

"Why? I mean, why should you do all that?"

He flushed slightly. "Like I said, I do feel that in a way I'm responsible. If you—"

She shook her head, experiencing the onset of growing distrust. "I can see that. But we might have started something anyway, even without what happened that time. Why should you want to pay out a lot of money you don't really owe?"

He shrugged nervously. "But it did happen because of what I did, that's right, isn't it? If you hadn't—"

She cut in on him again. "Maybe it is. But it didn't have to happen that way". She boasted a little, salve for her pride. "I could have gotten him without that. I just hadn't really tried up 'til then."

He didn't reply immediately, and she saw something that looked like dismay in his eyes. Then he looked away and began to talk, hesitantly.

"I didn't really want to tell you this, but I guess I have to. The fact is, when I passed out in the restaurant that time, it wasn't anything to do with having been ill. I told you I'd followed you there because you reminded me of someone I'd known. That was true, but what I didn't tell you was that it was my wife you reminded me of. She died in an accident, a month before she was due to have our first child." He paused, glanced quickly at her, then looked away again. "What you say could be true, of course. Maybe you would have got him without this business at the lodge, but that's something we're never going to know. The fact is that you and he got together because he wanted a sympathetic ear that night, and you're pregnant because that was how the relationship got started. That is right, isn't it?"

After a moment, she nodded, slowly. "I guess so."

He looked down at his hands, knotted between his knees. "Obviously, what you do about it is your business. If you decide to have an abortion, then that's it. But you don't really want to, you've admitted that, because you feel it would be a kind of murder. I don't want it to happen, either. I do have a share of responsibility in this, and if you have an abortion I'm going to feel that in a way my own child is going to die all over again. That probably sounds crazy, but that's how I feel about it." He paused, then grimaced, resignedly. "That's it, I guess. I know I shouldn't be pressuring you like this, but it's important to me, too."

So that was it, she thought. She felt a mixture of relief and sympathy. And it did make sense, of a kind. But there had been something there that momentarily intrigued her even more than the fundamental situation. Maybe she'd misinterpreted what he'd said, she thought, but she wanted to know.

"Was your wife black?"

He nodded. "Yes, she was. Pretty much your colour. I can see differences as well, of course, but you are very much like her in some ways. Quite a bit younger, though." He smiled, sadly. "I wouldn't want you to read more into this than I've told you, by the way. I may be a little crazy in one sense, but I don't have anything personal in mind, if you understand what I'm saying." He shook his head, dismissively. "Look, I've embarrassed you enough. Would you like to think about it for a day or two, and then let me know what you decide? It really would be a no-strings arrangement, I promise you."

She shook her head. "No, that's O.K., I've made up my mind. I'm going to have it."

He opened his mouth, then checked himself. "Which?"

She smiled. "The baby."

They both laughed, and she saw the relief that suffused his face.

She said she wouldn't need much money, anyway; she'd already decided to look for another job in a week or so, whether she'd had the abortion or not. Perry told her to take her time about that, not to look for anything until she really felt like it. If she got a job, she'd have to give it up a few weeks before the baby came, anyway, he said, and afterwards she'd probably want to see it through at least the first year or so without having to worry about how she was going to pay her way. They discussed the practical issues, the kind of things she'd need, and he asked her if she thought she'd be O.K. at the rooming-house; if she wasn't happy there, he said, she should look for something else, maybe a small apartment.

She told him she'd be fine where she was, for the time being at least. He's seemed sincere when he'd assured her that his interest wasn't personal, but he wasn't somebody she really knew at all, virtually a total stranger. She speculated, very briefly, on the likelihood of such a relationship, looking at it from her own side, and dismissed it immediately. He seemed nice, but he was at least twice her age, probably quite a bit more. She'd never really gone for older men, and anyway he wasn't really her type at all. He was white, too, of course. She felt a flicker of embarrassment at the thought, recalling the totally unselfconscious way that he'd talked about his wife, but she didn't want those sort of problems added to the ones she already had.

He told her that he'd have to give her most of the money the next time he was there, a few weeks from then; he'd only brought a limited amount with him, and he was currently short of ready cash, anyway, until he collected some that was owed him from a property sale. In the meantime he wanted her to take seventy-five dollars, to help tide her over and prove his good faith. His visits to Kansas City would probably be finishing pretty soon, but he'd make absolutely certain that everything was in hand before that happened.

She hesitated when he produced the money, but then she took it. It was a good thing her parents couldn't see her just then, she thought; they'd have jumped to all the wrong conclusions. They'd have to know the basic facts soon, though, and she'd have to think up some story eventually to explain how she was able to support herself and the baby without making it sound too bad. They certainly weren't likely to believe the truth, she told herself, wryly.

They were about to go, when he paused, suddenly a little awkward again. He'd just realized that he'd been taking something for granted, he said, but as she hadn't said anything to the contrary he'd assumed that she would be keeping the baby, not putting it in a home, anything like that. Whichever it was, his offer was still good; it was simply that he'd like to know.

It was her baby, she told him. If she was going to the trouble of having it, she wasn't going to give it away to anybody; she'd be raising it herself, he wasn't to worry about that.

He nodded, smiling.

29.

I'd laid awake a long time the night before, considering all the possibilities and working out the best ways of tackling them. If she'd already decided on an abortion, I realized I'd have to use a very persuasive line of arguement if I was going to stand any chance at all of changing her mind; the fact that she still hadn't come to a decision made it just as imperative, and the lie about Donna and the baby was the only thing I'd come up with that felt as though it might do it.

I didn't like the idea of trying to engage her sympathy in that way at all, but the issue was altogether too important as far as I was concerned for me to be squeamish about means. The truth is that after the first year we'd never even considered starting a family; a child would've been emotionally brutalised in that atmosphere, and at least we had enough sense of responsibility not to produce one as a kind of last resort, the way that some people with ailing relationships do.

Of course, I had no way of being absolutely certain that what I was doing was actually necessary to ensure Donna's eventual existence. Looked at logically, there might not have been any direct lineage between Foster's baby and her at all, but at least the family link existed, I'd found confirmation of that, and because it did the possibility had to be preserved. In fact, for a little while I wasn't totally happy about what I'd achieved, because in the long run it seemed to be guaranteeing our own meeting, Donna's and mine, and what had stemmed from it as well, what happened to her at the finish.

But I reminded myself that in any case it was all over and done, an ineradicable part of the existing future. Her birth and life were already facts, and it hadn't all been unhappiness for her, not by a long way. I know that she had a happy childhood and adolescence, and the only really bad times she suffered were during the final year or so as things fell apart between us.

Anyway, after Thelma and I finished talking I walked her back to the rooming-house and told her I'd be in touch in a day or so. She seemed quite calm by then; not exactly happy, but at least resigned to things, accepting that she'd made a decision and that fundamentally it was the right one as far as she was concerned. Although I didn't have any specific plans for the rest of the day, I decided it'd be best if I left her alone for a while. There was still obviously an element of embarrassment about the situation, and I don't imagine that she really wanted my company right then while she came to terms with what she'd decided, let it sink in. There was no real danger of her changing her mind, I was sure of that by then; she'd never really liked the idea of abortion, and the fact that she knew she'd have the means to cope with the pregnancy and what came afterwards had clearly clinched it for her.

Even though the focus of my interest wasn't there any more, I decided to visit the restaurant that evening. I felt I owed Williams at least some explanation; there was no way that it could've been a complete one, of course, but Thelma and Foster had both been employees of his when the situation had been created, and I decided he'd probably be curious about the outcome of my going to see her, anyway.

I got the usual welcome. He asked how things had gone with Thelma, and I told him as much as I dared, about everything, starting with my first visit to the restaurant and my story about having been sick. I'd been too embarrassed to tell him before, I said, but the way things had turned out I felt it was only right that I should come clean; after all, he'd gone to some trouble on my behalf at the time, and it had been on my conscience ever since. I finished by telling him what had happened that morning, and repeated everything I'd said to Thelma, including the lie about the baby, because there was always the chance that he'd see her sometime, and I didn't want to take a chance on them coming out with conflicting stories.

He was actually amused over my lie about having been ill; he said if that had been the worst thing anybody had ever done to him he'd have been rich as well as lucky. Now that I'd explained he could understand my interest in Thelma and why I'd done what I had; he'd realized very early on that I had a kind of special thing about her, he said, but he'd assumed that it had been something very different to what it actually was.

Although my relationship with him had always been pleasant and although I'd gathered that he liked me, I was never really sure why. I'd simply taken it for granted that there was a little snobbery involved, that the idea of mixing with someone from the academic world appealed to a private desire for respectable acceptance after his years of operating in a largely hoodlum-dominated environment.

But I decided then that I'd been totally wrong, and I felt pretty ashamed. He was far more worldly-wise than I was ever likely to be, altogether too mature to be bothered by that kind of parochialism. He simply took people as he found them, and even though much of our association was based on the lies that I'd been forced to tell him he really did seem to like me for myself, for whatever reason; not only that, I felt that he was the kind of person that I could go to in a crisis, and be sure that I wouldn't be turned away.

I know now that that's true, in part at least. Whether it goes beyond what he's already demonstrated is something that I'll probably be finding out very soon now, although I still haven't made up my mind whether I should actually test him that far or go for what would almost certainly be the trickier option. But whichever I decide on, I'm sure it's going to work out; I just can't believe that I've come this far only to have the whole thing collapse around my ears at the last minute because I've got it figured all wrong, or because of some technicality that I have no way of knowing about. Nothing like that is going to happen, I'm certain of it. In the broad sense I know where I'm going, although what's going to follow afterwards has to be a completely open question, of course, at least as far as I'm concerned.

I asked him if he'd heard from Foster, or anything about him, how he was making out with Valentine. He said that that reminded him of something; he had a note for me. Foster had left it with him when he'd given notice; he'd meant to give it to me the previous evening, but I'd taken off again so fast he'd forgotten about it. He took it out of his desk, a white envelope with the name 'PERRY' scrawled on it. While he poured us a couple of drinks I opened it, wondering why Foster would write to me.

It wasn't from Foster, it was from Buddy Henry. It started off by saying how much he'd enjoyed our playing together and he hoped that we could do it again sometime. Valentine would be on the road for another couple of months, and then they were booked into the Apollo in Harlem for a week. If there was any chance of my making it to New York while they were there he'd be happy to take me around, maybe get in a little blowing.

There was a P.S.. It said, 'We had a hot time, but nothing like the joint I've been staying at. Caught fire last night, a real mess. Lost some of my stuff, but at least I'm still breathing. Lucky we stayed with it as long as we did—I might have ended up toast if I'd sacked out early!!'

I sat there staring at it with my head spinning, reading it over and over, trying to make sense of what it said. It was like grasping at something that you know can't really be there, a kind of mirage that every instinct normally tells you is impossible. But it wasn't quite like that, because I felt something that I'd felt before, the same sensation I'd had when I was trying to persuade Thelma to keep the baby, and before that, too, when I'd played with Henry, a sense that there were dimensions to what was happening that somehow stretched way beyond what I'd already reasoned.

I hadn't queried it before, because on both occasions it had seemed to make its own kind of sense, *felt* right. So did Henry's note, unbelievably, despite the shock it had given me. But I still didn't understand it, and right then I was frightened as well as totally confused. I was still staring at it when Williams put a drink down beside me and asked if I was O.K. It was only then that I realised I was shaking, not just my hands, my whole body, like a palsy.

I said I was all right, but he knew I was lying, of course. He took the note from me and read it, and said he gathered that I hadn't known about the fire. It had happened around four in the morning, he said; several people had been killed, and there'd been a lot of damage. He hadn't realized that Henry had been staying there, though. Had I been picturing what might have happened if we hadn't played for as long as we did?

I told him, yes, that was it; suddenly finding out about the fire and realizing the implications if things hadn't worked out the way they did had really shaken me for a moment. It was close enough to the truth to be convincing, and Williams told me I shouldn't exercise my imagination like that. He'd heard that it had been quite a session, he said, and he was sorry that he'd missed it. We talked about it for a while, and then I finished my drink and said I'd be getting back to the hotel; I'd had a long day and felt that bed would be the best place for me right then.

When I got back to the hotel, I didn't go to bed. I prowled around the room like something in a cage, beating my brain and trying to make sense out of what had happened. Henry was alive; the fire had been on schedule, but he'd survived, hadn't been caught up in it after all. If anything had happened to him since, if he'd died in another fire somewhere else, word would surely have gotten back to K.C., and Williams would almost certainly have known, but the records were specific. He'd died in K.C., they said, in a fire at the Morrison Hotel during the early hours of December 15th, 1942, and the possibility of him being trapped in another fire so soon after that one would have been stretching coincidence to ridiculously unbelievable lengths.

Records aren't always accurate, of course, but if they were in this case then a tragedy that had been scheduled hadn't happened when it was supposed to, and on the face of it at least that was because we'd carried on playing through the night, past the time of the fire. I remembered the intensity of the interaction between us and the feeling that it somehow went beyond the music, and I wondered if that could possibly have been what it was about. But whether it was or not, he'd survived, and unless some other disaster had caught up with him in the meantime and news of it had simply failed to get back to K.C., his talent had survived with him, meaning that there was every chance of him eventually being acknowledged as another key figure in the evolution of the music.

I began to recall something that we'd been told at our induction interviews; that although some cosmologists were convinced that the concept of parallel worlds was theoretically sound, it was generally accepted that the laws governing the transference of matter meant that actually being able to move from one to another was out of the question, automatically ruling out the possibility that that was what the hole was about. Our comprehensive knowledge of the period hadn't detected any discrepencies with the recorded facts, either, they'd said, and in any case for quite a while there'd been a steadily growing conviction that travel to the past would become a reality one day. All of that had convinced them that what the hole represented was an unanticipated preview of a natural process that might eventually guide us to a means of entry that we could actually control as far as selecting particular times to visit and study was concerned.

At the time my total ignorance of such things meant that I had no real reason to doubt any of that, but right then what had happened meant that I wasn't sure about any of it any more. I couldn't get my head around it at all, so I went to bed, hoping that I'd see it a bit clearer after some sleep, but I had a restless night, and the next day I was just as confused, so I decided that the best way to approach it would be to chase up the Valentine band and see if anything similar had happened since.

I had no idea where they were by then; Henry's letter had just said that they'd be touring right up to their Apollo gig, so I called the El Torrean and got the name of the agency that had booked them in there, and then I 'phoned them and asked how the tour was going, if there'd been any accidents reported. I was a friend of Henry's, I said, and I'd heard a rumour that he'd been involved in a fire when the band had been in K.C..

They told me there was no need to worry; they knew about the fire, but none of the musicians who'd been staying at the hotel had been hurt. I asked if there'd been any similar incidents since then, and the guy said, no, he was sure there hadn't because the road manager had called in the previous day, but only about a possible cancelled booking; there'd been no mention of an accident or anything like that.

So that confirmed it; the fire had happened like the records said, but he was still alive, at least up until then. I wondered if it was possible that the standard reference material was simply incorrect because of inadequate research; that whoever was responsible for that particular entry had relied on information that they'd copied from earlier sources that were in fact faulty, something of that kind. After all, the belief that past events are bound to be set in stone makes complete sense, and I still fundamentally accepted what we'd been told about the inaccessibility of parallel worlds, if such things existed at all. I kept on trying to make sense of it, but the harder I tried the more confused I got, and eventually it got to the stage where I decided that if I didn't get it off my mind for at least some of the time it really was going to drive me crazy.

So I began to see Thelma more than I'd originally planned. She was understandably wary when I called on her and suggested that maybe she'd like to come out to lunch, but she'd shut herself off from her normal circle of friends and she was bored, so it didn't take me long to persuade her. We never talked about that side of it, any initial embarrassment she might have felt, and in any case she soon seemed to become reasonably relaxed in my company, didn't appear to suspect me of possible ulterior motives like she must have when I'd approached her about the baby, and I could hardly have expected her not to. After all, she didn't really know me except for what I'd told her, and virtually the whole of that had been lies. Something else we never talked about was the colour aspect of our relationship, but I'm pretty sure she never felt particularly comfortable about it. Male and female, one black and one white wasn't exactly commonplace then, and K.C. was still a cracker town in a lot of ways, not even as relatively sophisticated as the New York of the time, and mixing was still a risky business there.

I think it was the fact that I'd told her that Donna had been black that persuaded her to accept the situation as much as she did. To that extent it became a matter of pride with her, wanting to show me that she wasn't afraid to stick her neck out in the same way that another Afram female had, part-way at least. I don't know how she'd have felt if she'd known that Donna's and my relationship had taken place in a future where racial intolerance had become relatively diluted, in our part of the world, anyway, and I guess there'd be no point in me denying that there was a considerably bigger element of risk in what we were doing then than there is now, even though the separatist survival movement is doing its damnedest to reverse that in our increasingly panic-stricken present.

It wouldn't surprise me too much, Phyl, if you're seeing all of this as an act of pure selfishness on my part, using her to make my own situation more tolerable and simply ignoring the fact that I could have been endangering her to some extent. I accept that there has to be an element of truth in that, but she was getting some benefit from the arrangement as well, and there was another side to it, too, because in a low-key kind of way what we were doing was staging a protest, quietly giving the finger to racism.

Because of that I always made sure that we didn't take any unnecessary risks. There were a few occasions when I detected hints of disapproval, but I took care to stick to places where the dividing line looked to be relatively blurred, and I imagine our mutually unromantic demeanour helped us to avoid any open unpleasantness, anyway.

She turned out to be pleasant company in her limited way; pretty naïve in many respects, not particularly well-educated or conscious of the world beyond her own immediate experience and her generally romanticized view of it provided by the movies, not at first, anyway. After a while, though, I began to detect some evidence that parts of our conversation had begun to stir her curiosity beyond that. It became evident that she was paying at least some attention to the news bulletins and reading the papers past the funnies pages, and the sheer enormity of a lot of what was being reported must've at least temporarily taken her mind off her own problems.

I still wonder how she'd have reacted if I'd been crazy enough to blurt out the truth; how and why I was really there, and the seemingly terminal sickness of our own time. My guess is that she'd have put as much distance between us as she could, which would've been totally understandable. But even if she'd believed the part about how I got there, I don't think that for one moment that she'd have been prepared to accept my account of the future, the way things are right here and now. Even though the war reports played some things down for obvious reasons, there was still enough in them to have convinced her that we must've reached the limits of human idiocy and brutality, so what we've achieved since would almost certainly have been beyond her comprehension, a nightmare that she simply wasn't able to conceive.

Just think about it, Phyl. How do you imagine you'd have reacted if you'd existed at that time and been told that in less than a century from then our own stupidity and greed were going to be major factors in helping turn our jewel of a planet into an over-heating and very probably uncontrollable furnace where the total insanity of fundamentalism persisted despite its obvious irrelevance, supplies of food and drinkable water and other essentials were shrinking even faster than the inexorably drowning continents and people were increasingly being driven to extremes of violence to try and ensure their basic survival, never mind such high-flown aims as liberty and the right to free speech and all the things that we've liked to think of as the inalienable rights of humankind?

Existing like she did, in a society that still believed in itself and its future, how could she possibly have come to terms with a scenario like that? Not that she'd have had to, of course, because there was no way I could ever have exposed her to such a terrible truth. What Cora had told me about her early death underlined the obvious fact that there'd have been no point in souring the time she had left with things that'd never concerned her. Besides, despite the business of the baby and the gradual broadening of her horizons she was still basically an innocent, and as well as not being prepared to erode that any further, for me to have told her what the distant future held and how I knew it would've convinced her that I was seriously unbalanced, someone she'd be wise to stay well away from after all.

Anyway, she gradually became a little more relaxed and easier to talk to, and I think she got to like me fairly well. But she wasn't Donna and never could've been, even as a purely physical substitute, and we both knew it without ever openly acknowledging the situation. Despite that, we became quite good friends, as close as could be reasonably expected, given the circumstances and the fact that I was living a pack of lies and had to keep on lying a lot of the time I was with her. Whatever, it helped to break the monotony as far as she was concerned, and it worked for me, too, because it helped to keep me from fretting too much. The Henry mystery didn't go away, of course, but I found that our time together and what I'd been told about Artie counter-balanced it to some extent, so I was able to handle it without letting it worry me to distraction, the way it had originally.

When I'd returned to base from the previous trip I hadn't detected any particular signs of tension during my time in medical. I guess there must have been some, because they had to know about Artie not making it back; I can only think that I'd been too exhausted and wrapped up in my own concerns to notice. But I definitely felt something off-key when I got back and checked in that time, a sense of general unease, mixed in with an undercurrent of excitement. Everybody was very close-mouthed, uncharacteristically evasive, restricting themselves to necessary conversation and nothing else.

The psych session had something of the same atmosphere to it. The guy who dealt with me was the same one that I'd seen after the previous trip; you probably remember me telling you about how he'd spent a while wrongly diagnosing my depression, but this time he didn't do much more than go through the motions, simply asked a few standard questions and didn't pursue any of the answers.

It was a relief in a way, but it certainly added to my curiosity about what was going on, and I was still puzzling over it when I got to the section office and almost collided with somebody who was just on his way out. I knew him by sight; Roache, one of the security people; a tall, light-skinned Afram with high, wide shoulders. I caught his eye as I stepped to one side to let him pass, and I thought I saw something there that immediately set an alarm-bell going inside my head; what looked like a quick, searching glance that couldn't have lasted more than a second before he nodded and passed me, but at the time it felt like a real somebody-just-walked-on-my-grave moment that left me really uneasy.

I watched his back as he walked down the corridor, wondering if I really had seen what I thought I had, or whether it had just been my conscience instinctively reacting to a close encounter with somebody like that. He didn't turn round, though, simply kept on going, so I told myself that that was what it had been, a guilty reflex on my part, nothing more serious than that, but the bell rang even louder when I went into Walden's office and saw who was sat by his desk. I'd never spoken to him, but he'd chaired a question-and-answer session for new inductees towards the end of our training period; Urich, who ran security, a gimlet-eyed individual with the kind of face that never gives anything away, and my heart skipped a couple of beats when I saw him there.

He turned his head in my direction as I went in, but I couldn't tell anything from his expression, and although Walden nodded, that was it; no real greeting, none of his usual affability. He looked angry, and he was drumming a hand on his desk-top, clearly having trouble reining himself in.

I realized that my turning up at this point could've been pure coincidence, of course, but I had more than enough on my conscience to make me wonder if in fact the obvious bad vibes actually concerned me in some way, maybe even to the extent of being the cause of them. I suddenly felt as though I was presenting a picture of guilt that a one-eyed person could've spotted a mile away, because the encounter in the corridor had already knocked me off-balance a little, and the atmosphere in the room had abruptly stoked that up to point where the words 'lie-detector test, lie-detector test' were hammering away inside my head like a shouted threat.

I wondered if that was what it was all about; that quite simply my luck had run out and what I'd feared ever since playing at the lodge session was actually going to happen, with the inevitable result; my removal from what was left of the programme and goodbye to my one and only chance to at least partially straighten myself out by completing my commitment to Thelma.

It was another situation where I could feel myself teetering on the verge of panic, but I knew that I still had to appear as calm as possible until what was really happening became clear, and there was only one thing I could do that might help me achieve that, even if it was only momentarily; I had to take the initiative, get a shot in first, and just hope I could handle the reaction it got.

30.

___

If anyone was flustered, it was Walden, Urich decided. But that was because he was fretting over the latest reduction of his gradually dwindling survey team. It had already been decided that it was far too late to recruit and train a replacement for Mastin, and now he was angrily querying Forrestal's removal from the programme. He was understandably sore about the way it had been dealt with, but the implications involved had made it imperative that they kept as tight a clamp as possible on what had happened. The cover story that they were in the process of concocting was unlikely to contain the rumours that were already circulating for long, but the inevitable confusion might just hold things together until the closure that was now only a few weeks away.

He reflected on Lohmann's entrance and subsequent demeanour. There might have been a touch of shocked nervousness at first, but now he seemed simply surprised and curious, which was to be expected.

Lohmann said, "Do I take it that there's some kind of problem? They seemed a little edgy in medical just now."

Urich smiled, humourlessly. "Did anyone say anything to you about it while you were there?"

"Nobody said anything much at all." He returned Urich's stare. "Should they have?"

"They're under instructions not to." He hadn't anticipated involving Lohmann at this stage, but this unexpected encounter could be useful. He hesitated, briefly. "Lohmann, isn't it? I understand you knew Artie Mastin pretty well."

Lohmann nodded, frowning. "Yes, I did."

"How well?"

"We met in college and we've been friends ever since then." Lohmann grimaced slightly. "I guess I should have said were."

"Close friends?"

"We kept in touch. Yes, I guess you could say pretty close."

"Were you surprised to hear about his disappearance?"

Lohmann frowned again, patently puzzled. "'I don't follow you. How do you mean, surprised?"

There's nothing there, Urich decided. It had been a long-shot anyway. But he had to chase up anything at all that might provide a lead.

"Would you say that he was a careless person? Reckless, forgetful, anything like that?"

Lohmann continued to look at him curiously. "If he had been it would have showed up during training, and he wouldn't have been allowed to go out on survey duty."

Urich nodded. 'That's right. So he wasn't reckless or forgetful, but something still happened that prevented him from making it back here. That's what I meant when I asked if it surprised you."

Lohmann said, slowly, "I still think surprised is the wrong way to put it. I was shocked, naturally, but we all realize that it's something that can happen to any of us. He knew the risk, so obviously he must have found himself in a situation that made it impossible for him to get back in time; an accident, or some kind of illness most probably." He shrugged. "It might not have been that, of course. Maybe he had some trouble with the law, something like I ran into a while back. Or maybe his medication let him down."

After a second, Urich said, curiously, "How do you mean that?"

Lohmann shrugged again. "He might have developed a kind of tolerance for it. If he did, that could have meant that his dosage wasn't strong enough and eventually it didn't protect him because he didn't start back in time." He stared at Urich questioningly. "That kind of thing has to be at least a possibility, doesn't it?"

31.

——

I was looking Urich in the eye just then, and I saw something happen there as I was going through the bit about the medication. It was as though he'd suddenly slammed down a shutter, closing off any expression that might've been there for somebody to read, and then he shook his head and said that it was something that'd been considered, but the medical people didn't think it was at all likely. Appropriate dosages were calculated to fit individual physical profiles and medical histories, and the chances of tolerance build-up were extremely small. They'd learned a lot since the early days of the programme, he said, and the process was continually being monitored and refined to reduce any potential risk of that kind.

I didn't really accept that. His reaction had hinted that he didn't, either, and in any case we were talking about territory where unforeseeable consequences were bound to factors, but I didn't see any point in debating it, not right then. Anyway, that seemed to have put a stop to his questions, and I was just about to ask him why the interest in Artie when Walden cut in. I'd obviously walked in on a pretty heated situation, and it was equally obvious that the head of steam he'd been building up while Urich had been ignoring him and talking to me had just about reached boiling-point. He said he'd see me later; he and Urich still had something to sort out, and I could freshen up before I gave him my report.

Even though I was really itching to know why I'd undergone the quizzing about Artie it was plainly no time to argue with him, and I'd barely closed the office door behind me when I heard his raised voice. There was nobody in the outer office, so I could've eavesdropped, but I decided it'd be better to wait and get the whole story, so I went to the accomodation block and cleaned up and hung around there for half-an-hour or so, wondering what in God's name Artie had to do with what was happening, if anything. I couldn't see Urich as someone who'd waste time on conversation that had no real point to it, though, and I was really chafing at the bit by the time I got back there.

There was still nobody in the outer office, but things seemed to have quietened down in Walden's room as far as I could tell. I still took the precaution of knocking before sticking my head around the door, but Urich had gone and Walden was obviously cooled down by then, looking more thoughtful than mad, so I asked him what was going on, why security's sudden interest in us and Artie.

He told me that he hadn't known about the Artie connection at first. As far as he was concerned the whole thing had started when he'd heard a rumour that my New York replacement, a guy called John Forrestal, was being held incommunicado by security. He'd apparently followed normal procedure and reported in to medical when he'd gotten back, but as soon as they'd finished with him security had rushed him out of there and were still holding him, he had no idea where. When he'd approached them about it he'd been told that it concerned a breach of regulations that they were looking into, but he hadn't considered that enough of an explanation, so he'd carried on nagging at them until they'd sent the Roache guy around to try and smooth things over. All he'd gotten from him was a hint that Forrestal was being viewed as a security risk, he wouldn't say why or how, so he'd demanded to see Urich, and he'd just showed up when I'd walked in.

On the subject of Artie, he'd assumed that Urich had simply been using my presence to try and deflect the conversation away from the Forrestal business, but he said that he'd subsequently found out that there was a lot more to it than that. He hadn't made any progress with Urich, he said, but after he'd left an unexpected visitor had shown up, one of the doctors that he'd gotten to know quite well. She'd told him that she'd been the one who'd dealt with Forrestal when he'd reported in, apparently very preoccupied, and just after she'd given him his shot and as he was dozing off he told her that he'd seen Artie in New York the previous evening, passed him on the street! That was all he said before he blanked out, and the medical people were still trying to decide how seriously to take it when security suddenly showed up, so she assumed that somebody in the department had immediately gotten in touch with them, although she had no idea who. Before Forrestal came round and was hustled out of there they'd been given strict instructions to keep it to themselves, but she'd eventually decided that since he and Artie were both on Walden's team he had the right to know.

I hadn't sat down when I went in there, but right then I had to, and pretty damn quick, too, before my knees gave out. I didn't believe it, of course, not really, but just the idea of Artie still being alive had made my head spin. That was all she'd been able to tell him, Walden said; she didn't know if Forrestal was supposed to have approached him, tried to speak to him, anything like that, but the fact that security had been in a big hurry to put him under wraps seemed to give at least some credence to it, however crazy the whole idea was.

I didn't really hear much of what he said during the next couple of minutes, because I was trying to make some sense out of it, wondering if it had simply been some kind of misunderstanding, that she'd misheard what Forrestal had said, but there was no getting away from the fact that security had taken it seriously enough to try and stop it from spreading around. It was already too late for that, of course, but I didn't see how it could possibly have been a genuine sighting. Unless Artie had somehow miraculously solved the blood component problem I couldn't for the life of me think of any other way that he could've survived there that long, and security knew that he shouldn't have as well, so their reaction was just plain baffling, at first, anyway.

After we'd talked about it for a while, though, we very reluctantly decided that if Forrestal had claimed to have seen him it had simply been a mistake on his part, most probably based of a fleeting glimpse of someone vaguely similar, the kind of thing that often happens after a family member or friend or close colleague dies or goes missing, especially if no actual body turns up as confirmation. As far as the security angle was concerned, paranoia's an occupational hazard in that game, and the magnitude of what we were involved with must inevitably have meant that they'd have been under the kind of pressure that would've kept them very close to the edge ever since the start of the operation, so we eventually concluded that that had to explain that part of it at least; that in effect they'd toppled over the edge and were fantasising at the slightest hint of trouble, no matter how flimsy the evidence.

We carried on talking for a while, but didn't get any further with it than that, so I turned in my recordings—a very thin batch that time, cobbled together during my last couple of days in K.C.,—told him my prefabricated story about 'Shaddick's' absence, and then took off to get some rest.

I still hadn't told him about Henry, and I wasn't really sure why; something held me back, though, and even now I'm not altogether clear in my mind why that was, although the likeliest reason has to be the rumour about Artie, the way it seemed to echo what had happened to him. They both *should* have died, but Henry had survived and by then it was being speculated that Artie might have, too, although for the life of me I couldn't imagine how that was possible. The conclusion that Walden and I had eventually reached was the only explanation that made any sense, but it didn't answer the Henry question at all, and somehow I just felt I was doing the right thing by keeping quiet, at least until I got my thinking into some semblance of order.

During the rest of that break period I kept on fumbling with it, but all I did was keep on hitting the same old frustrating dead ends. There were occasions when I found myself thinking about what the controllers had told us about parallel worlds and the impossibility of transferring from one to another, but since their actual existence hadn't even been proved in any material way I didn't dwell on it. In any case, whether they existed or not I felt safer sticking with the opinion of people who at least had a better understanding of such things than I did, and on the question of Henry I still favoured the incorrect entry idea, even though I was never really comfortable with it. I had the business of figuring out what to do about the money for Thelma as well, of course, but even without that distraction I suspect that I'd still have ended up going nowhere on the same merry-go-round, unable—or maybe subconsciously unwilling—to get off it and stretch my imagination beyond the more reassuring option, for the simple reason that that was something I could understand.

As far as the money was concerned there was never any question that the only way to handle it would be to take something negotiable; jewellery was the obvious choice, but there were a couple of equally obvious problems with that. Problem number one was that part of the procedure we had to follow immediately prior to going through the hole involved being checked over for items that weren't on our approved lists, and that included a metal-detection scan, so there was clearly no possibility of taking complete items; stones would be O.K., but the mountings would have to go.

That created problem number two, of course. Approaching legitimate dealers with unmounted stones would be tricky, so I eventually decided that Williams would be my best bet as far as disposing of them safely was concerned. As far as I knew he was totally respectable by then, but I'd deduced from what my friendly bartender had told me that he'd sometimes skated on thin ice in the past, so he probably still had contacts that could help in that kind of situation. I realised I'd have to have a story ready if I was going to approach him like that, which I wasn't exactly happy about, but looked at realistically our whole relationship was based on a lie, and it obviously would be a lot safer dealing through him rather than attempting to with total strangers.

Anyway, after I cleared what I had to do at base, I went down to Baltimore for a couple of days. Most of the first day I shopped around the jewellery places and ended up buying two second-hand diamond rings, quite nice stones in not particularly expensive-looking mountings. Because I couldn't think of anything else that looked as though it'd work better, I used one of the oldest concealment tricks in the book; back at the hotel, I loosened the heel of one of my shoe's inner soles, dug a hole in the heel, took the stones out of the rings and wrapped them in tissue, then wedged them in the hole and stuck the inner sole back down. I walked around for a while and it felt O.K., so I just prayed that I'd stay lucky when I was checked over before going out again.

Next morning, before I went back to base, I spent a couple of hours in a cyber café, researching the Henry business, seeing if I could trace a press retraction or a correction to public records regarding the reports of his death, but I got nowhere with it. I tried every contemporary source I could think of, right from the time of the fire through the following three months; the K.C. papers and the local register of births and deaths, the Wichita papers and records, the jazz press, and if there'd been anything

I'm sure I'd have found it, but all I turned up was confirmation that he'd died the night we jammed together.

When I got back to base that time, Forrestal still hadn't reappeared; security had issued an unspecific statement about the supposed breach of regulations, but there was still plenty of talk about the Artie rumour by then, none of it particularly surreptitious, either. I still couldn't decide whether or not to tell anybody about Henry, but eventually I decided I'd left it far too late, which was a relief in a way, although I think now that I'd subconsciously made up my mind as soon as security came into the picture. I still wonder just what would've happened if I had spoken out, how much it would've influenced this whole thing, but the fact that I didn't isn't weighing on my conscience at all, not now that everything's worked out the way it has.

As well as not clarifying the Henry mystery I didn't manage to come up with any answers to the other things I didn't understand, but while I was there I at least sorted out my thinking sufficiently to make a mental list of what I saw as the key questions. In addition to the one's I'd brought back with me, the reception I'd gotten had raised others, and I decided that what I needed to know had to be specifically connected to that. Even though Walden and I had ended up agreeing that security and Forrestal must have both been simply over-exercising their imaginations, I'd gradually grown less and less sure about that, and if security wasn't just jumping at shadows after all then it could only mean one thing as far as I could see. They had to believe that there was a genuine possibility that Artie really had been seen; that somehow he'd made it past the three-week limit and found a way to survive, at least until the time that Forrestal claimed to have seen him.

The implications of that were staggering, of course, in a whole lot of ways. As far as Artie himself was concerned, if he *was* alive and hadn't reported in that had to mean in effect he was on the run from our own people; that he'd opted to stay there and that they were after him. Somehow, the miracle that I'd longed for had happened to him, but because it had he'd become a renegade, someone whose continued presence might still actually disrupt history if their beliefs about its inviolability were wrong, and they were desperate to find him before the closure date so that he couldn't do any more damage than he may already have done.

But whether they were right or not about the undesirability of any effect he might have, it would still mean that he was blessedly alive, that somehow he'd adapted to the conditions there. I wanted to believe it, but I still didn't see how it could be possible, because I remembered my own early experience on the other side, my first trip in particular, the symptoms that had jarred me into the realisation of what would happen if I didn't make it back to Leyland in time. Nothing as bad as that had happened since, although like I told you earlier I'd still felt the beginnings of the same kind of thing on a couple of occasions, when I'd cut it a little fine.

I didn't feel I was really any closer to finding the answers to any of it when I got ready for my last trip. The questions were still nagging at me the whole time, though, and I knew that that was going to be the one opportunity I'd have to figure them out, and that my only real chance of doing that would be if I went to New York. Buddy Henry was going to be there with Valentine, and if Artie was alive and heard about it I knew he wouldn't be able to resist checking it out, even though he was on the run. During his last time at base we'd discussed Henry, mutually mourning his premature death after I'd gotten confirmation of it from the records, and the fact that he'd survived past the accepted date would draw Artie like a magnet, I was absolutely certain of it. He'd be there; at the Apollo, or in the after-hours joints that Henry would be frequenting after the job finished, somewhere.

The whole idea was like a bizarre dream, of course; truly nightmarish in some respects, because he and I would both be doing the same thing, seeking out someone who should have been dead but apparently wasn't, and that made no sense at all. But it was what made it irresistible, too, why I was prepared to stick my own neck out and go back to New York, despite the fact that the element of risk was going to be even bigger in some respects than it had been up until then.

The beard and glasses and different persona were a pretty effective disguise, though, and I decided that as far as the New York police were concerned by then there was at least a reasonable chance that they'd pigeon-holed the problem that I'd left them with anyway, the business of the soldier who'd broken jail and what had developed from that; either that, or they'd actually caught up with him and refused to accept his inevitable protestations as far as the hotel incident was concerned. Another thing was that with

Artie and Forrestal both out of the programme, that meant that we'd been reduced to six operational surveyors including me, with only three of us out at any given time. It would be assumed that Henry was dead by then, too, which automatically knocked the Valentine band back down the priority list and meant the Apollo gig probably wouldn't even be covered by our people.

Security was my big worry. After what had happened at base it seemed certain that they'd be out looking for Artie, so I realised I was still going to be taking a real chance. I had an excuse all ready if they did grab me, but I couldn't really see it satisfying them if I had to use it. 'Joe Shaddick' hadn't returned to K.C. as I'd been led to expect, I'd say; when I gotten back there I'd been told that he'd gone to New York instead, and because of my brief and his importance to our part of the programme I'd decided that I had no real choice about following him there. I was sure Walden would have wanted to back me, but I knew I couldn't count on it after such a flagrant breach of the regulations; even so, it was hard to see just how I could be penalised at that stage of the game, although I'm sure I'd still have ended up with problems of one kind or another.

There were no hiccups when I went through on what was my last official trip; nobody gave my shoes a second look, so I headed back to K.C. feeling pretty pleased with myself and able to relax a little for the first time in weeks. I still had to unload the stones, of course, and I wanted to sound Williams out about that as soon as possible, so after we got in and I'd checked into my hotel I went straight over to the restaurant.

Williams was in his office when I got there, and after we'd chatted for a while I said I wanted to ask his advice on something. I took the diamonds out of my wallet and showed him them, and told him that they'd been in the family a long time, part of an inheritance my parents had received about the time I'd been born. They'd hung onto them for a rainy day and that had happily never arrived, so I'd inherited them when they'd died. On the question of Thelma, I was short of ready cash, so I'd decided that her rainy day was sufficient justification for selling them.

The problem, I said, was that no longer had any documentary proof of ownership; I'd lost my copy of my parents will, and the solicitor that had handled it had gone out of business years ago. That meant that if I was to take unmounted stones to a jeweller it could raise all kinds of problems and complications, instigate a whole crop of enquiries, and because of Thelma's situation I couldn't risk having that happen. I'd taken on an obligation and made a promise, and I had to be able to keep it without getting involved in what would almost certainly turn out to be long delays.

I asked him if he knew anybody who might be able to help me with it, possibly suggest a potential buyer.

32.

———

There'd always been something cagey there, Williams thought; a hint of permanent caution, a looking-back-over-his-shoulder quality. He hadn't expected this, though. Whatever else he might have been, he'd always figured him to be clean, right with the law. But at least they had to be genuine. He was obviously intelligent in his slightly academic way, too bright to imagine that he could unload that kind of thing without them being properly checked out first.

Some kind of set-up? He weighed the idea carefully, delaying his answer, continuing to finger the stones on his desk-top. No, it didn't figure. He'd always trodden an amiably circumspect path, right through the old days and up to the present, and he had no real enemies, he was pretty sure of that. As always, his relationship with the police was an affable one, his contacts there carefully maintained. In any case, Perry didn't fit into that kind of scenario at all, not in any way. There was a naivete beneath the furtiveness, a kind of innocence that he sensed was genuine, despite the implications of what was happening.

He studied him across the desk. You really do interest me, baby, he thought. There's a whole lot more to you than you're probably ever going to tell me, but whatever it is it doesn't smell like a fix.

He picked up the biggest stone and lifted it closer to the light, squinting against the refracted brilliance.

"This is only part of it, you say?"

Perry cleared his throat. "Yes. There are a few other pieces. These are just a couple of odd items. They're obviously out of rings or brooches, something like that. I've no idea what happened to the mountings."

Williams studied the stone for a few more seconds, then replaced it on the desk-top, making his decision.

"Would you like me to handle them for you? I know one or two people who might be interested."

Perry blinked. "Really? I'd appreciate that very much."

"I'll get a price, and if it's O.K. with you I can fix a sale. It probably won't quite match what you could get at some of the retail houses, you'd better know that now." He looked down at his desk again, giving the statement time to fully register.

Perry cleared his throat again. "I'm sure it'll be fair. I'll expect you to take a commission, of course."

He shook his head. "Not this time. Usually I'd expect a cut, but we'll skip it on this one. She's a nice kid and I'd like to help out a little. Besides, I told her ma I'd look out for her that time, so I guess I owe something." He shrugged, and poked at the stones again. "O.K.? If you leave them with me I'll get back to you in a couple of days."

Perry nodded, smiling eagerly. "That would be fine."

He smiled back. "Sure. Any time."

33.

——

As well as the obvious relief I found the whole business rather touching, because quite apart from the question of his unanticipated generosity and acceptance of at least a share of the responsibility for Thelma's situation, we'd both moved past the bounds of casual friendship to an extent that was unique in my experience. Although neither of us had come right out into the open, we'd been mutually prepared to reveal that there were sides to our lives that wouldn't stand up too well under close legal scrutiny, and even that limited degree of confidence made me feel good. In my own case I hadn't had any realistic option if I was going to fulfil what I saw as my obligation to her, but he'd had a choice and still gone along, and I was truly grateful for that. Right then I'd have given a lot to have repaid his trust by telling him the truth about myself, but even though we'd reached another plane in our relationship I knew that was never going to be possible, and it's something I shall always regret.

He didn't even ask me to keep it confidential, but I raised the point anyway. I told him that I really appreciated what he was doing, and that as far as I was concerned it would stay strictly between the two of us. There was no reason for Thelma to be told the facts about how the money had been obtained, I said, but I would like to make it clear to her that he'd made a contribution, a kind of good-will gesture. He shrugged and said that was up to me, and we shook hands on it. Neither of us mentioned a receipt, but as far as I was concerned that was my way of reciprocating, showing that the trust really was mutual. He put the diamonds in the safe and we had a drink, and then I left, glad that I'd had at least one load taken off my mind.

I called on Thelma the next day and took her out to lunch; she seemed pleased to see me, and while we were talking she never raised the question of the money at all, which was something else I found touching. She trusted me, too, and I knew that whatever happened after that I'd always have good memories of what I learned during those couple of days. I mentioned it myself, though, when I took her back to the rooming-house; I told her that the property sale had reached the completion stage, and that I'd be able to let her have the money in a day or so. She said she still had most of the seventy-five I'd given her and wouldn't actually need any more for a while, but I told her not to deliberately skimp, that there was no need for anything like that. We batted that one around for a while, but in the end she said O.K., still a little reluctant, genuinely so, I could tell, and I said that I'd be seeing her again when everything was tied up.

I'd already decided to go to New York as soon as the money question was settled. I didn't see any point in delaying it; Valentine was already at the Apollo, and the longer I gave myself to try and check out the question of Artie's possible survival the more likely it would be that I'd find the answer, if it was there to be found.

I covered a lot of ground during the next two days. In the evenings I did the rounds of the places where the better music was being played, stocking up on stuff to present when I got back. There was at least a chance that I wouldn't run into any of our people in New York, and although I was prepared to take the consequences if I did I still wanted to duck that kind of trouble if at all possible, so that side of it had to be covered.

I spent most of the afternoons just trailing around on my own, because I wanted to concentrate on soaking up impressions and visual memories of the place, really absorb them, leave clear images in my mind. It was a town with a lot of attractive features; plenty of parks, wide boulevards that were a pleasure to walk along. I'd decided that it was almost certainly my last sight of it as it was then; if I ended up stretching the New York visit to the limit in my attempt to find Artie I simply wouldn't have the time to go back there, and I wanted to take as many memories of it with me as possible, because it was the setting of the turning-point in my life that I'd desperately needed and never dreamed I'd find when I went there.

I 'phoned Williams on the Tuesday, and he told me he'd gotten a price, fourteen hundred and fifty. It was quite a bit more that I'd expected, because I'd worked out what I'd paid against the current value of money and I'd figured no more than eleven or twelve hundred at the most, even allowing for his own contribution. It made me wonder just how realistic a price it was, whether in fact he was being considerably more generous than he'd already shown himself to be, but I decided not to ask. His money and what he did with it was his business, not mine. I said that was fine, and would he please go ahead with the sale. He told me he'd have the money there that evening, so I said I'd see him then.

So that's what I did, and we had a meal and talked, mostly about music, but about Thelma, too. It was the closest I got to being completely at ease with him, and I wished again that I could have told him the whole truth, but obviously still recognising that my situation made that impossible. I just had to accept that the circumstances of my being there at all had meant that his own trust had been abused right from the start, and that despite his knowing at least part of that he still seemed prepared to accept me without question. But it hadn't all remained lies, not quite, and I was glad that I'd come clean as much as I'd been able to.

I was feeling a little down when I went back to the hotel. I hadn't let it show, though, and before I left the restaurant I told him that although I was sure I'd see him again sometime, right then I wasn't able to predict my future movements; my K.C. research was going to have to be put on hold for the time being because I'd gotten involved in another project that was going to keep me busy for a while, so would he mind occasionally checking on Thelma, make sure she was O.K.? He said he would, and that seemed to tie everything up, because I didn't want either of them to think that I'd deliberately disappeared without any kind of explanation, even though I realised that when I failed to reappear at all they'd be bound to wonder why eventually.

I collected Thelma for lunch again the next day, and gave her the money when I took her home afterwards. She was still hesitant about accepting it, especially when she saw how much it was, but I told her that I might not be coming back to K.C. for quite a while. I really had no idea how long it would be, I said; I'd become involved in some business that could keep me away for a long time, so it was even possible that the baby would come before I was able to be there again, and I wanted to be absolutely sure that she had enough, especially for later, until it had reached an age when she felt O.K. about leaving it in somebody else's care. I kept it as cheerful as I could, but it was a particularly sad occasion because of what Clara had told me about her, a twisted echo of what had happened to Donna. It was another of those times when foreknowledge can become an unwelcome liability rather than an asset, and I hoped again that her marriage to the man Fry worked out and that she'd be happy during the time she had left.

It's still too early to judge how much the episode is ultimately going to affect my feelings about Donna and me. Even though what's happened since has thrown the whole thing wide open again in some ways the dreams have definitely faded and I'm sure I'm a little less uptight as far as my memories of our relationship are concerned, so I guess it has been beneficial in the way I hoped it would. Complete atonement was never a serious possibility, of course, but peace of mind and I have been strangers for so long that even the partial respite I'm experiencing now is more that I'd ever dared hope for before I met her.

Anyway, I wasn't altogether sorry when I left for New York the next morning. The business of Artie had never been far from the front of my mind, and during the journey I pushed my personal affairs to one side and got back to speculating about it, trying to find some kind of lead that might make sense of it all. I got nowhere, of course. Whichever way I approached it I ended up in the same cul-de-sac, the point where my imagination simply couldn't take it any further. All I knew for sure was that there had to be an answer somewhere, but I was no nearer finding it when we pulled into New York than I had been at the start of the trip.

It cost me an extra ten bucks to remind my cab driver that there was a room available up in the West nineties, but I guess that was the going rate. It was almost midnight when I checked in, so I decided to make a start the next day, but sleeping wasn't easy; it was a pretty noisy place, with doors slamming into the early hours and occasional racket in the corridor, and I didn't really drop off until almost daylight.

I stuck around the immediate area for most of the day, then went up to the Apollo in the evening to catch the last house. Despite the evidence of Henry's note and what I'd been told by the booking agency I couldn't really convince myself that he was going to be there, but he was, clearly visible at the end of the trumpet section.

Even then a tiny part of my brain resisted the idea that it could be him, but he had half a chorus to himself on one number, and that clinched it. It was him, without any question, incontrovertibly alive and still making music that had that indefinable promise of greatness in it. Watching and listening to him then was a very strange experience, because in a sense it made me feel totally isolated again, despite the packed house and the proximity of all those people. But as well as that I felt relief and exhiliaration, almost a sense of triumph, because what I was seeing and hearing was confirmation that I really had played a role in his survival, maybe even the pivotal one, and despite the reports and what the records said his unique musical poetry blessedly hadn't been silenced by death after all.

Foster was there as well, among the reeds; he took brief solos on two fastish numbers, and in its way that was a revelation, too. It was only a couple of months since the second K.C. session, but already his playing had taken on a new authority. There wasn't much of the old Foster about him at all; he sounded purposeful and alert, none of the casual coasting that had weakened his playing a lot of the time, and I felt a touch of something that I guess was akin to parental pride, because it was me that had planted the first seeds of dissatisfaction that had eventually dragged him out of his rut and steered him in the direction he was going, really beginning to use his talents in a worthwhile way at last.

One of the Valentine band's near-misses had been recorded just before the union ban came into operation; it had been selling pretty well for a while, and they closed the programme on the strength of it. I made a quick move out of there just as the show was ending, to make sure I didn't miss Henry afterwards; I checked the audience over as far as I was able to with my head tucked down, but I didn't see anyone who looked anything like Artie. I realised that what I was doing was risky, drawing attention to myself by quitting early, because if anybody from security was there the chances had to be that they'd have recognised me without me recognising them, but I wanted to be absolutely certain that I caught Henry before he took off.

I waited by the stage entrance, and eventually he and Foster came out together, both of them carrying their instrument cases. Henry was all smiles as soon as he saw me; Foster was a bit more circumspect, but he seemed friendly enough as far as I could tell. His attitude at the end of our second musical encounter had implied a touch of belated maturity, a tacit acknowledgement that in fact I'd done him a favour after all, and I guess he was still feeling more or less the same way towards me. I wondered how he'd react if I was to tell him about the baby, but Thelma hadn't wanted him to know and I wasn't going to go against her wishes; there'd have been no real point, anyway.

It was obvious that to some extent Henry and he had become buddies, although whether that extended beyond the purely musical side there was no way of telling. We strolled across town, both of them hopefully waving down passing cabs, and I told Henry that the news about the fire had come as a real shock, but I'd been relieved to hear that he was O.K. and that he'd missed being in it because of what we'd been doing.

It had been pretty bad, he said; some people had been killed, although most of them had made it out safely. He'd lost the stuff he'd had in his room, but he wasn't worried about it because he was claiming on the hotel's insurance; there hadn't been anything worth much anyway, and this way he was getting new clothes and luggage out of it. He was obviously just happy to be alive and unharmed, which certainly echoed my own feelings, although of course there was an extra dimension to it all from my point of view. A couple of empty cabs came along just then, and they grabbed one of them; Foster got in and Henry asked me if I'd like to go along. They were heading over to Minton's to let off some steam, he said, and if I came there might be a chance for us to blow together again.

I'd made a decision about that before going to New York. The last thing I wanted was to draw attention to myself, and that had to mean that playing publicly was out. In any case, although white players were more or less tolerated at Minton's then, it was only as embryo disciples, people who were prepared to accept that the new directions were a black prerogative and that they were there to learn, not lead. The K.C. session had been a one-off, not something that had happened in a setting where the same kind of ground-rules had been tacitly established, so it hadn't provoked any ripples in that sense, but I knew that Henry would be hoping for an encore of what I'd done then and there was no way I could have risked making myself that conspicuous anyway.

But it would have been embarrassing for both of us if I'd offered that as an excuse, so I told him that it wouldn't be possible because I'd wrenched some ligaments in my right wrist; I could use my hand for everyday things as long as I was careful, I said, but playing was too painful just then and would probably have made it worse. I told him I'd still like to go with them for a while, though, just to listen and take a few pictures, so we went over there.

Minton's was pretty busy, a lot of people on the stand and off it. The quality of the music was variable, despite there being several established people in the room, including a couple of genuine comers who were due to make it in the not very distant future. Henry and Foster played after a while and did O.K., Henry in particular, but one or two second-raters were sitting in that evening and stubbornly refusing to quit, so the overall results were fairly patchy. I stayed well in the background and kept an eye open, but I didn't see anyone who looked as though they might have posed a threat. There was no-one who looked like Artie, either, but I decided it would have been too much to hope, anyway; if he was around, my chances of finding him on my first night in town had to be pretty small.

Henry pulled out unexpectedly early, pleading fatigue; he'd played quite beautifully for some of the time, but there'd been a few fluffs creeping in towards the finish. I was a little beat myself by then, so we left Foster and rest of them to it. On the question of Artie the evening looked to have been a bust, but I'd gotten irrefutable evidence of Henry's survival and there were another eight days before I was due back at base, so I still had plenty of time to find him if he really was there.

It was raining when we got outside, coming down quite steadily.

34.

There was a cab parked a short distance away, but as they approached they saw that it was already taken. They retreated to the club entrance, Henry genially cursing the inaccuracy of the evening weather forecast.

Initially he'd played pretty well back there, he knew, but after a while the creeping onset of tiredness had begun to delay his reactions, blurring the co-ordination between thought and execution. Before that happened, though, there'd been several occasions when he'd felt himself drift into that area where tension and relaxation achieved a balance that temporarily freed his imagination and transmitted its product through lip and fingers with the kind of effortlessness that he always hungered for.

He glanced at Perry. He was standing beside him, wiping his spectacles with a handkerchief and peering out at the now thinning traffic gliding along 118th Street. It really was too bad about his hand. When he'd shown at the Apollo, he'd gotten a real lift, anticipating another chance to feed off the kind of backing he'd given him that time in K.C.

Maybe in a day or so, he thought, but it would have to be soon. They'd be back on the road on Sunday, and that didn't leave much time.

Perry caught his eye, and smiled his slightly cautious smile.

"It seems a pity to quit so early. You were going really well for a while."

"I guess so." He shrugged, pleased at the compliment. "I got to catch some sleep, though. We were blowin' 'til eleven yesterday a.m., up on 145th. It's too bad about your wrist. That Monk plays foxy piano, but it's you I'm waitin' for, man."

They both laughed. Perry said, "I'll have to see what I can do, but I wouldn't bank on it, not this time." He flexed his right hand, self-consciously. "It's still pretty touchy."

He ducked his head. "Sure. Don't take any chances with it." A cab pulled into the kerb, and some people got out. He nodded towards it. "You take it. You got further to go than me."

Perry thanked him, said goodnight, and climbed into the cab. It pulled away, and another slid to a stop a few yards down the street, disgorging a solitary passenger. Henry tugged up his jacket collar, and headed towards it. As he did so, someone passed him from behind and moved hurriedly across the pavement, getting there just ahead of him.

He slowed as the other man opened the cab door and began to climb inside, turning to stare at him as he did so. For a split second it was as though he was about to acknowledge him, an implication of recognition that was tinged with something else that could almost have been fear. Then he was inside, slamming the door behind him.

Well, he thought. What was that all about? He'd never seen the guy before as far as he knew. He sure wasn't going to get into a hassle over whose cab it was anyway, especially with a cripple. The limp had been very noticeable, not that it seemed to have slowed him down any.

He wandered back to the club entrance. The cab moved away, and seconds later the occupied one that was parked down the street followed it.

He watched them disappear, idly curious, then shrugged. Maybe he really did have something to be frightened of, he thought. Maybe I just gave him a little more time. He sure couldn't have run very fast, if that was his problem.

He looked up and down the street, but there were no more cabs in sight just then. He lit a cigarette, mentally damning the weather with slightly less good humour than before and listening to the faint sound of the music that continued in the building behind him.

35.

___

I'd just collected my key from the desk clerk when a bunch of Aframs, a couple of them noisy drunk, came into the hotel lobby from off the street. The elevator wasn't available right then but I was only two floors up, so rather than risk finding myself sharing it with them I used the stairs, and was sticking my key in the door to my room when somebody said my name, my real name.

It was just the one word, Alex, and it hit me like a thunderbolt, and it wasn't simply the shock of suddenly being hailed like that, because I knew straight away who it was that had said it. I looked back down the corridor and saw him walking towards me from the direction of the stairs. The lighting was dim, and even though his face was shadowed by a wide-brimmed hat, I knew it was Artie. The voice had told me that, and the walk was confirming it, a splay-footed shamble that I'd have recognised anywhere, although he was limping noticeably, too. I didn't say anything, just waited by the door as he came up and said, hi, with a kind of nervously exaggerted casualness.

It was the most ridiculously understated greeting imaginable under the circumstances, and I almost burst out laughing, although it wouldn't really have been laughing, more a kind of pent-up hysteria, a mixture of agitation and relief and total bafflement. He'd grown a Mexican-style moustache and a small semi-goatee beard; he was wearing shades, too, and his face was definitely thinner than when I'd last seen him, but I think I might still have just about known him if I'd passed him in the street and looked at him directly. But even allowing for all of that, I got a funny feeling just then, because there was something recently familiar about him that I couldn't quite place.

He nodded at the door and said we should go inside, but that I mustn't switch on the light. I still didn't say anything, just did what he'd told me to. We went in, and I locked the door, then turned around and looked at him, not knowing what to say. I couldn't really see him properly, just a blurred impression of him standing by the bed, but there was a street light almost opposite the window, and after a few seconds my eyes adjusted to the gloom and I saw that he was pointing a pen-gun at me.

I asked him why he was doing that, and he said he had to be sure. He told me to take out my own pen-gun between my finger and thumb, then lay it on the bedside table. So I did that, very carefully, and then I backed away and sat down on a chair in the corner, moving very slowly the whole time. Neither of us said anything for a few seconds after that, and then I said I was glad to see him.

He seemed to relax a little then, because he sat down on the bed and took his hat off and lowered the pen and held it on his knee. It was when he took his hat off and I saw the light reflected on his skull that the something recently familiar about him clicked into place. I'd looked at the same shaved head earlier that evening, sitting in the shadows at the back of the room at Minton's, and I simply hadn't recognised him. He'd always had a very full head of hair before, and without it the whole proportion if his head was different, and because of that and the other changes I hadn't given him more than a passing glance when I was there.

I still couldn't see his face all that clearly, but the overall impression that I got was a kind of tired wistfulness. Then he shrugged it off, and said he'd followed me from 118th Street. He'd tacked himself onto the noisy bunch that had come in just after me, he said, and while the desk man was trying to quiet them down he'd sneaked past and tailed me up the stairs.

I told him what had happened at base, the story that had gone around about Forrestal and his report, and the business with security. He said he'd seen Forrestal at the corner of 48th and Broadway one night, but he hadn't known whether Forrestal had seen him or not; the beard and moustache were only half-grown then, so he'd realised that it was possible that he'd been recognised. They'd literally been within a couple of yards of one another, walking in opposite directions; he'd crossed the road immediately after that, just before the lights changed, so he'd been able to lose himself before Forrestal had a chance to come after him.

A couple of days ago he'd had the feeling that he was being followed, he said; he'd ducked into a store and left by the side entrance, but nothing had actually happened and he'd put it down to imagination. Now he wasn't so sure, though, after what I'd told him. The business about not switching on the light had probably been unnecessary, but instinct had warned him to tell me that. The room fronted onto the street, and a light going on in there could have given our location away to anybody out there who might have been interested.

That shook me almost as much as finding out that he was alive. If he *was* being followed, then it almost certainly had to mean that security had found him, and in that case I had to assume that they were tailing me by then, too. So I asked him if he'd seen anybody that evening that he thought might have been following him, and he said, no, he hadn't, but he didn't really know any of the security people; a man called Wells had been his security instructor during training, but he and Urich were the only people he could positively identify. If somebody was after him, it could be almost anybody on the street. I got up and took a careful look out of the window, but there was nobody obviously loitering down there that I could see. So I sat down again and asked him how it was he was still alive.

He told me it was because of an accident he'd been involved in. He'd just started back to base when somebody had collided with him on an escalator, and he'd fallen down practically the whole length of it. When he eventually woke up in the hospital he'd been told that he had a hairline skull fracture and that his leg had been broken; the bone had actually emerged, severing an artery on the way. Massive transfusion had been necessary, and they'd told him that he'd been lucky to survive. When he asked how long he'd been unconscious, they'd said it had been eight days.

If he really had been there that long then he knew that accident or no accident he should have been dead for at least five days, maybe longer. But since he obviously wasn't, then something had equally obviously contrived to save him. When he'd come round he'd been feverish for a while, but apart from that and the state of his leg and the nagging remains of a headache that gradually faded along with the fever, he'd felt reasonably fit; there'd been occasional spells of vomiting, but they'd gradually stopped, too. So while he was laying there he considered all the possible explanations he could think of, and eventually he'd figured out what logic told him had to be the answer. What he came up with really shook him, he said, but he admitted that after thinking about it for a while he could at least understand the reasoning behind it.

What he'd concluded was that we'd been lied to. The truth was that there was nothing at all in the climate of the period, or the fact that we were out of phase with our own time, that was going to harm us in any way. What we'd been told about the loss of two preliminary scouting surveyors had been pure fiction. The three-week limit was a contrivance, something that had been cooked up, most probably by security, to ensure that none of us made a break for it, become so desperate to escape the inexorable decay of our own time that we simply ignored our sworn undertaking to leave the past as undisturbed as possible and deliberately lost ourselves there until the hole closed and sealed us safely away on its far side.

Whether the controllers believed that they really understood the hole's relation to the past or not, they were still clearly wary of the possibility that after allowing for existing restrictions there, long-term relative freedom of action by any of us might harm the future somehow, accelerate our own problems, so they decided that only the fear of certain death would deter anyone hoping to make a run for it. But they also decided that the only way to absolutely guarantee that the temptation was removed was to ensure that anybody who stayed beyond the specified period actually did die. If they should overstay accidentally, as he had, that still couldn't be allowed make any difference; they still had to die, to prevent the continuation of their presence there and to dissuade others.

The way that this had been achieved had been obvious, he said, once he'd arrived at his basic premise. The injections we were given before each trip weren't a safeguard at all, at least not as far as we were concerned. They were some kind of delayed-action poison that began to take effect when the three weeks were almost up, and the gradual onset of heart irregularity and all the rest of it were the signal that it had become active. When we got back to base and went through medical, the shots we were given neutralised it. He was sure he was right, he said, because of the circumstances of his own survival. He'd gone past the three-week limit, but he hadn't died because most of his poisoned blood had been replaced by the transfusions that they'd given him in the hospital; the fever and vomiting he'd experience afterwards had been the residue working its way out of his system. Now that the poison was no longer there, he could stay where he was permanently, not that he had any real choice by then, he said, although it was what he'd have chosen to do if the option had been offered.

Listening to what he was telling me was like having a bucket of iced water slowly tipped over me, but as well as the shock and the cold and the fear I felt real anger, too, because along with all the other surveyors it suddenly put my relative value in perspective, and I saw the whole business as something altogether more sinister and ruthless than I'd ever suspected it might be. What he'd told me was horrific, of course, but it all fitted together too neatly for me to be able to reject it, even though I desperately wanted to. I began to wonder just how far the people behind the programme were prepared to go, the kind of limits and values they saw as admissible in that situation, and I'm still wondering. Going right back to the beginning, for instance; what if the people who found the hole hadn't agreed to keep their mouths shut and go along with the story that was cooked up to explain their sudden move to new premises, some nonsense about dangerous wiring and insurance? If they hadn't been prepared to play, would it have started there with them; a convenient 'accident' or unexplained disappearance, something of that sort? There's a whole bunch of questions like that that I'll never know the answers to, which is maybe just as well, but telling you about it now still gives me chills.

Something else I wondered about was whether the medical people at base actually knew what it was they were injecting us with, but in view of subsequent events I've decided that even if the senior staff did, not everybody there was in on it. Anyway, I hadn't really understood Artie's last remark, so I asked him why he believed he had no choice but to stay there.

He said it was because he was bound to be at serious risk if he did go back. If they were searching for him, it might not simply be because they believed that his continued presence there might pose a threat to the pattern of the future. After all, there was no way that they could know just how firmly he'd committed himself to the idea of staying, and that would only add to the problem as far as they were concerned. If he was alive, there had to be at least a chance that he'd figured out why. But even if he hadn't he'd still be a threat, because as long as the hole stayed open they could never be certain that he wouldn't change his mind and automatically blow the whistle on the poison thing by reappearing at the last moment.

There was no way that they could keep it quiet if he did turn up and actually managed to get back to base, he said. If they didn't find and eliminate him in New York it was his guess that they'd be waiting for him to reappear in Leyland, grab him before he could get anywhere near the hole and then kill him, because as far as they were concerned that would be the only way that they could guarantee re-stabilising the situation.

In its own way it would be understandable, he said, just like the poison business. From their point of view they had to protect the past from the possibility of interference, and on the other hand they simply didn't dare let him return to our own time, or even get anywhere near base, because once it got out that he'd suddenly reappeared, months after he'd been pronounced dead, there'd be no way of engineering a cover-up. Far too many people were involved for there not to be a leak, especially from close associates of Carrie Bethal and the man Glass, the two surveyors who'd gone missing earlier, and as well as the general uproar it'd provoke when the hole's existence and the way it had been kept under wraps became public knowledge, it'd inevitably lead to demands for a public inquiry into the way it had all been run. He couldn't see the kind of arguments that they'd offer in their defence cutting much ice, either, not in view of the global situation, but even if they did, quite apart from the effect it would have in the broader sense, there'd still be a bad aftertaste, messy legal proceedings, a whole lot of repercussions that they'd be desperate to avoid.

What all that had to mean was that they really wanted him dead, rather than simply found. He wasn't overly concerned about it, though, he said; there were less than two weeks to go before the hole was due to close, and he'd make sure he laid low until it did. It didn't look as though anybody had spotted us that evening, so as long as he kept his eyes peeled and stayed off the streets as much as possible he was pretty sure that he'd be O.K.; it would mean giving the music a miss for a while, but that couldn't be helped. He'd find a cab when he left, he said; although his leg hadn't mended altogether cleanly and he'd been slowed down a little as a result, he still liked walking around town at night, something that was normally possibly without feeling that he was at any real risk, but in view of what I'd told him it would be a sensible precaution.

36.

The tall man in the hat and dark trench-coat moved slowly along the still-moist pavement, a solitary figure among the other pedestrians that periodically drifted past him.

Traffic had gradually thinned since his arrival, but there was still a sporadic flow, mostly cabs or trucks, an occasional police car. Each time a police car passed, he mentally noted its number, comparing it with those of earlier sightings. On one occasion, a patrolman approached from the opposite direction. The tall man carefully maintained his pace, passed him, and walked to the corner of the block. He waited there until the patrolman had disappeared in the distance, then retraced his footsteps and continued his back and forth coverage of the strip of pavement opposite the hotel and a little way beyond it.

After a while, the pedestrian traffic in that part of the street temporarily petered out. He looked searchingly in both directions, then retreated into an adjacent alleyway, soon merging with a patch of deep shadow there. In the shelter of the near-darkness, he twisted the mounting of the signet-ring on the middle finger of his right hand, then held it to his mouth, his eyes fixed unblinkingly on the alley entrance. He spoke towards the ring in a quietly urgent voice, twisted it a further notch, then raised it to his ear. He did this several times, his brow creased, cursing under his breath with steadily increasing vehemence at the lack of response.

Earlier that evening, from his observation point beside the window of the diner on Lennox Avenue, he'd been startled to see Lohmann walking past, in conversation with two other men. In his haste to follow them, he'd thrust out a hand to prevent the door closing behind another departing customer who'd just preceded him, briefly trapping it. The ring had partially cushioned his fingers, but it had borne the brunt *of the blow. With his attention focussed exclusively on Lohmann's unexpected presence and despite the discomfort this caused the incident barely registered on his consciousness at the time, and it was only after eventually arriving at the hotel that he'd attempted to use the communicator and been dismayed by its failure to respond.*

Despite his repeated attempts to activate it since then, the situation had alarmingly remained the same. He'd have discovered the problem earlier if circumstances had permitted, but his cab-bound vigil outside the club that Lohmann and his companions had gone to had made it far too dangerous, with the driver's curious eyes frequently on him in the rear-view mirror. Now that he'd decided that the limping occupant of the middle cab in their ostensibly unrelated caravan must have been a disguised Mastin, though, the matter had become even more urgent, forcing him to a reluctant decision. It was possible that he'd leave again during his absence, he acknowledged, but not all that likely; the fact that he hadn't reappeared so far indicated that he'd established contact with Lohmann, rendering it improbable in the immediate future.

He'd have to risk it. He twisted the ring-mounting back to its original position, and re-emerged onto the street. Shortly afterwards, a man with a package under his arm appeared, walking briskly in an uptown direction. The tall man approached him.

"Excuse me, do you know if there are any pay 'phones near here?"

The man with the package slowed to a halt. "I guess so." He puckered his mouth thoughtfully, then turned and pointed down the street. 'The nearest one's back there, round the corner. First left, then about four hundred yards, I'd say."

"None closer than that?"

"Not as I know of", the man with the package said. He glanced across the road. "You could try the hotel. Should be one in the lobby. Worth checking out, anyway." He moved on.

The tall man hesitated, then crossed the road and entered the hotel. Apart from a bald-headed man propped behind the desk reading a newspaper, the lobby was empty and the only visible telephone was beside where his elbow rested on the counter. The tall man hesitated again, then approached the desk.

"Excuse me, do you have a pay 'phone? I need to make an urgent call."

The desk clerk looked up from his newspaper. He stared at the tall man appraisingly for two or three seconds, then returned his attention to his newspaper. "Out of order."

"Do you have another 'phone I could use?"

The desk clerk shook his head without looking up. "Sorry."

"It really is important."

The desk clerk jerked his head towards the entrance. "There's a pay 'phone round the corner. Downtown, first left."

The tall man tapped the counter lightly, his smile bleakly polite. "Right. Thanks for your help."

He'd briefly considered offering a bribe, but the man's reaction to his presence had clearly implied prejudice rather than avarice, and on reflection using the desk 'phone would have presented its own problems. Coherently wording what he needed to say without arousing suspicion would have been difficult, if not impossible. He went out onto the street again, thinking hard. How long would it take him to get to the pay 'phone round the corner, use it and get back? Five minutes, ten, longer? It could be in use, or broken. No, it would be too risky. Despite his earlier speculation about the unlikelihood of Mastin's imminent departure, he didn't dare take a chance on losing him.

Looks like you're on your own, buddy, he told himself grimly. He swore again, and resumed his perambulations, this time staying on the same side of the street as the hotel and restricting himself to a shorter length of pavement, carefully ensuring that he couldn't be seen from inside the lobby.

People entered and left the hotel at irregular intervals, none of them disturbing his measured pace for more than a second or so. As the traffic continued to thin, he retreated to the alley on the far side of the road again and continued his surveillance from the shadows there, periodically attempting to coax a reaction from the signet-ring, each time further frustrated by its relentlessly stubborn silence.

37.

—

I asked Artie if the prospect of staying bothered him very much, and he said it didn't, not really. There were obviously things and people that he'd miss and the racial climate was pretty hard to take at times, but he'd always been adaptable, able to adjust to most circumstances he'd found himself faced with, and he was sure he'd have found it hard to turn the opportunity down if it'd been offered. Until very recently his biggest worry had been about his situation as it related to the future, the possibility that he'd become a foreign body in the destructive sense, causing irreparable damage somehow simply by being there permanently.

But now other things were happening that could be confirming something that he'd suspected for a while, he said. He'd followed me back to the hotel partly because he wanted to tell me what he'd deduced about the medication business and to reassure me that he was O.K., but also because I obviously knew things that he didn't and he'd wondered if they might help to clarify his own ideas.

At first he'd been appalled by his conclusions about the medication, but he admitted that eventually he'd come around to accepting that the programme controllers probably hadn't had a realistic choice if the basic theory that they were working to was right. Subsequently, though, he said, he'd started to have doubts about whether what we were involved in really was the way they believed it to be.

The three-week limit to our field-trips had still given us enough time to get at least some feel for the general atmosphere of the period, he said, but since he'd been stuck there he'd gradually become conscious of a subtle difference, a sense of change that was somehow askew, not quite natural. He couldn't describe it any better than that, he admitted, but by then he was quite sure that it really was happening, that it definitely wasn't just his imagination playing tricks, and now the Buddy Henry thing felt as though it was somehow slotting into it all, convincing him that he wasn't simply developing some kind of phobia as a result of his enforced stay.

Like me, he knew that he was supposed to have died in a fire in Kansas City several weeks ago, an accident that had been reported in the press at the time and was confirmed by public record, but that morning he'd heard that he was in town with the Benny Valentine band. At first he'd assumed that his informant had made a mistake, but somebody else had backed him up, sworn that it was true; a trumpet–player called Buddy Henry was with Valentine at the Apollo and playing the joints afterwards, he'd been told, blowing stuff that was making quite a few heads turn.

Although he realised he could be taking a pretty big risk, he'd decided to check it out, because if it *was* true it seemed to be proving that contradictory events were taking place that he couldn't possibly be personally responsible for, he said. But even if they weren't linked to him directly there was at least a chance that they could be tied to his situation in the broader sense. He'd been at the Apollo that evening and he'd been startled to see me leaving just before the finish, but even though he'd realised that he might lose me he hadn't dared follow straight away because it would have meant drawing attention to himself. When he got outside, though, he saw me again, but I was with Henry and someone else, so he hadn't been able to approach me with them there.

He'd followed us until we went off in the cab; he'd been beaten to another one that had come along just then so he'd lost us for a while, but he'd decided that our most likely destination was Minton's, and luckily he'd been right. He kept as far away from me as possible while we were there, because he'd decided that approaching me in a public place would be far too risky, but although I'd looked directly at him a couple of times the changes he'd made to his appearance had obviously fooled me. He'd followed us when we left and waited just inside the building until we'd split, and then he'd sneaked ahead of Henry, grabbed another cab that had just turned up and tailed me to the hotel and up to my room. It had been clear that I knew Henry quite well by then, he said, so I had to have some idea of the circumstances of his survival. He asked me what had really happened back there in

K.C., how much it was to do with me sticking my neck out and coming to New York like I had.

I wondered if I should ask him if he'd seriously considered the possibility of some kind of parallel world being involved, but I decided to wait and see if he volunteered anything like that without my prompting. So I just told him everything, condensing it as much as I could; about Donna and Thelma, Henry, Williams, Foster, 'Joe Shaddick', all the things I'd taken a direct part in and helped to shape by my actions, and the way that I'd justified what I'd done by persuading myself that the planners were being over-cautious and that the reality of the situation was that it was bound to be more flexible than they'd decided it had to be.

But the Buddy Henry thing had changed all that, I said, which was one of my reasons for being there, although the principal one was the rumour about Forrestal and him, the possibility that he might be alive and that the two things might be linked in some way. There was obviously no way of knowing how much his continuing presence would affect the future, but what had happened to Henry seemed to prove that meaningful change was possible. I agreed that his deductions about his own survival made sense, so that wasn't really a mystery any more, but it still left the question of Henry unanswered. *His* survival flatly contradicted the official records, and unless that was the result of a mistake of some kind being made somewhere along the line I just didn't see how it could have happened, I said, and always assuming that he continued to survive I didn't see how it could fail to distort the future, either, particularly as far as the music was concerned, and quite possibly in appreciably significant ways.

He hesitated for a bit, and then he looked me in the eye and asked me if I thought it possible that we were in a different past, one that was going to lead to a future that might turn out to be very different from our own. The programme people had firmly dismissed the idea, citing the laws of physics and what they'd told us was the current line in cosmological thinking, but when all the facts were considered he didn't see that any other explanation really made sense.

After all, our own past was an accomplished fact; it had happened, and facts can't be changed, he said. But changes that contradicted the records of that past *were* possible where we were. The fire that should have killed Henry had happened on the recorded date, but he hadn't been in it, and given the circumstances it was reasonable to suppose that my ideas about why he hadn't were right, and he'd survived because of our musical encounter, my unscheduled presence and deliberate participation in events. The records of the time categorically stated that he'd died then, and my research hadn't found anything to refute that, but it simply wasn't true. He accepted that under normal circumstances an incorrect entry could've been a feasible explanation if it had concerned an isolated incident, but it wasn't, and in any case the circumstances had been far from normal. When it was added to the things he'd told me, a picture that had already seemed to him to be gradually forming became even clearer, he said. He admitted that it was still a long way from being complete, but as far as he was concerned there was already enough there to confirm what he'd suspected, that we'd moved away from our own time-line onto another one that no longer consisted of an exact replica of our own history and was changing all the time, almost certainly as a result of our presence there.

So although we'd apparently started out by visiting our direct past—the recorded existence of T.& M. Research and the fire that eventually broke out there seemed to confirm that, anyway, he'd reasoned—at some point there must have been another shift of some kind that had taken us onto an adjacent time-line, one that most likely had initially been a duplicate of our own but was at least partially different now, and after that our journeys back and forth had been a sort of diagonal process instead of the direct connection that'd existed at the beginning.

It'd probably happened when the operation had been going for a while, he said, maybe just before my first trip to K.C., but whenever it was it seemed pretty obvious that nobody on the survey teams had reported the kind of changes that he'd detected, almost certainly because the three-week limit to our visits was too short for it to have really registered. Whatever the reason the controllers didn't seem to know anything at all about it, because if they had they'd have called an immediate halt to any more trips while they tried to decide what to do. Even before I'd told him about Henry he'd pretty much decided that the evidence pointed towards what he'd been telling me, but hearing what'd happened to him had clinched it as far as he was concerned, he said.

Ever since finding out that Henry was still alive I guess my imagination had simply become seized up with a mixture of confusion and ignorance and fear, but listening to Artie released a flood of questions and possible answers that came so fast I had trouble keeping up with them. For instance, when we'd been told about the impossibility of transferring from our world to a parallel one, that could've been because the controllers genuinely believed it, of course, but what if they didn't, not altogether, anyway? What if the truth was that they'd been understandably terrified of letting us interact too directly with a setting that they suspected might be revising the laws of physics in ways that were beyond their imagining, the real reason for the stringency of the regulations governing our time there?

I wondered about the time we'd spent in our own past, if it'd actually been more influential than anyone'd figured it'd be, just how much effect it might've had. The controllers obviously didn't really understand any of what'd been happening, so what if our ostensibly innocuous day-to-day activities intermingled with the present in a way that was far more influential than anyone realised, to the extent of at least partially re-shaping it in a critically destructive way?

The whole concept of time as a purely chronological process had already been thrown into turmoil, of course, but what I'd just arrived at completely petrified me, and I wondered if the controllers had considered such a possibility but eventually decided that anything like that had to be so improbable that it needn't stop the programme from going ahead. Anyway, what I was feeling clearly showed, because Artie asked me what was wrong, so I told him, and he said it was something he'd been wondering about, too, ever since he'd arrived at his fundamental conclusion, but it was only a possibility, and in any case the evidence to support this time-line switch theory seemed to be pretty conclusive by then, he said, so the way he saw it we could take at least a little consolation from the fact that we'd eventually arrived at a cut-off point. Neither of us had actually broken any rules while we were visiting our direct past, either, he pointed out, and nothing we'd done since could possibly have affected events there, so any damage we might've been doing to it stopped when the switch happened.

Considering the state of our present I didn't really find that particularly consoling, but I did feel better about my deviant behaviour, enough to make a decision I'd been dithering over for quite a while. I'd never told him or anybody else about the occasions when I'd seemed to sense a pattern to what was happening to me, and even wondered if it could possibly have some kind of spiritual basis, for the very good reason that to the best of my knowledge nobody else on field-work had come up with anything like it, and I obviously didn't want to run the risk of being seen as delusional or unstable or whatever.

I decide that this new situation was the time to come clean, though, so I did, and although like me he'd drifted away from religion in his early teens he didn't dismiss it, simply suggested that we put it on hold until we'd gone into things sufficiently to be able to decide whether something like that might slot into anything we hit on that could be reinforcing the idea. Anyway, although we'd both had a cursory brush with quantum physics during school and college what we'd mutually retained could've been written on a postage stamp, and before being recruited into the programme what we knew about other worlds and dimensions was strictly derived from science fiction, but we still gradually got into a debate that took in everything we could think of that looked as though it might relate to what was happening; how time really worked, multiverse and chaos theories, anything at all along those general lines that we could dredge up.

The most important question was obvious enough, of course; was the hole simply a motiveless tear in the continuum that'd presumably self-repair at the time of closure, or did it actually have intent behind it, some specific purpose to suit the requirements of the powers of creation—whatever *they* might be—and if so, what were those requirements? Because of the awesome implications of such a concept we concentrated on that to kick off with, discussed the possibility of it being something that really had been consciously provided and would benefit us in a limited way, but existing primarily so that we could help shape a world where future events needn't follow the same destructive pattern as ours if our foreknowledge was used to change that.

That sounds absurdly pretentious, I know, Phyl, but in that situation and thinking about everything that'd happened all I can say is that right then it didn't seem foolish at all, but in any case we quickly ran into problems with it. I'm not going to go into the details of everything else we touched on, either, because it'd take far too long, but I still need to at least give you an outline so that you understand why we reached the decisions that we did.

Anyway, as far as the escape-hatch and rescue idea was concerned the principal stumbling-block was Artie's apparently valid theory about switching to another time-line, of course, because if the preservation of humankind was what it was really all about it was only logical to assume that when the hole opened it would've led directly to where we were and simultaneously provided a clear pointer to what was possible, not wasted time by taking us to our own past first. If I hadn't belatedly found out that I'd played a key role in extending Henry's existence and Artie hadn't been there long enough to arrive at this own conclusions we'd never have known that we were in a different past, which automatically seemed to rule out pre-planning or thought of any kind and at the same time knock the spiritual angle squarely on the head. As things stood, we'd run out of time before either of those things had happened, anyway, so even though the chance to at least try and lay the foundation of change had been there, seemingly inadvertently, and even if we'd managed to convince the controllers of what we believed it was obviously far too late to take advantage of that as far as choosing the right people and making all the necessary arrangements was concerned.

What we eventually decided was that if the changes that we've been responsible for there are going to prove beneficial it'll more than likely have been down to pure luck. Maybe our presence had actually helped things, although we mutually admitted to finding it impossible to feel any real optomism about what looked to us like an extremely remote chance. On the other hand, we wondered if anything we'd done would turn out to have a negative effect on the war, maybe even influence its eventual outcome, and Artie said that something else he'd been wondering about was if in fact other holes existed, and if they did whether anyone had stumbled on them the way we had ours. If that was so, he said, and if they'd subsequently been as closely guarded as ours had been, there'd be no way of knowing about them or how they'd been used; it could've occurred anywhere, maybe in hostile territory, and the implications of what might result from that were obviously extremely alarming.

It was another sobering possibility, of course, but clearly light-years away from our own sphere of influence, so we focussed on the question of what might be feasible, if there was anything at all we could do to help the situation there, and on the face of it there was one course of action left open to us was obvious enough. Even so, although the idea of contacting people in high office and persuading them to let us demonstrate the hole's existence and what it represented, give them a sight of our future so that they realised the urgent necessity to change course as soon as possible sounds fine when it's summarised like that, the reality would obviously have been a far trickier proposition.

For one thing, everybody there was far too preoccupied with their current problems to concern themselves with a warning of what could happen in the relatively distant future, especially coming from a couple of total unknowns like ourselves. Even if we'd managed to reach someone at the necessary level of authority and weren't simply dismissed as a couple of cranks, the chances had to be that we'd have been detained as subversives or worse, trying to peddle a crackpot idea that'd only distract them from the hard facts of their situation if they were foolish enough to take it seriously.

If that happened we'd both have been in real trouble, especially me, because I still had the poison inside me. That sounds criminally selfish, I know, but even if they did take us seriously enough to look into our claim and met with our people, Artie and I would've needed to persuade the controllers that our reading of things was correct, and there simply wouldn't have been time to compile the kind of verification they'd have wanted before they were prepared to lower their guard, accept that we really had become linked to a duplicate of our past where corrective change truly was possible. In any case, if our hole should turn out to be the only one after all, by the time the war was over the rest of the world would only have had our government's word for it that it'd ever really existed. At the very least everybody else would've reacted with extreme scepticism, seeing it as a spectacularly clumsy political gambit that was designed to further our own interests in some oblique way, a dangerously naïve ploy that could only lead to an upsurge in international tension.

The more we thought about it the more improbable it looked, and eventually we agreed that we just had to forget it, because what we were considering was clearly an unworkable dream, and I hope you're prepared to accept the logic of what we decided and take my word for it that we didn't allow the personal risk element to colour our judgement, Phyl. Believe me, we were acutely conscious of the magnitude of what we were being forced to do. If we'd seen even a sliver of a chance of helping the situation in any way at all we'd willingly have stuck our necks out, but we couldn't, so all we could do was hope that during our collective time there what we'd actually been doing without realising it was laying the groundwork for the kind of change that was needed, that'd eventually help steer them right before it was too late.

Just to say it was frustrating probably makes that the biggest understatement of all time, but we really couldn't come up with anything more right then, and the conversation simply petered out and left us sitting there, thinking our own thoughts. I was feeling pretty much knocked out, anyway, completely drained, and Artie obviously was, too; it was after 5 a.m. by then, and we'd been stretching our imaginations to the limit for at least three hours, maybe four, so it was hardly surprising that we'd run out of gas. Despite the inevitable feeling of deflation, though, it was still the most engrossing and stimulating conversation I'd ever taken part in, and although the whole thing was ludicrous in a lot of ways it was magical as well; two not particularly bright people sat in a seedy hotel bedroom, wondering if they'd just discovered one of the keys to existance. The sudden rush of questions and possible answers I'd experienced when Artie's and my own ideas had meshed still had me convinced that I'd been on the verge of grasping reality for the first time in my life, and although we'd failed to arrive at anything like a solid conviction even my memories of my time as 'Joe Shaddick' didn't really mean very much just then.

Eventually, Artie said he had to go; someone was expecting him, he said, and she'd worry until he got there. Although I knew he'd accumulated plenty of acquaintances that was the first indication he'd given that he'd started to develop a more substantial private life, something that simply hadn't occurred to me. He asked how long it was before I had to go back, and I told him I had eight more days; because of the hole's imminent closure the trip had been cut to two weeks that time. Saying it got the cold sweat going again, because it was a reminder of what I was carrying inside me, poised to become activated and eventually kill me if I didn't make it back to base before it was too late.

He said he'd see me again the following day, when we weren't so tired. It'd have to be at night because of the security threat, and even though we seemed to have exhausted all the possibilities it'd give us time to let what we'd discussed sink in and maybe come up with other ideas.

So we agreed that he'd come to the hotel again the next evening, around eleven. We hugged, something I very rarely do, but right then it seemed totally natural and the only appropriate way of expressing what we were both obviously feeling. I took him downstairs and saw him past reception and out of the building, and then went back to my room and watched him from the window, walking uptown on the other side of the street.

38.

There were no cabs around when he left the hotel, and the only other people visible were a man and a woman standing beside a parked car some distance away on the other side of the street, their poses and gestures graphically depicting argument.

He heard the querulous note of their exchange as he approached, and moved quietly past, looking straight ahead. If it was going to escalate into something more than just a quarrel, he didn't want to be in the vicinity when it happened. He looked for a cab again, but the only other vehicle in sight was a delivery truck that drifted disinterestedly past.

If no cab happened along before he got to Broadway he'd be able to catch one there, he reassured himself. It wasn't far; around the next corner and then straight up ahead, a couple of minutes away. He looked back down the street, and saw the man and woman still beside the car, but the man had his hand on the woman's shoulder now and their joint demeanour was altogether more conciliatory, suggesting that some kind of compromise was under negotiation.

He caught a glimpse of other movement back there, directly behind him. It was a tall figure, a man, fifty yards or so away and moving in the same direction as himself. There was no urgency in his movements as far as he could tell, no hint of pursuit. Even so, his own pace instinctively quickened a little, accompanied by the same stirring sensation at the nape of his neck that he'd felt a couple of days before, when he'd resorted to precautionary evasive action.

Take it easy, he told himself. Not everybody out on the street's gunning for you. He checked inside his jacket, feeling the reassuring bulge of the pen under his fingertips.

Despite his tiredness, he was still warmed by the relief and excitement that he'd felt at the recent encounter, his head continuing to whirl with a kaleidoscope of dazzling visions. In many ways his future represented a challenge that he welcomed, but when Lohmann left that would be the end of his contact with the era that in some respects at least he still thought of as his own. There'd be no way that he'd ever be able to indulge the same kind of confidence with anyone, he knew that, no-one to share the wonder of this new consciousness of reality with. Despite the friends he'd already made, it would be a singularly lonely existance, a life of unique solitude.

If only it had been possible for Alex to stay as well, he though longingly, somehow contrive to have his blood purified, the poison removed. But there was no realistic way of achieving that that he could see, none at all. However it was attempted, it would be bound to involve enormous risks, a multitude of unforeseeable dangers that there'd simply be no way of safeguarding against. After all, the circumstances of his own survival had been freakish in the extreme, and there was no genuinely plausible way that he could see of duplicating them.

But if it was impossible, and he really was destined to be the sole representative of that other, discarded time, his situation would still have its full quota of fascinations, endless points of interest to note and compare. Many of the changes that their presence had initiated would escape his notice, of course, perhaps not even become evident during his lifetime; after all, he reminded himself, he had no way of knowing how long he was going to survive there,

Deep in thought, he reached the corner of the street that led up to Broadway and the broken line of traffic that moved across its far end.

39.

He hadn't gone very far when another man suddenly appeared from an unlighted alleyway on the other side of the street and started to move in the same direction. He was totally anonymous at first, just a dark figure in the general dimness outside, but then he paused and looked across towards the hotel, staring at the upstairs windows, and for a second or two I saw his face.

I still hadn't switched the room light on and I was mostly masked by the curtains, so I was pretty sure he couldn't see me, but he was directly under the street light just then, and I could see him clearly. He was wearing a hat, but he'd tilted his head back, and just that quick glimpse was like an almighty kick in the stomach, because it was Roache, the security guy I'd almost collided with outside Walden's office, right before I'd gone in and found him arguing with Urich and then had Urich quiz me about Artie.

I didn't think at all, I simply reacted. I shot downstairs again, gabbled something about having to speak to my friend as I passed the night man, and then out into the street, bracing myself to shout a warning to Artie. I'd only gone a few yards, though, when I slammed on the brakes, because I suddenly thought of something that was another kick in the stomach, and for a few seconds I just stood there, not knowing what the hell to do.

It was obvious that Roache must've latched onto me earlier in the evening, probably at Minton's and even if he hadn't recognised Artie when he'd tailed me to the hotel he must've seen us together when I'd taken him past the desk and out onto the street. That could only have meant one thing, of course; that he'd taken it for granted that while we were together Artie had told me the details of his survival, so as well as violating orders by going to New York I'd automatically become another threat that'd have to

be dealt with. Right then he was on his way to kill Artie, and as
I saw the situation my sudden re-casting as an additional problem
had to mean that there were other security people out there by
then, waiting for an opportunity to kill me, too, and because I'd
rushed from the room without thinking my pen–gun was still on
the bedside table where Artie had made me put it.

In fairness to myself, despite the fact that that meant I was
completely defenceless I did still try to shout a warning, but to my
eternal shame I was almost choking with fright by then and I could
barely raise a whisper. I kept on trying while I looked around, but
my throat stayed locked tight, even though the only other people I
could see were a man and a woman talking beside a parked car and
seemingly taking no interest in Artie who'd already passed them
on the other side of the street. Roache was still a fair way behind;
he looked to be just pacing him, not hurrying at all, obviously
not daring to make himself conspicuous just then, and because he
wasn't closing on him that persuaded me to do what I did.

Anyway, I turned around and rushed back to the hotel.
Mercifully, the night man had disappeared somewhere, so I ran
upstairs, grabbed the pen, slammed the door behind me like the
first time, and then raced back down and onto the street again.

It can't have taken more than a minute, maybe even less, but
it'd been long enough for the whole scene to have changed. The
man and woman and the car had gone, and there was still no sign
of anybody hanging around the hotel, waiting for me to come out
again. The only person I could see was Roache, stood motionless
at the nearest street junction about two hundred and fifty yards
away but still clearly visible in the concentrated lighting there,
looking down at something dark that was laying at his feet.

I don't expect you to understand this, Phyl, but in a way that
was an even worse moment than when I'd learned that Donna
was dead, because I knew what I was witnessing, and that it was
my cowardice that had let it happen. I didn't go any further, just
stood there feeling helpless and sick and utterly ashamed, and
then I heard a faint shout and saw that he was staring up in the
direction of Broadway. It was only a split second before he turned
and started to run back towards me, but he'd barely begun to move
when I heard a gunshot. He staggered, but he didn't fall, and he
was leaning on the railings there and fumbling in his coat pocket
when there were two more shots, and then he did go down, and

the way he hit the ground convinced me straight off that he was dead.

I'd only been outside the hotel for a matter of seconds, but in that time the whole thing was over. I just carried on standing there, totally numbed by it all, and then I saw a uniformed policeman appear and kneel beside Roache and immediately after that a patrol car drove around the corner and pulled up alongside them. That instinctively unfroze me, so I ducked into the shadows and watched what was happening from there.

Lights went on in a few windows and a handful of people appeared, but all the interest was concentrated up at the corner, so after a minute or so I went back into the hotel again. The night man was just coming back into the lobby from somewhere at the rear when I got there; it was obvious that he hadn't heard any of it, so I just said goodnight again and went up to my room. I locked the door and sat on the bed, covered in cold sweat and shaking like a leaf in a gale, half-expecting to hear sirens outside, a knock on the door and demands that I open up. I'd been there maybe five minutes when I did hear a siren, but it was obviously some distance away, and after about an hour I decided that I probably was in the clear, as far as the police were concerned, anyway.

I wondered what had happened to any back-up people who'd been with Roache. Even though I hadn't actually seen anybody who might have been one of them it was only logical to assume that they'd been there, because he'd had plenty of time to call in help and it would have made no sense for him to have tried to tackle the situation on his own, especially as there'd been two of us and he knew we were both armed. The most likely explanation seemed to be that they'd discreetly faded away when the police nailed him, but although he was out of the picture I decided that they wouldn't have gone far and were probably already back, covering the hotel and waiting for me to try and make a break for it, so it looked as though I was still in very deep trouble.

Right then, though, I was simply too shaken up and confused to think straight, try to assess the situation objectively. All I knew for sure was that I had to figure out a way of getting out of there without running into anybody who might be waiting for me, and then try to find somewhere safe where I could re-group and review my options before deciding what to do. I automatically thought about sneaking out through the service quarters, the way

I had the previous time, but I decided against it because the rear might have been covered, and in the dark anything could have happened. Travelling in the daylight would be dangerous in other ways but on balance a safer bet as I saw it, so I wedged a chair under the doorknob and tried to settle for what was left of the night.

I didn't actually get any sleep at all, just lay on the bed or paced around when I couldn't stand that any longer, still in shock and sick to my stomach over my part in what had happened to Artie. If I hadn't gone to New York the chances had to be that he'd have survived, but because I had and then unwittingly helped Roache find him I had to accept that the responsibility for his death was at least partly mine.

The thing that really obsessed me was the business of going back for the pen-gun, of course. I kept on fretting about what might have happened if I hadn't done that, even fantasised that maybe a cab would have come along and I could have passed Roache in it, snatched Artie off the street before he had a chance to get to him, utterly futile nonsense like that. I didn't really believe any of it, though, so I tried to persuade myself that the fact of my choking up and not being able to shout to him had made my retreat into the hotel the only practical option at the time, but I knew it was a lie, that I should have carried on running, made some kind of noise, warned him somehow. But I hadn't because self-preservation had become my first concern, despite there being no real evidence that I was at immediate risk. I'd chickened out, it was that simple, and because I had Artie was dead, and even if I somehow managed to survive in the long-term I knew that that was something else that was going to haunt me for the rest of my life.

Anyway, I eventually decided what I was going to do, and around seven-thirty I went down and settled my bill and asked the guy to arrange for a cab for me at eight and let me know when it was there. I went back to the room and kept an eye on the street while I waited, and by the time I got the call there was plenty of traffic out there. I hurried downstairs and straight into the cab, taking my case with me, told the driver I needed it with me to check some stuff, and gave him an address in Melrose.

I kept looking behind as we headed uptown, but the roads were so busy I had no idea whether we were being tailed or not. After we'd been going for a while I told him I'd changed my plans, to drop me off at the next elevated station and then take off again straight away. I told him it was worth an extra five if he'd do that, and he just nodded and told me the fare and reached back for the money, and after we'd reached the end of the block that was what happened. There was a downtown train coming in as I got up on the platform, and I rode it through the next couple of stations, then got off and took another cab to Penn Station, caught a train to Philly and then switched to a bus that was going down to Cape Charles. All the way there I kept looking out for anybody who might have been following me, but there was no sign of anything like that, so eventually I decided that I really had slipped them, that all the toing and froing had worked and that for a while at least I could breathe a little easier again.

I've been down to the cape a few times since Donna died, when I wanted a complete break; I have some friends living locally, a writer and his lady, but needless to say this was before either of them were even born and the place they live in hadn't been built yet. I booked into a rooming-house; the people seemed pleasant enough, not too curious, and apart from them I had the place completely to myself.

The area wasn't really all that different to the way it is now, and finding it like that came as a blessed relief. The weather was reasonable for the time of year, and the day after I arrived I went for a long walk to try and clear my head sufficiently for me to consider the situation in a rational way, the dangers and responsibilities I'd suddenly found myself stuck with and what if anything I could do about them.

The obvious priority was survival, of course. It looked as though I'd managed to lose anybody who might have been following me, so at least that meant that I had time to weigh my options, and it didn't take me long to realise that fundamentally there were only two, both of them terrifying.

If I stayed on that side of the hole, the poison would get me, because I simply couldn't see any way of emulating what had happened at the time of Artie's accident without putting myself in a situation where there'd be an enormous risk of ending up dead anyway. The alternative, which was only marginally less horrendous, was to try and get back to base without being snagged by security on the way there—and that didn't seem very likely in itself—but if I did actually make it then I'd have to bank on my arrival being seen by a friendly face, so that even if I was grabbed immediately and hustled away, maybe even prevented from getting back through the hole, there'd at least be a chance that the word would get around about it, the way it had when they'd placed John Forrestal in quarantine.

If that didn't happen, though, and they managed to keep it all under wraps, I couldn't seriously picture a very prolonged personal future. As I saw it, it was inevitable that whoever had been Hurran's back-up when he'd killed Artie would already have turned in a report that would convince the programme controllers that I'd become a dangerous liability who could bring the whole business crashing down around their ears if I wasn't permanently put out of the way before I got the chance.

They couldn't be absolutely sure that I knew about the poison thing, but it would be only logical for them to assume that I at least suspected the truth as a result of my get-together with Artie, either because Artie had already got it figured, or because we might have worked it out between us then. If I hadn't actually been seen outside the hotel when I chased after him, they couldn't be certain that I knew about his murder, either, but I reluctantly decided that my hasty departure and disappearance next morning must surely have convinced them that I did, and there would be no way that they'd be prepared to give me the opportunity to tell anyone about it.

The only way of guaranteeing my permanent silence would be to kill me, of course, and they'd already demonstrated just how far they were ready to go if they felt it was justified. They obviously couldn't rely on my word to keep quiet, even if I was prepared to swear it on a stack of bibles a mile high that I would. My only chance in that situation would be to stall for as long as possible, admit that I'd been stepping out of line long before I went to New York that last time—omitting anything about either the poison or Artie's murder, of course—and then stretch out an account of all my rule-breaking for as long as they'd let me before they strapped me to a lie-detector or injected me with whatever it is they use so that they could check whether or not I'd been telling them the whole story.

I fantasised about how I might wriggle out of it, of course. Trying to 'phone Walden was out of the question; even if I'd known what to say to him, all calls were monitored by security, so I'd simply have been put on hold while they got a fix on me. The only glimmer of hope was my idea that I might be seen by a colleague when I arrived, a possibility that'd be dependent on coincidence to a totally unrealistic degree, but it was all I could come up with. In any case, as I saw it they needed me dead because of the scale of threat I posed, so whatever happened they'd still get rid of me somehow, regardless of any suspicions it might stir up. The poison angle meant I had no acceptable option, anyway; I had to go back and take my chances, and if I actually did manage to get there without being caught en route I'd just have to hope that a last minute miracle saved me, although for the life of me—an apt turn of phrase if ever there was one—I couldn't picture what form it could possibly take.

I kept as active as I could during the next few days; did a lot of walking despite the by then indifferent weather, but it didn't matter how many miles I covered, I couldn't get away from the God-awful oppressive feeling that time really was running out for me and the knowledge that all the distance in the world couldn't prevent that. Once or twice I tried to concentrate on the things that Artie and I'd talked about, but each time I'd barely gotten started when I instinctively shied away again, because the memory of what'd happened to him took over and tormented me for the rest of the day.

Despite spending so much time in the open while I was there I still felt that I was inside a cage that was shrinking with every passing second, and in a bleak kind of way it was almost a relief when I eventually took the bus back to Philly, the whole while wondering what I'd find waiting for me if my luck held long enough for me to at least reach base and report in.

40.
—

The man behind the desk said, "So you think he's in the clear. How sure are you really?"

Urich shrugged. "If you're asking for a cast-iron guarantee, of course I can't give you one. All I can say is that it definitely looks that way, given what we've got. We know that he got himself a lady-friend of sorts, but Ashby says there was nothing at all to suggest it was anything more than just a friendly relationship. The how and why of it's a mystery, of course, but we've got no reason to believe that it added up to anything significant. The rest of the time he stayed solo, including his evening rounds, and he went straight back to his hotel when he was through."

The man behind the desk ruminated, briefly. "If that's all that happened, I guess we can just forget it." He fiddled with the report in front of him. "I can't help wondering if three days was long enough, though. Wouldn't it have been better to have covered him at least the whole of the first week, just to be sure?"

Urich held back his impatience. "If Mastin was going to show in K.C. at all, the odds have to be that it would've happened during the first couple of days. He knew when Lohmann was due, and it's my guess that he'd have been there already, if he intended to get together with him at all. You know what I think about that, though."

"But you could be wrong."

Urich smiled, humourlessly. "There's always that possibility, but given the circumstances it's highly unlikely. The fact is that Lohmann was never more than a long-shot, anyway. If it really was Mastin that Forrestal saw, and he suspected that he'd been recognised, he'd be very conscious of how much at risk he was, the fact that he couldn't really trust anybody else on the programme. There were always going to be a few people who might've let the situation seduce them into jettisoning all sense of responsibility and make a run for it if they'd thought there was a realistic chance of getting away with it, of course; not too many, though, I'd guess, and he couldn't even be certain that Lohmann wouldn't have turned on him if he wouldn't listen to reason. Although he'd be itching to let him know he'd survived—and how, if he knew how, naturally—I think he'd stay under cover until the hole closed down. Friendship could turn out to be a very fragile thing in a situation where the issues are as big as this, and he was certainly smart enough to realise that."

"So you'll keep on trying to dig him out, if he's there."

Urich said, "Now that Forrestal's dithering, that's taken the heat off the local situation, but we still have to accept that he just might have been right. It's hard to figure out how Mastin could be alive, but if he did make it past the effect of his injection somehow there's no particular reason why he shouldn't be, so we have to keep on looking, and the more people there are on it the better our chances of finding him. Always assuming that he actually is alive, of course. If he is, he could be anywhere, I realise that, but my hunch is that he'd be reluctant to leave his natural habitat altogether, which is why everybody I can spare's in New York now. It might well turn out to be a total waste of time and resources, but we have to at least try." His expression soured. "I just hope it doesn't cost us anybody else, that's all."

The man behind the desk nodded, sombrely. "Roache, yes. That's not looking good, I must admit." He frowned. "Is it possible that his shot took effect prematurely, something like that? After all, he hadn't been out for quite a while. Maybe his system just couldn't take it."

"Not according to the lab. They tell me that they're sure they've got that side of it figured by now."

The man behind the desk demurred, cautiously. "I wish I shared their faith, but poison is still poison. If we had a total understanding of human chemistry and what happens when we tamper with it this way I might be prepared to go along with them, but we've still got a long way to go there. It's too bad we've had to use it on your people at all, of course, but they're only human. At least none of them have made a personal issue of it, started sounding off about their integrity."

"That's because they're trained to be realists. They know we can't afford to take any chances, even with them."

After a pause, the man behind the desk said, "How Mastin could possibly have beaten it's still the big question, of course. Is it remotely possible that he could've wised up somehow, got hold of some of the antidote and used it before he left, after he'd been given his jab?"

Urich shook his head. "I see no reason why he should've figured it out, or how he could have, and we've already chased the lab up on the antidote. There's no way he could've helped himself without leaving traces, and the stock checks out, anyway. None of it's been diluted or tampered with, they're absolutely certain about that."

Following another pause, the man behind the desk said, "You know, I'm still not sure we handled that right, as far as the field operatives were concerned, I mean. If we'd been open about it, told them what we were doing and why, emphasised the absolute necessity for a watertight safeguard against any of them deciding to take off, I think that there was a good chance that they'd have gone along with us, been prepared to accept the risk. We might never have lost Bethal and Glass if they'd fully appreciated the importance of sticking to the regulations, that cutting it fine really could be a life and death thing because we'd been forced to make it that."

Urich shook his head again, dismissively. "No way. For one thing, if they'd known that long-term survival actually might've been possible, how could we have guaranteed that they'd always have kept their mouths shut about it? In any case, most people will only stick their necks out just so far to get what they want, even when they want it pretty badly, and believing that you're voluntarily risking your life on a regular basis is a lot to handle under any circumstances. Don't forget how nervous most of them got when we told them the blood component story, what it could mean if they didn't follow official procedure to the letter and get back here in time. Coming clean would've been a non-starter psychologically anyway. Being injected with so-called protective medication's one thing, but poison is something else entirely. If they'd known what we were actually going to pump into them, most of them would've backed off the minute they were told, which would've been awkward, to say the least. We'd never have gotten this thing started at all if they'd known what they were really going to be taking on board."

The man behind the desk grimaced. "You're probably right. There'd be no point in debating it, anyway, not now. That takes us back to the subject of Roache again, I guess. I still can't help wondering if he found Mastin and got beaten to the punch somehow. But you don't buy that either, do you?

Urich shrugged. "Not really, no. It's possible, but I can't picture it. As far as I'm concerned the most likely explanation is that he ran into something he couldn't handle with some of the locals. Harlem always was a tough patch, and they've never cared too much for strangers who come around asking questions."

The man behind the desk nodded, slowly. "You could be right. If you are, that's been a hell of a waste." He chewed his lip. "Still, it looks as though we're going to come out of this not all that badly overall. We're not in a position to close the books just yet, of course, but four out of two hundred and eight over a thirteen month period is a pretty respectable close-out figure, all things considered. Let's hope it stays at that." He paused." It really does look as though we'd be wasting our time bringing Lohmann in for questioning, so just let that one lay. There's nothing to be gained by letting him know that we've had someone on his back."

Urich agreed. The man behind the desk said, "You'd better leave your people out there as long as possible, just in case. Maybe Forrestal was just seeing things, but if he wasn't and Mastin's still around we have to assume that he poses a risk, I suppose. Whatever, we'll have done as much as we can, and after that history's simply going to have to take care of itself. Let's hope it's able to do that." He tapped his fingers on the desk top, restlessly. "You know, we might be sweating over nothing at all. Even if he is there and we don't find him, whatever he gets up to might turn out to be no more than a drop in the ocean. After all, we don't really know how long it's possible to survive there, and he'd be a stranger in a strange land, anyway. Just about anything could happen to him there, maybe something along the lines of what you think might've happened to Roache."

Urich rose. "If he is there and we don't find him, I sincerely hope you're right."

41.

—

By the time I was only an hour or so away from base I started to wonder if I really was going to make it after all. I had no sure way of knowing whether or not I'd been spotted and was being tailed, of course. For all I knew somebody from security could have been sat in the next seat, but as far as I could tell nobody had even taken the slightest interest in me, on the bus or the train. I decided that even if I was in the clear up until then they'd still be bound to have the Leyland station covered, so I got off at a place about fifteen miles down the line and took a cab the rest of the way. Even after that precaution, by the time we got there I was pretty close to sheer panic, but I took a few deep breaths and said one last prayer and announced myself while I was still capable of it.

Nothing remotely unusual happened while I was being checked in, and that only made me more nervous in a way. On the surface at least, everything seemed normal; nobody hanging around who looked as though they might have me in their sights—no familiar friendly faces, either, which didn't help—no-one new in medical, and they really did seem genuinely concerned about my shakiness and agitated breathing.

I wondered if we'd all been steered into that situation, with them the unwitting executioners, but either way I was convinced by then that my last idea on how it might be handled was almost definitely right, and that that really was it as far as I was concerned. Whether they were in on it or not I was sure that they'd simply ignore my apparent ravings and force me to take the usual shot, but even if they didn't I'd die eventually. It was a total nightmare, but of course I had no real choice. Anyway, I let them go ahead, scared out of my mind and instinctively fighting the effect, but before I knew it I was awake again and feeling fine, physically at any rate.

My first reaction was unadulterated relief, of course, but I was totally confused when I left there and reported to psych, still expecting security to appear and drag me off, but nothing like that happened. What was even more extraordinary was that I detected nothing remotely threatening during the interview, no blip of any kind. It was all utterly baffling, but I acted my way through it as best I could, and then went to the section office, wondering what the hell was going on this time, just what kind of game they were playing with me.

The first thing that Walden told me when I saw him was that just after I'd left on my last trip Forrestal had reappeared, admitting that he could have been mistaken about seeing Artie. There'd been a strong similarity, he'd said, but there'd been differences, too, and eventually he'd decided that he must have been wrong. After the initial unrest most of the staff had already come around to the same conclusion anyway, Walden said, so there'd been no point in security hanging onto him. They must have breathed a big sigh of relief at his turnaround and things had pretty much quietened down again, but they'd kept a very low profile since then, he said, presumably because they were still embarrassed by their over-the-top reaction to Forrestal's claim.

I wondered if Forrestal's change of tune and the general concensus had been reached voluntarily or cultivated by security the way I'd speculated before I went back, but whichever it was it'd obviously done the trick on all counts. Either way, it still didn't explain their apparent total lack of interest in me, and of course there was no way that I'd have dared tell Walden the truth after my own part in what had happened. Anyway, I decided I had to get out of there for a while, give myself more time to get my head straight, so I told him I was feeling really tired and needed to rest, and he said we could do the de-brief the next morning.

So I went to my room and flopped onto the bed, still finding it hard to believe the way things had gone. Taken at face value, it was almost as though none of it had happened at all; that it had all been some kind of terrible dream that my subconscious had dredged up and somehow convinced me that it was real.

But it hadn't been, of course, because Forrestal had been right. Artie had been alive, but now he was dead, largely due to me and my rule-breaking, and even if Roache hadn't died at the time as well he'd been caught committing murder, so he'd be finished too, especially after they found his pen-gun and phoney ID and any other equipment he might have been carrying.

What I simply couldn't understand was how it was that security didn't seem to know about any of it, because although it was still hard to believe I was halfway convinced by then that they didn't. I threw that one around for a long time, and eventually I decided that there was only one truly plausible explanation, bizarre as it was; that for some reason I'm never going to know the answer to Roache hadn't notified anybody else that he'd found us! It *had* to have been that, because if he'd called in support they'd have swarmed in from all directions and even if the police had picked up one or two of them because they'd decided they were acting suspiciously and then held them because they hadn't been able to explain away their own bits and pieces, it was highly unlikely that they'd have grabbed all of them.

After all, there'd been no indication at all that I'd been followed the next morning, and now this, no sign whatsoever that I was under any kind of suspicion. Anyway, whatever the reason it really did look as though I was in the clear, and when the full implications of that suddenly hit me it knocked me completely sideways, because without the poison in my system I knew that I could survive on the other side, and of course that had already been neutralised.

The first thing I felt was pure elation, but it didn't stay pure for long because almost immediately I remembered Artie again, so a lot of guilt and remorse very quickly got mixed in with it. In effect I was being offered what he'd accidentally been given before I turned up and provoked the situation that had led to his death, but even though I knew that what had happened that night would harass my conscience for as long as I live, the truth is that as soon as I realised what had become possible there was never a second's doubt in my mind about what I was going to do.

Quite simply I decided that I had to figure out a way of getting back through the hole and then pray that security kept their distance until it closed, because despite my mixed feelings it was still what I'd been desperately longing for ever since joining the programme. Some of the things that had already happened to me meant that I wasn't blind to the negative side of what I'd be committing myself to, either. It would be bound to involve a whole raft of complications and dangers that I'd never be truly free of, but if it worked out it'd mean the realisation of my original dream, and I was fully prepared to take whatever risks were necessary to try and achieve that.

There's very little for me here now anyway, and I have no serious responsibilities that I'd be ducking. Since Donna died I've become more and more reclusive, and the truth is that for most of my life I've felt out of step with the world I was born into. I'm hardly alone in that, I know; there are millions of people who desperately wish that they could get back to an earlier time when life was less complicated and hope was still alive, although as I know from personal experience the reality isn't as straightforward as most of them fantasise that it would be. Even so, I've been granted the chance to have that particular dream come true, and I'm going to take it, because it's the rest of my life I'm talking about, and it would be just plain madness to let guilt over something that can't be put right anyway deprive me of it.

Thinking about the risk factor, I realised that I'd already laid the foundations of a solution to the financial aspect when I'd approached Williams with the diamonds; it had been established inadvertently, but it was there, and I still can't see any reason why I shouldn't be able to make use of it again. I won't be faced with the problem of unloading unmounted stones this time, because there's nothing to stop me from taking complete items now, but I'm still a bit uneasy about the idea of trying to sell stuff in the open market, at least until I'm established somewhere. After all, I'll be a non-resident initially, and anyone legitimate is likely to treat me with caution, so selling through Williams has to be the safer option.

There'll be the question of identity documents as well, and I guess he might be able to help me there, too. I don't like the idea of involving him in something like that, but I think it's what I'll have to do; admit that I'm on the wrong side of the fence and in a situation where I need false papers. He already suspects me of something shady, but he's demonstrated that he'd be prepared to help out when things aren't exactly legal, so I guess the chances have to be at least reasonable that he'll do it again. I'll have to have some kind of story ready, I suppose, just in case he wants to know how serious a fix I'm in. As long as I don't confess to being guilty of something like a capital offence I think it'll be O.K., although his image of me is certainly going to take another beating. I really do wish I could tell him the truth, but I still don't see how that's ever going to be possible, and that's a shame.

As far as the break itself is concerned, a couple of things very quickly became obvious. The first was that there's only going to be one logical time to do it, and that's as near to the time when the hole's due to close as possible. The second was that there's no way that I'll be able to make a move as long as the building's occupied, which automatically means that it'll have to be a virtually last-minute thing, when everybody on both sides has been pulled out and there's no-one actually left in either set of premises.

The whole of that end of the estate is going to be empty, I already know that much; there'll be a phoney report of a gas leak issued early tomorrow morning, and after it's been evacuated the street will be sealed off, with a special services fire unit standing by. Most of our personnel are already out of there, and even if they still have people on either side looking for Artie and Roache they'll be bound to withdraw them in plenty of time, too, although they'll probably leave somebody in the building for a while. They have no idea at all how the fire's going to start, of course; nothing was said in the papers about an explosion, but it's accepted that the closure might involve something like that, so I'm sure the place'll be empty when I make my run.

What actually happens is going to be watched and recorded, and I felt a bit squeamish about that at first, the fact that I'll be on record, sneaking away like a thief in the night, but I'm reconciled to it now. It'd be ridiculous to claim that self-preservation's a secondary issue as far as I'm concerned, of course, although in a sense that's true, because even if the future here looked to be bright I'd still have gone back given the opportunity, so I see no need to feel guilty about it, not really.

Anyway, something else I had to consider was the question of having enough contemporary money to get me to K.C. and tide me over until I can organise the disposal of at least some of the jewellery I'll be taking. I did actually become a thief at that point, I'm afraid, but I obviously had no choice, so I took what I figured I'd need from what was left of the money I'd taken with me and stashed it in the pocket of a spare shirt, solving that problem at least. It still left me with the big one, of course, how to get back into the building once it had been emptied, because although I started out by wondering if it'd be possible to find a hiding-place and simply stay behind when everyone else left I soon dropped the idea, because everybody's going to be checked out, and if I was still unaccounted for they'd just dig around until they found me. Getting back in after I'd officially left and after the place had been cleared meant that the time element was bound to be very tight, but I decided that despite the risks the tighter it was the better, because at least it would act as a deterrent to anybody who might be tempted to come after me.

Walden wasn't particularly happy with the report I turned in, but for the time being he still believed that we'd briefly unearthed a totally unsung pioneer, a previously undreamed of link in the chain; he actually told me that even though my last trip had been something of a bust he still felt that what I'd been doing in K.C. had turned out to be a genuinely invaluable exercise. I did feel a small, pointless flicker of conscience just then; he's been very supportive, but the lies have all been justified by events, maybe even inevitable, and I don't mean from just my own point of view.

During the day I made excuses to visit every part of the building; the basement, upstairs, everywhere, and I drew a total blank. The place was fitted out to be sealed up as tight as a bank vault; all the windows and skylights had steel shutters fitted behind them, the ventilation openings were far too small, and the rear and side doors were fitted with alarms and locks you couldn't have dented without using gelignite. I even considered the sewage tunnel, but the inspection panel's fastened with bolts and padlocks and a security check would have been bound to spot something so obvious if I'd somehow managed to leave them in an open position.

I began to panic a little as I ran out of possibilities; I even wondered if it might be necessary as a last resort to get hold of some kind of heavy vehicle, drive it through the street barrier and literally smash my way into the place. The limitations and dangers of something as wild as that were so obvious, though, I didn't stick with the idea for long, and it was only when I went outside to get some air and try to clear my head that I totally unexpectedly found what I was looking for.

During the past few years a more conveniently sited industrial estate's gradually developed on the other side of Leyland, and because of that the Bush Hill estate never actually extended beyond the point where what used to be the Weatherby and Stolz's place is located, which means that it's still at the far end where the road terminates. There's a single-strand wire fence there, and on the other side it's open country that gradually slopes down into the river valley that leads into Leyland. What I hadn't noticed before is that there's a ditch on the far side of the fence, running parallel with it; most of it's almost hidden by long grass that's grown in and around it, but I could see through a couple of gaps and there's no water in there.

As soon as I saw it, everything just seemed to slot straight into place. The local weather's set fair for the next few days, so staying dry won't be a problem, and nobody's going to see me arrive there because while it's still dark I'll approach it up the slope, stay down until everybody's out of the place and back behind the barrier, and then make a run for it. I'll be hidden by the building when I start out, and when I hit the open it's only fifteen or twenty yards to the front entrance; I'm no sprinter, but I can cover that in around five or six seconds—I know that, because I've already timed myself over that distance—and even if I'm spotted I'll be inside before they can get near me.

It might be necessary to shoot out the door locks, although I doubt it. Even though the sprinkler system'll be triggered as soon as the fire starts the fire crew will want immediate access, so it's only logical that it'll be left open. I'm taking a gun, though, just in case, a .38 revolver that I've owned ever since Donna and I were burgled that time; I suppose there's always the chance that someone'll come through the hole after me, too, although I don't imagine it's very likely, not that close to closure time. God forbid that I should even have to threaten anybody with it, but I do at least have to be prepared for a situation of that kind.

And that's it. You probably see it as almost too simple, but that's its virtue, because the fewer things there are to go wrong the better, and I really do believe absolutely that it's going to work. I'm sure you're instinctively labelling that as nothing more than recklessly naïve over-optomism, but I don't accept that at all, and it's not just because I don't want to, either. It might even be confirmation of the predestiny idea, I suppose, although I have to say that since Artie and I threw that one around I've carried very strong doubts regarding such a possibility. Even so, I still can't be certain, because whatever it implies I have this really firm conviction that nothing's going to happen now that'll prevent me from getting back there.

Anyway, I spent the rest of the afternoon tidying up the immediate things I had to do, and then I looked in on Walden and asked him if he'd have any objections to me taking a couple of days off. I was sorry to leave it so close to the end of the programme, I said, but I really was completely bushed and felt that I'd be able to handle my part of the final wind-down with a much clearer head if I had a short break first.

He didn't argue, which wasn't all that surprising, because apart from the time I took off after my first outing when I'd fretted more than I'd relaxed, my visit to Aunt Clara and my jewellery-buying trip, I hadn't used any of my leave allocation at all, simply hung around at base between trips. He actually thought it was a good idea; he'd suspected for a while that my virtually non-stop involvement must have been creating some extra tension, he said, and he agreed that a couple of days off would be bound to be beneficial, help me focus better on what there was left to do. It was another occasion for guilt, I suppose, but I was so completely wrapped up in what I was planning that my conscience never even stirred that time, and bearing in mind that the catalogue of lies I'd been feeding him ever since the lodge session it was far too late for that kind of nicety anyway.

Next morning I came straight down to Philly and checked out the local jewellers, and spent virtually everything I had in my accounts on an assortment of rings, bracelets and whatever, all of them quite old and the kind of not too expensive items it should be possible to trickle into the market without creating problems for myself. Even though I'll probably lose out a little dealing with Williams again—I obviously can't expect him to be as generous as he was the first time—I don't imagine it'll be by much, and all in all I should have enough to see me through the first year as long as I watch my spending.

I'm going to have to make a living eventually, though, and the best way I can think of is to try and work my way into the record business, and if you see that as just another pipe-dream it isn't as crazy as it might sound. A whole crop of shoestring independent labels sprang up towards the end of the recording ban, and I know that there'll be a market for the stuff that I'll be catching, even if it's only a small one at first.

It means I'll have to get hold of some contemporary equipment, of course. Tape is still a few years in the future, and although there are a few wire recorders around actually getting hold of one could be difficult. I might have to settle for a disc-cutter, I'm afraid; the sound quality's adequate, but they're bulky things, and I could have wept when I handed in my 'camera', but even if I'd managed to hang onto it somehow I'd have had playback and transfer problems. It also means that I'll be forced to operate openly now, of course, but at least that'll help to authenticate my researcher role. I won't be the first of the amateur recording engineers to appear on that scene, but I'll still be one of the early birds; even so, there are enormous gaps to be filled, so I'll still only be able to scratch the surface, working on my own. It should be enough to give me a start, though, and with any luck it'll build from there.

As far as the piano-playing's concerned, I haven't made up my mind about that yet. I had strong personal reasons for doing it on the two occasions that it happened and for playing the way I did, but that no longer applies and I don't really feel I have any justification now to carry on doing the same kind of thing, deliberately exerting that kind of influence when it's no longer necessary. Maybe I'll just be more circumspect about it, make sure I only keep in step with the natural evolutionary process instead of running ahead of it. I really don't know, though; it's a tricky issue, and I'm going to have to think about it very carefully before I decide.

Of course, things that I've done so far have already re-shaped events beyond my own situation, particularly as far as Henry's concerned. As long as he doesn't fall prey to some other disaster there has to be at least a possibility that his contribution'll nudge the music onto a subtly different track now, and even Foster's change of direction could be a part of something like that; I can't really picture him having any kind of major effect, but he's so fired up right now by what he's learning I guess I shouldn't rule it out entirely. I was speculating a while back about whether what's happened to the two of them as a result of me becoming involved in their lives was going to be my bequest to this new future, and

I suppose it could actually reach that far when I really think about it, so that what I'll be hearing and recording is going to be quite different from what I've been anticipating, not the virtual re-run I've assumed it would be at all.

On the subject of re-runs, you may find this particularly hard to believe, but something that only hit me a day or so ago is the question of whether or not another version of me's ever going to appear in that other future. For various reasons it doesn't seem very likely, but I suppose I must have at least considered it before, even if it was only subconsciously; I certainly don't remember doing it, anyway. In any case, now that I had given it some thought I find it a disturbing idea in several ways, and one of the major ones is that it raises the possibility of Donna and I doing a repeat performance of our destructive time together.

Somehow, though, I can't really picture that, and I guess the principal reason is that I'm going to be there well before then, and events are obviously going to be amended all the time, anyway. Maybe my family line is going to be broken or steered in another direction entirely, and I don't appear at all. A great deal's going to happen to that in the next fifty or so years, and in any case it's possible that someone on the programme's already done something that will rearrange that particular piece of history; I could very easily have done it myself, in some way that I simply haven't recognised.

If that really is the way of things, it could mean that Donna's going to be all right after all, maybe even live the long, full life we all want for ourselves. I can't tell you how much I hope that that's so, Phyl; there could never be any actual guarantee, of course, but at least the chance would be there, and that's the most any of us can reasonably ask for. I'd like to think that it'd work that way for Thelma, too, but to be honest I can't persuade myself to get very optimistic about that. The fact that I prolonged Henry's life might have been purely inadvertent, and in any case the circumstances of that were entirely different, so it'd need some kind of freakish outside chance that had nothing to do with me to help her survive. I guess such a thing is possible, although it doesn't seem very likely; even so, it is a different world, and somebody there might come up with a medical development that could save her. It might even be another instance where one of our own people's been influential, deliberately or accidentally helped to steer current research in a direction that might do it; another day-dream, I know, but one's just come true, so why shouldn't that one, too? And as far as her private life's concerned, who knows? Maybe the existence of the baby means that however much time she has left it's going to be very different in this other version of events. Even if she still meets the preaching railroad man called Fry and he wants to marry her, he might not be prepared to take on an illegitimate child as part of the package; a pretty un–Christian reason if that was to be so, of course, but general social attitudes were still pretty uptight back then. Whatever, the implications of things working out that way as they relate to your own family line are disconcerting to say the least, but that's something else I really don't have time to get into now.

I don't think there's much more I can tell you, not of immediate importance, anyway; if I had the time I could go on speculating indefinitely, of course, but most of it would just be aimless rambling. In any case, I'm going to be glad to give my voice a rest; apart from occasional breathers and taking time out to eat I've been talking for around eight hours now, but that's something you already know, because it's taken you as long to hear me out, always assuming that you've had the patience to stay with me this far.

What you do with all of this is your business, of course, and I admit that strictly speaking I'm abrogating my responsibility there, but that's the way it has to be—again, I could be meaning that quite literally, I guess—and like I said at the beginning, I don't know what should be done, anyway. Maybe everyone should be told, maybe not. If what's happened truly has been unique, a once-only thing that won't ever happen again, then I suppose no constructive purpose would be served by telling anyone else at all, whether what I believe about it's true or not.

I don't have time to rationalise it all sufficiently to make a decision of my own, anyway, which is why I'm passing it on to you; the address and 'phone number and names of the people in charge of the programme are with the accompanying documents, by the way. I guess that in fact I'm paying you a compliment here, because despite our differences I've always respected your level-headedness, and that's what's wanted in this situation. Predestined or not, my own actions confirm what a hopeless romantic I am in some ways, and I have to admit that a very large part of my life has been directed by emotional instinct rather than reason, all too often inadvisedly.

Apart from my vocal chords I can't really say I'm tired; too keyed-up, I guess, but I daren't risk driving up to Leyland without at least trying to sleep for a few hours. I'll have to allow myself some leeway, but as long as I'm there an hour or so before dawn I'll have plenty of time to position myself without any serious risk of being seen. I'm not really worried about any of that, though, because I know that when the time comes I'm going to make it through the hole.

Like I say, I don't know why I'm as sure of that as I am; it's as much a mystery as the rest of it, but I *am* sure somehow. I can't truthfully claim any kind of precognition beyond that, though; that's a complete blank, but there's no reason why I should know what's going to happen, anyway. Maybe in the event it's going to turn out very differently to what I've sketched out for myself, not remotely like it, even; life often works that way, after all. Whichever way it takes me, though, I'll have hope, and that's what really sustains us, even when things look as if they've reached a point where it's become irrelevant, the way it does here, tragically.

There is one other thing I have to mention before I finish. Because of some of what's happened recently I made a new will a few weeks ago, but now that I'm still going to be alive in the strictly technical sense I've instructed my legal people to replace it with a deed of transfer that covers the same ground, to take effect from the first of next month; you may have already seen the copy that's with the rest of the papers. Just in case you haven't read it yet, apart from the stuff connected with my work everything that's left will be split equally between you and Clara; I hope that doesn't come as too big a shock on top of everything else, but you're the nearest I have to family now, and I'm just happier doing it this way. The savings don't amount to much now, but the apartment and contents should realise a reasonable amount. What you do with the proceeds is your business, of course; it wouldn't surprise me at all if you feel that I'm trying to buy my way into your good books and decide not to keep any of it, but whether you do or not's of no real importance now. I shan't have any use of it myself, anyway, because by the time you get this it'll all be over and I'll be sealed away in my new world, separated from all of this by a barrier that probably won't ever be breached again.

I'd still like to believe that in one sense at least I'm way off track, and that this edition of us and our environment isn't really fated for the kind of ending that looks to be increasingly inevitable now. Unless Artie and I were right about us unknowingly laying the groundwork for salvation in this other past I just can't convince myself that our presence there, or anything I do after I go back, either, is going to affect the course of events in any significantly remedial way, because I simply don't believe that humankind has the collective will to commit itself to the kind of restrictions that'd be necessary to avoid a repeat of what's happening here. I could be wrong about that, of course, and I hope to God I am, but it's hard to picture; after all, the need for drastic change here's been glaringly obvious for the best part of a century and we've still largely ducked around the issue, so why should it be any different in that other future?

Of course, looking at it in a strictly objective way, if in fact we're involved in a multiverse situation that kind of gloomy prognosis would be totally irrelevant. It's such a mind-numbing concept, though, I have to admit to hoping that where I'm going's simply a single duplicate, although I suppose that could be an appallingly selfish way of seeing the situation. The truth is I can just about handle the thought of one extra edition of us, but the multiverse business absolutely throws me. I've never personally had any desire to have life handed me on a plate, but presumably that's what it'd mean whenever a particular formula shaped things that way. I'm sure there are plenty of people who'd relish the prospect of a world tailored to their own specification, although come the reality I think most of them would soon find life without any sense of surprise or achievement a disappointingly empty experience. Exactly where good and evil and kindness and cruelty would fit into a process where every conceivable permutation's possible brings in some worryingly complex issues, too, and I can't say that I'm at all keen to pursue them.

That's something else I mustn't get started on; besides, the whole thing's still only theoretical, for the present anyway. Maybe it'll be confirmed one day, but as things stand I'm more than happy to settle for a version of events that's going to provide me with what'll at least be a partial realisation of my own dream.

For obvious reasons it's a much darker one now than it was at the start of all this, but despite its tragic aspect I guess I still have to count myself lucky that this much has worked out for me the way it has.

I'm not blind to the special problems I'll always have to contend with, either, and in other respects as well I don't have any illusions about what I'm getting myself into. It's still a world with countless flaws, not least the fact that it's engaged in a war that's going to cost untold suffering and millions of lives before it ends, and as far as the personal issues are concerned I've already accepted they they're permanent parts of my life wherever I am. Although Donna's ghost seems to have retreated to the sidelines now, Artie's never will, because there's no way that I'll ever be able to compensate for my part in what happened to him. But at least I'll be facing an open future—at least, I guess I will—and experiencing consolations that simply don't exist here, and knowing him like I did I really don't think he'd have begrudged me that kind of mitigation.

I hope that's true, anyway. I probably don't deserve forgiveness for that and the other lamentable things I've done, because even though I was able to make some kind of positive contribution to Thelma's situation I realise that it's more than likely that she'd never have gotten into it in the first place if it hadn't been for me. That's something else I'm never going to know, though, and maybe it's just as well. In any case, what's done is done, and I only hope the consequences don't cause too many problems for any of the people concerned.

And that's it, I guess. I can't help suspecting that in some ways at least you see me now in an even worse light than before, and I've probably got it coming, but I still hope you respect my honesty, despite the fact that I'm offering it to you from a position where I'll be safely distanced from any recriminations you may want to confront me with.

So long, Phyl, good luck, and whatever your feelings towards me are I hope you can at least bring yourself to wish me the same.

——

42

It was a bright morning, with traces of mist lingering in the still-cold air. The guard was revolving slowly, beating his arms around his body and momentarily facing away from the blocked-off end of the estate when he heard the fireman's startled query.

He spun around, and stared across the barrier to the far end of the road. He saw the man immediately, an angular figure, close to the front wall of the final building there, sprinting clumsily towards the entrance, his progress plainly hampered by the holdall that jolted at his side. Before he could react, the man reached the entrance, dropped the holdall, and began fumbling with the door. Something glinted in his hand.

The guard swore, vaulted the barrier, and raced towards him, unholstering his gun as he ran. He'd only covered a few yards when the figure snatched up the holdall and disappeared into the building.

The guard picked up speed. Behind him, he heard other running footsteps, shouts, the sound of a revving engine. He reached the building, and swerved inside. The vestibule and the corridor beyond it were empty. Half-way down the corridor, a door was slowly being closed by its unseen safety hinge.

He threw himself down the corridor, and shouldered his way into the room beyond. Some way to his right a wide, heavy-looking door gaped open, revealing another corridor, this one an apparent cul-de-sac, illuminated by a lifeless fluorescent glare and with no doors or windows punctuating its white–painted walls.

The man was there, more than half-way down, his flight seemingly blocked by the featureless wall at its end. As the guard entered, he glanced back over his shoulder, then stumbled, simultaneously swivelling towards him. The guard saw his pale, panicky face staring at him with terrified eyes as he backed away, hunched and visibly shaking. There was a revolver in his right hand, wavering uncertainly in his general direction.

The guard said, breathlessly, "Take it easy, and hold it right there." He continued to move forward, slowly now, his own gun aimed rigidly at the retreating figure.

The gun in the man's hand fired, the bullet ricocheting wildly from the wall beside the guard and thudding into the door-frame behind him, the sudden welter of noise deafening in the enclosed space. He flinched, instinctively dropping into a crouch and jerking his head away, at the same time squeezing the trigger of his own weapon.

In the second or so that his eyes were averted, the man was gone. The guard ran forward, continuing to fire at the suddenly unoccupied end of the corridor. Before he reached it, he stopped, inches short of the bright red line that stretched across the floor and continued up the side walls to ceiling height, several yards from the blank wall that faced him.

He hesitated there, cursed explosively, then backed a couple of steps, jabbing his gun out in front of him. He recommenced firing directly at the wall, keeping the gun level and moving it in a steady arc from left to right. After several seconds, it clicked emptily. He paused briefly, cursed again, then lunged forward.

Beyond the red line, light appeared, a sudden glare that stretched vertically from the floor to a point roughly three feet from the ceiling. At the moment of its materialisation it was flatly leaf-shaped, but it expanded almost immediately, extending a serration of flames beyond its outline and simultaneously blooming towards him.

The guard rocked to a halt in mid-lunge, lifting his hands to his face. He spun away from the advancing rush of heat and light, screaming, his hair and uniform igniting as he fell.

The outer door burst open again and other people crowded into the corridor as water sprayed from the ceiling, rapidly extinguishing his burning clothes and hair and soaking his writhing body.

As abruptly as it had materialised, the flaming leaf-shape retreated, shrinking rapidly to a point of light that flared once with blinding ferocity, then vanished, the charred figure of the guard and a pall of acrid smoke the only evidence of its brief existence.

43.

CODE ONE

FOR THE ATTENTION OF
DEPUTY CONTROLLER ONLY –
ADDENDUM

Well, there you have it. I imagine your reaction's been pretty much the same as mine, but whatever we might think you can bet your sweet life that the fur's going to fly with a vengeance when this gets to Washington.

Anyway, you can see now why I've been stressing the security angle as much as I have. Some of his and Mastin's speculations were rational enough – none of them really went over any ground that we hadn't already covered ourselves, of course – but can you picture the scene if their big idea was to reach the public domain? Even though it's nothing more than a prime example of ignorance combining with imagination and reaching a nonsensical conclusion, given the global situation and knowing how readily a large slice of humankind's prepared to accept beliefs and rumours as facts, there's no way that we could avoid ending up with what'd amount to the final nail in civilisation's coffin, and I really don't think I'm exaggerating when I say that.

Trying to convince people that travelling back to our own past really was on the cards for quite a while before the hole appeared, and explaining that in any case if other universes did exist the laws of physics make it quite clear that interference phenomena simply wouldn't allow matter of any kind to be transferred from one to another wouldn't get us anywhere, not after they found out what Lohmann and Mastin became convinced was the truth. Just how they'd figure the hole could've been used as an escape-hatch on any kind of scale would mean completely ignoring the practicalities, but grasping at straws in desperate situations in a natural thing to do, and the fact that there's no realistic reprieve for us anywhere in sight would certainly make it understandable in this instance. Of course, sooner or later it'd dawn on them that the existence of multiverses would have to mean that predetermination ruled and free-will was only a myth, but by then it'd be too late to simply do an about-face. A realisation of that magnitude would turn what'd already become an even worse situation than the one we're in now into an uncontrollable nightmare, so keeping the lid on it as tight as we possibly can really is vital.

On that point we're obviously going to have to trust Waters and Kennway to keep their mouths shut, but fortunately I don't think we have a problem there, not now. Come the finish we were in broad agreement as to what it was really all about, but they still both plainly appreciated that if any of it leaked the outcome would be bound to be catastrophic. Kennway covered their backs before they came, of course, but after we talked he said he'd be destroying his copies when he got back, which is a pretty good indication of his degree of committment, so I'm sure they'll be keeping it to themselves without us having to lean on them in any way.

To be fair, I can understand why Lohmann and Mastin got around to believing what they did, although when it's analysed objectively it's easy enough to dismantle. Although the Henry business undeniably contradicts what's on record, the press reports of the hotel fire say that the building was more or less reduced to a shell afterwards, and, significantly, that most of the bodies they recovered were charred beyond recognition. The fact of him losing all his stuff must've meant that his room burned out, so in the general confusion – and with him leaving town that morning as well, of course – it was obviously assumed that he'd been in it at the time. Forensics was still a relatively unsophisticated field back then and incorrect identification of corpses wasn't exactly unique, especially when it involved transients, so given all the circumstances it clearly adds up to a simple case of mistaken identity.

After all, there's no question that he did survive then, but if Lohmann's views on his musical potential were right, and I think

we can accept that they were, the reason for him not going on
to make any kind of recorded mark at all afterwards is an open
question that I think we should look into, just to clarify things.
In any case, it's worth bearing in mind that Lohmann painted a
picture of a pretty frail-sounding individual, so given the chaotic
way that a lot of jazz people obviously existed then it could easily be
that he was a victim of that kind of disorganised life-style, maybe
very shortly after their last meeting. It's clear that he regularly
burned the candle at both ends, and Lohmann acknowledged that
hard drugs had begun to play a larger role in the jazz community,
too, although we have no way of knowing if he'd fallen into
that particular trap, of course. Anyway, it's possible; it's widely
documented that quite a few of them terminated prematurely as
the result of acquiring a habit, but even if drugs didn't enter into
it, and even if he didn't actually die around then his health could
very easily have broken down not long afterwards and forced him
to quit playing, simply vanish off the radar.

As far as Lohmann himself was concerned, his idea that he
might somehow be the central figure of some kind of cosmic
excercise was clearly nothing more than a rather sad ego-trip that
he'd been gullible enough to let circumstances kid him into taking.
Meeting the Woods girl like he did was a pretty extraordinary
coincidence, I admit, but the fact that his wife's people came from
K.C. means that it was still well within the bounds of reasons.
Add to that what happened to his wife and Henry's survival and
you've got a formula for fantasising that'd have its own kind of
twisted plausibility for someone in his situation, although of
course it was really only a scenario that he'd pieced together from
a bunch of random events, with no real pattern there at all. As for
Mastin, his talk about sensing an overall change of atmosphere was
totally unspecific, so that can hardly be treated seriously as actual
evidence of what he believed was happening. After his near-miss
with Forrestal he knew there was a chance that we'd have people
out looking for him up until the time that the hole closed, so one
way and another he was in a situation that could very easily have
induced paranoia or a generally delusional state of mind.

We're still stuck with a few unanswered questions, of course,
although they're relatively minor ones, this business of Roache
playing it the way he did, for instance; after all, he clearly needed
help in that situation, and he'd had plenty of time to call it in.

Urich's adamant that he wasn't the reckless type, so it's unlikely that it was from choice, and communications swear by their equipment, so unless they're considerably over-rating its efficiency it's difficult to imagine what else it could've been.

What exactly brought about the closure's another one, and I know I'm taking a chance on sounding as though I'm sticking a toe into Lohmann's cosmic plan territory here, but there's undeniably a touch of chick and egg about that as I see it. It might simply have been due to happen then without any kind of assistance, of course, but what if it was a gradual repair process that wasn't actually due to finish for a while but had reached the stage where some kind of final boost would accelerate the completion? A concentrated burst of gunfire generates a lot of heat and energy, and there's no argument that the flare-up signalled that it shut directly after the security guy emptied his gun through it, so I can't help wondering if that was what actually triggered it and maybe closed it prematurely, that the shooting was an essential part of what happened then.

Well, maybe, although considering the relative forces involved I guess I could be accused of over-stretching things just a little on that one. Anyway, at least we're certain that he missed Lohmann with his first shot; the CC footage shows that the angle of fire was way off target, but we have no idea whether or not he scored after that, of course. The rest of the bullets definitely got through; there was no trace of them when we checked the corridor out afterwards, so there was only one place they could've gone. Even if he wasn't hit, though, or was hit but only wounded, I think he terminated at the time, and there's a very good reason for me believing that.

Instead of simply re-sealing the hole, isn't it logical to assume that it was restoring the natural order as well, repositioning that segment of time back where it belonged, back to its chronological location on the time-line? If that is what happened then surely it's also logical to assume that it'd automatically revert to its natural components and nothing else, making it incapable of accommodating any kind of foreign body? Mastin and Roaches' deaths had already removed a couple of potential complications, and with Bethal and Glass obviously long gone Lohmann's attempted re-entry was the only remaining factor that could've caused problems, so in the event there was simply no place for him to go. He'd have been erased before he could disrupt the pattern, and that would've had to mean that instead of ending up where he thought he was going, he died, too, somewhere between here and this other place; an ironic end as well as a cruel one, but at least he'd have gone out believing that he was headed back to what he admitted was still his dream-world, even though it'd be a constant reminder of his part in what happened to Mastin.

And that's it, I guess, end of story, because I somehow doubt that we'll be accessing that particular scene again in a hurry, if at all. Whatever, there's no denying its tragic aspect, but despite the predictable element this was always going to be a high-risk operation, even discounting the security aspect of it. At least learning what Lohmann's been up to's been instructive in its way, and like I said earlier, it isn't hard to understand why he and Mastin interpreted things the way they did, especially when you consider the situation here and the one they found themselves in; after all, there's no denying that even without those specific ingredients being thrown into the pot this whole thing's created a particularly intriguing set of circumstances as far as playing the "what if" game's concerned.

I don't need to spell out what our first priority'd be, either, but if multiverses really was what what it was all about, just think what it could've meant if it was applied to that particularly grisly piece of our history, too. The obvious example's worlds with no Hitler and no war at all, of course, but even in instances where he was still trying to impose his lunatic ideas on the rest of humankind there'd be ones where, say, the Tehran conference massacre never happened, and Roosevelt and Churchill and Stalin survived and steered us through the whole hideous business a lot faster than it actually took. Seven-and-a-half years was a hell of a long time to be at total war, and it's easy to see how losing them all in one fell swoop like that must've taken the edge off the impetus we'd been building up for a while, especially after the Germans grabbed their chance to regroup on the Russian front. And while I'm looking on the gloomy side, how about ones where we didn't just beat them to it with the bomb? When you think about what losing that particular race would've meant, it puts even narrow squeaks like the air war over Britain in the shade. Frankly, I've never been able to understand the objections to using it against them and the Japs, not when you think about how close they were to producing their own, and the scale of the losses we'd have been bound to suffer if we'd been forced to invade the European and Japanese mainlands hardly bears thinking about.

The truth is that we were darned lucky to come out of it the way we did, and it's our eternal shame that we've fouled up as catastrophically as we have since then. In any case, although the idea of versions of us that made the most of their chances is enormously appealing, the prospect of there being limitless universes and situations has it's downside, too – something that Lohmann acknowledged, of course – so despite our own situation I guess it's just as well that Occam's razor still cuts it, right?

You know, it's just occurred to me that as I've been speculating about an existence that'd offer every conceivable variation I haven't exactly been over-taxing my imagination, but sticking close to home seems to be all it's capable of at the moment. That being the case, and in view of what's prompted all of this, I suppose I might just as well have envisaged a benevolent version of events where Lohmann made it back to his idea of Heaven on earth after all, totally unscathed and soaked up his beloved jazz again, his hand-me-down piano playing occasionally steering the music to places it's maybe never been before and might never have visited if it hadn't been for his nudging, still not really sure what his being there had to mean in the overall sense and facing a life that's as happy as he could reasonably expect, given the tragic associations he'll always carry with him.

I'm sure I have a pretty good idea of the various lines of argument that'll be pursued in Washington, but even if they come up with something I haven't thought of I'm prepared to guarantee that nothing quite like <u>that's</u> going to enter into their considerations! Anyway, that's got to be it for now; I've just been told that the transport's on its way in, and I have to collect Waters and Kennway and speak with Mal before we go. I just hope they save the interrogating for when we get there; what I need more than anything else right now is a couple of hours with my head down, so this really would be a very bad time for anybody to start firing questions at me.

Don't forget to wipe this, and I'll see you when I see you. I can't seriously imagine that anything really useful's going to come out of this trip, but we'll have plenty to chew on when I get back, that's for damn sure.

END